THINGS SLIP THROUGH

BY KEVIN LUCIA

EDITED BY JOE MYNHARDT

Paperback Edition

Crystal Lake Publishing
www.CrystalLakePub.com

In order for the light to shine so brightly, the darkness must be present.

FRANCIS BACON

There are more things in heaven and earth, Horatio,

Than are dreamt of in your philosophy.

SHAKESPEARE, *HAMLET*

For now we see through a glass, darkly . . .

I CORINTHIANS 13:12

COPYRIGHT ACKNOWLEDGEMENTS

"Lament", *Anthology: Year One*, Shroud Publishing, 2012

"Way Station", Editor's Choice Award, *The Midnight Diner*, 2008

"Water God of Clarke Street", *Abominations,* Shroud Publishing, 2009

"Lonely Places", *The Midnight Diner, Volume 3,* 2011

"The Gate and the Way", *The Midnight Diner, Volume 4,* 2012

"The Sliding", *Morpheus Tales,* Issue #1, 2009

"Bassler Road", originally Darkness Road, *Next Gen Pulp*, Issue #1, 2009

"A Willing Donor", *Raw: Brutality As Art,* Snuff Books, 2010

"On A Midnight Black Chessie", *For the Night is Dark*, Crystal Lake, 2013

"Mr. Nobody"—previously unpublished

"Monster"—previously unpublished

PRAISE FOR *HIRAM GRANGE &THE
CHOSEN ONE, BOOK FOUR OF THE
HIRAM GRANGE CHRONICLES*:

*"In the mood for a wild ride of a book? Something
smart and scary and exciting? Kevin Lucia's HIRAM
GRANGE & THE CHOSEN ONE fits the bill to
perfection. It teems with monsters and demons, with
arcane lore, black magic and narrow escapes. What
could be more delicious?"*
**Robert Dunbar, Bram Stoker Nominated
author of THE SHORE and MARTYRS &
MONSTERS**

*"HIRAM GRANGE & THE CHOSEN ONE moves fast,
fun and furious . . . I couldn't put it down! If you've
always thirsted for James Bond to have a serving of
Lovecraft—you'll eat this one up."*
**John Everson, Bram Stoker Award Winning
Author of COVENANT**

*"Brilliantly paced and with very few moments for the
reader to stop and catch their breath, Hiram Grange
and the Chosen One is an adrenaline drenched jaunt
through the realms of horror, fantasy and dark
humor. Violence and gore abound, presented expertly
by Lucia in a way that not only shows his raw talent,
but the ruggedness of Hiram's character as well."*
Apex Publications

INTRODUCTION

DARK AND HUNGRY

I guess the first thing to deal with is how I came to be here, in this place, at this time, writing an introduction to a collection of stories written by a young guy who lives in the same town that gave us another talented teller of strange tales, Rod Serling.

And so . . . a story of my own.

For the past ten years, Elizabeth and I have been conducting the Borderlands Press Writers Boot Camp during that cold, dark internecine week-end between the conclusion of the NFL Conference Championship games and the Super Bowl (*Yes, we like our football as well as our books . . .*). And each session brings us between twenty and thirty writers willing to undergo the harsh critiques of grizzled veteran writers and New York editors, as well as suggestions from their fellow grunts. It's always a splashy combination of personalities, ages, and skills. Some of the attendees take their lumps and are never heard from again; others return for several additional injections of criticism and instruction; and an alarming number go on to create careers for themselves as professional writers.

It was at one such gathering that I met Kevin Lucia. I can't remember the year because I need to use my failing memory for more important stuff these days, but that's okay because I'm sure Kevin remembers and would be happy to tell you. Regardless, I can tell you I *definitely* remember seeing him for the first time—whatever year it was.

It was at our usual Friday Night warm-up session in which the Instructors for the week-end introduce themselves, each speaking a few minutes about the areas of the writing craft on which they will concentrate (*Such as Plot, Dialogue, Characterization, Voice, Setting, Grammar, Style, etc.*), and wrap up with a great exercise that increases not only awareness but also the need for honest, if sometimes brutal, criticism. As I looked out over the assemblage, I could see the usual wide-eyed anxiety in the faces of the grunts. A familiar expression that suggests they are all thinking: *what the hell am I doing here?!*

All but one.

There was this one guy in the second row who looked tall and rangy even when sitting down. He was leaning forward in his chair, his dark eyes sunk into his angular face, and staring at the front table of Instructors as if we were there to challenge him to a bar-fight (*And in a way, we were*). I remember thinking that if I were casting this guy for a part in *Julius Caesar*, he'd have Cassius nailed down so tight nobody could ever pry it loose.

And his prose is as lean and hungry as his aspect. It's a pleasure to read because it carries you along with the effortless pace of a massive freight train on seamless titanium rails. His initial submission to Boot Camp took quite a pounding, and Kevin did nothing but learn from the experience. He had a steely determination to improve his writing skills and it shows in this collection.

Ah yes, finally, we get to the book held in your hands. As I read this worthy tome, I quickly realized it was not just your usual, normal collection. In the tradition of Bradbury's classic *The Illustrated Man* or *The Martian Chronicles*, Kevin Lucia has created a clever frame in which to hold the assemblage of tales—some of which seem to be related, while others do not—all taking place in the same general locale. He even gets away with the greatest crime writers can commit—writing about characters who are *writers*. Because writing is what we do, we naturally believe such people make great protagonists—although most readers seldom agree with us. Writers spend a lot of time by themselves, not talking, barely moving. That's interesting?

But soon you will meet a chap named Gavin who will disabuse you of that notion.

He is a storyteller thinly disguised as the author of these tales and you will grow to love him as have I. This will happen because you will meet some Clifton Heights townsfolk who are gritty and real and not always likeable . . . but they are always believable. Gavin/Kevin peels back the onion layers of his town and explores some of the horror genre's most venerable themes and settings—the small, weird town; the phantom hitchhiker; the old creep house where kids break in; the hospital of horrors; and of course the reluctant-to-believe authority figure. We've been down roads like Bassler Roads before, but somehow, Lucia makes it all not just palatable, but energizing and compelling.

Some of the stories connect and repeat and kind of

fold back into each other, each one expanding on the larger persona of the town and its inhabitants. The deeper we travel into this collection, the more we get the feeling Lucia is creating a subtle gestalt—an ultimate moment when we realize all the individual elements have gathered themselves together in a spinning maelstrom that is far greater than the sum of all its parts.

In the intensely revealing portrait of Gavin Patchett in "Way Station," I found myself nodding my head in approval of Lucia's straight-ahead confidence in his words. And I wondered how many of his readers would pick up on the sly implication of Gavin's need to read "the handwriting on the wall" had they not known the origins of *mene mene tekel*. This Lucia is a smart guy.

His "Water God of Clarke Street" captures the cadences of high schoolers. Their needs and fears ring true, underscoring the writer's gift for getting the ambience of his settings exactly right. This was a key element of this tale and the one that follows it. He seems concerned with examining the ghosts and demons of our childhoods, and wondering why some of them never faded off into the oblivion of the adult world the way they are supposed to do.

Sometimes Lucia is playful such as his nod in the direction of the town of Arkham and all the attendant mythologies that dwell therein. Sometimes, as in "Mr. Nobody," he writes with a flensed-to-the-bone honesty that leaves you with a terrible taste in your mouth. But in all cases, he writes with a clarity that is stark and real and you are left with images and emotions that do not leave you when you turn the page. In other words,

Lucia writes tales that stick with you, that are memorable.

And believe me, they are the best kind.

Wrapping things up, I must make one last reference to the framing narrative that contains all these excursions into a singular community's madness. With subtle dialogue, we realize that perhaps our Kevin Lucia is more the skilled manipulator than we could have first imagined. He leaves us with a quiet ambiguity that leaves us with a decision we may not wish to make—a kind of literary chicken-or-egg dilemma that succeeds in giving this collection that added layer of complication, that unexpected frisson.

I'm never sure about the purpose of Introductions like this one. I feel like it's just me getting in the way of your primary intention which is to read the stories of Kevin Lucia, and that's not a good thing.

And with that, I must urge you to turn the page.

—Thomas F. Monteleone
Baltimore April 6, 2013

ACKNOWLEDGEMENTS

As always, I want to thank my loving wife Abby for her continued support and tolerance. Being married to a writer is a tough gig and an often thankless job, and I wouldn't be anything without you.

Also, several other folks deserve mention for their help and friendship: Michelle Pendergrass, Ben Culbertson, Tosca Lee, Robert Liparulo, Phil Tomasso, Greg Mitchell, The Four Horsemen: Tim Deal, Danny Evarts, Johnny Morse and Mark Wholley, The Hiram Five and Richard Wright especially, Kelli Owen, Bob Ford, Ron Dickie, Mandy DeGeit, Jacob Haddon, Alethea Kontis, Maurice Broaddus, Brian Keene, Ron Malfi, Norman Prentiss, Rio Youers, Dan Keohane, Mort Castle, Tom Monteleone, F. Paul Wilson, Gard Goldsmith, Tom Erb, Susan Scofield, Matt Blazi, Savage Mouse and OF COURSE Tad, Nikki Graybeal, Norman Partridge, Robert Dunbar, Lawrence Santoro of *Tales to Terrify,* Brian Freeman of *Cemetery Dance*, Tina Corbin, Joanna Patchett and Claudia Gabel Lindvall. You've all helped in so many ways, some of you just by being the coolest folks ever.

Also thanks to editor Joe Mynhardt for believing in this collection. And, here's the clichéd thanks to my

12th Grade English teacher, Mrs. Lida Bassler, who was my first official reader, and the first person ever to say: "Go get published." Hope you don't mind what I've done with your last name . . .

Finally, to the folks of the Adirondacks, especially the Old Forge/White Lake area. I adore the Adirondacks and will always find my way back there, and humbly ask your pardon for taking some heavy liberties with your geography and locations.

AUGUST
5:00 PM
CLIFTON HEIGHTS, NEW YORK

I.

IT'S POKER TUESDAY. My daughter Meg is at the sitter's and my friends and I are relaxing on my front porch, enjoying a few quiet drinks after we wind down from our respective afternoons. Father Ward stands beside me, Fitzy leans against the railing at the porch's end and Gavin sits on the railing across from me. I'm sitting in my favorite Adirondack lounge chair.

The warm summer air is quiet and still, save for the distant buzz of cars easing their way down Henry Street. Usually, this is my favorite night of the week; an evening of carefree leisure, when the world's troubles are held at bay by camaraderie and friendship, and beer and pizza, too.

But tonight is different. Tonight, everything may fall apart because the things I've ignored for so long can no longer be dismissed and I must speak, risking at the very least our friendships, at the very worst this place I've come to call *home*.

And the others sense it too, I think. At least Father Ward seems to, as his gentle hand squeezes my shoulder. "I don't mean to pry, Chris . . . but how are you tonight? You look tired."

Fitzy sips from his beer and says with a grin, "What the good Padre means is, you look like *shit*, Chris."

I shrug but say nothing, while Gavin says, "Y'know Fitzy, most the time you manage a passable imitation of compassion, but every now and then? You're an ass."

He offers a jaunty salute with his root beer. "Just sayin."

Fitzy waves. "Oh, bullshit. I say what everyone is thinking and you know it."

He takes a long pull on his beer.

"It's your tone, Fitzy," Father Ward offers. "You don't realize it, but sometimes you sound . . . flippant. Insensitive."

Fitzy scowls. "The hell you say. Insensitive? I have a goddamn loving soul; I'll have you know. Ask any of my patients."

Gavin's smirk widens. "Maybe the coma patients. Anyone else, though . . . "

Everyone laughs and we relax some. But I still wonder if by the night's end we'll be able to recapture this levity, or if things will be changed forever.

Fitzy shrugs and grins at me. "Okay, we'll play things their way, even though I figure you can handle yourself, being a big bad cop and all. BUT, to make the touchy-feelies happy . . . Chris, you look *sad*. What's up? Women troubles? Too many of them, or not enough?" He winks. "Tell Dr. Fitzy the truth, now."

I laugh, not unkindly . . . but not happily, either.
Truth.
It's a precious commodity.

Especially between friends. It's essential in building trust and dependability. The problem, however, lies in how *much* truth do we share? How honest can friends be with each other, really?

I've come to believe that layers of truth exist. How far we peel them back depends on an infinite combination of variables: time, place, audience, mood, and intent. All factors are weighed multiple times a day and often in a heartbeat when considering how much we want to share with those closest to us.

For example, when my wife Liz was still alive, it went something like this: "Chris, please be honest. Did you find your partner attractive?"

One layer of truth: "Honey, she could never be you, could never raise our children and take care of me like you have."

Which of course isn't the same as saying "no." It's a truth that subtly replaces a deeper truth: "Yes, I am attracted to her. Because she's young, and she's a cop like me, and she likes the same things I do, and that's why I requested a new partner, because the more I looked into her bright green eyes the less I thought about you and Meg and that scared the hell out of me."

Or it went like this:

"Liz . . . you okay? Look a little pale this morning."

"I'm fine. Tired from working those late shifts. Just a little headache, is all."

Which had been a lie. Working in the oncology unit at Binghamton General, having seen dozens of patients with the same symptoms: dizziness, blurred vision, headaches, nausea, chronic fatigue, she knew too well her probable diagnosis.

Brain cancer.

A truth she shared with us much too late, because she'd understood a deeper truth: in the end, it wouldn't make a difference *when* we found out.

She was still going to die.

I think all this and then say, "Fitzy, you're right. I don't want to play poker, tonight. What I want is the truth, for once."

His jovial manner fades, his eyes taking on an odd, somber cast. I glance at Gavin. His face hardens also. "The truth about what, Chris?"

I've only lived in Clifton Heights for little over a year; have only known Fitzy and Gavin and Father Ward for about the same time. We all met around a tragedy last fall involving one of Gavin's students. I was first officer on the scene. Fitzy was the ER doctor who'd treated the shooter afterwards. Father Ward visited her in jail regularly until she was moved downstate to the Riverdale Psychiatric Institution for further treatment.

And out of that awful incident, our friendship slowly bloomed. We hung around each other for several weeks and somehow Poker Tuesdays developed and we became friends. Good friends, even.

But a wall has grown between us since then, a wall built from a subtle evasiveness preventing us from becoming *close* friends.

That wall?

The truth.

About this town and the strange things that happen here. Last September's shooting was tragic and heart wrenching but in some ways ordinary. Turn on the television and you'll see the same thing happening all over the country: bigotry, persecution and cruelty everywhere. Eventually, people are pushed past their limits and they lash out.

Other things have happened here, however.

Strange things. Unexplainable things. Like average people quitting their jobs mid-shift for no reason and vanishing into thin air. Mothers removing their children from school with no warning and taking off for parts unknown, entire families sneaking away into the night, clergy and veteran teachers resigning their posts unannounced, experienced hunters disappearing into the forests never to be seen again.

Of course, some of these things have been more . . . memorable. Grotesque, even. Like cannibalism. *Maybe*. Hard to tell, when the town coroner says bite marks "might've been made by human teeth" but all his tests come back "inconclusive," which has happened more than once around here.

And that's not all, by a long shot. There have been suicides. A LOT of them. Missing kids, more than you'd expect in a small Adirondack town. Also, patients in our small hospital are often mysteriously "transferred" to special recovery facilities "downstate."

What it all comes down to?

The truth.

What *really* happened in those cases? What's hiding in the dark corners of this town? This whole past year, I've tried unsuccessfully to wrest answers from my friends with probing questions like . . .

Has it always been like this? Did you ever imagine that he or she'd be capable of doing this? How'd you guys not see this coming? You've known this or that person all your life. How'd you miss the signs?

And as the year has passed their answers have

grown increasingly evasive, offering shades of half-truths, nothing more.

And I'm tired of it.

Especially after this last one.

"The truth?" Fitzy mutters, face oddly blank. "About what?"

I reach under my chair, pull out a stuffed manila folder held shut with several rubber bands and toss it at Fitzy. It hits him square in the gut, and he somehow manages to trap it there with one hand without spilling his drink.

I point at the folder. "That's our most recent case. Ellen Danvers and her missing son. Happened two weeks ago. You've all heard about it by now, I imagine."

A knowing silence.

One I've heard too much of this year.

Finally Gavin says, "Sure we've heard. Everyone has, and it's terrible, thinking her boyfriend did something like that."

"Right," Fitzy adds too quickly, nodding sharply. "Danny Tremont. Grew up with him. He's a sonnuvabitch. Always has been. Not surprised he—"

"Bull*shit*."

I look at every one of them in turn. If I weren't so annoyed, I'd find their shocked expressions at my rare use of profanity amusing. "That's not what *she* says, not now. At first she was hysterical, claiming *something* took her son Timmy. Of course, everyone just figured she was distraught and a little out of her head, especially the state police department's grief counselor. But then three days later she calls me at the station, asking me to end the search, saying we don't need to look for Timmy anymore because he's gone on to a better place."

Father Ward pats my shoulder again and says softly, "Shock and denial, Chris. Surely you've seen similar reactions in cases like these."

I shake my head. I've been put off by Father Ward's affable, man-of-the-cloth routine before. Not tonight. "But the physical evidence also doesn't match up. There was no time in the incident's chronology for *anyone* to have abducted Timmy Danvers, least of all Danny Tremont."

I look at each and every one of them again, then say, "Two weeks ago, Timmy Danvers effectively disappeared off the face of the earth and his mother doesn't seem too upset by this, now. And neither does anyone else in this town, with the exception of my guys and the state troopers."

I nod at the folder. "There have been other disappearances this past year, a recent one very similar to this. A month ago, seven-year-old Anne Marie Hauer from Utica vanished from her bedroom. No forced entry, no forensic evidence. She's just GONE, like Timmy Danvers.

"And you know what, fellas? I'm tired of this. I really am. All the time, you act as if you don't know anything, that you're just as mystified as me, like everyone else in this town. But I call, fellas. I call BULLSHIT."

And now a deep silence grows between us. I let it fester for several minutes before saying, "Here's the deal. We've reached a crucial juncture. If you want to continue as friends, you're going to tell me what the hell's going on in this town, or at *least* tell me what you know. We'll order some pizza, go inside, pour over the whole thing together, so I can do my job the way I'm supposed to."

"And if we don't?" Father Ward asks gently, but firmly. "Some things aren't meant to be known, Chris."

My answer is just as firm. "Then we cancel Poker Tuesday. I start looking for a new job somewhere far away from here, take my daughter and get the hell outta Dodge."

More silence.

And I see it in their eyes.

They're debating it. Weighing the pros and cons of telling me what they know or letting me walk away. And to be quite honest? A part of me, the part that never grew up, that little boy inside who's still afraid of shadows and wind rustling through leaves wishes they *would* let me walk away.

Because maybe that would be better.

But Gavin takes the folder from Fitzy, then nods down the street. "The Skylark Diner is open twenty-four hours. And its owner is very . . . discrete."

"In other words," I whisper, "he knows how to keep his mouth shut."

Fitzy nods sharply, dispensing with all pretenses. "Damn straight he does."

Gavin tucks the folder under his arm and gives me an odd, penetrating look. "I need to grab something from home first. Meet you there?"

I wave toward my long, winding drive. "After, you folks."

And as we thump off my porch, I wonder.

How much truth do we tell *ourselves*? What layers are we willing to face? And is there a place to stop?

THINGS SLIP THROUGH

A safe place where we can say: "Enough.
"I know enough."

THE SKYLARK DINER
5:30 PM

2.

SOMEHOW I'M NOT surprised when Gavin walks into The Skylark alone. No one said much as we left my place, but I sensed—through body language, maybe—that this was Gavin's job, telling me the truth or whatever passes for it in this town.

A *nice* town, dammit, in spite all of this. Picturesque, a postcard-beautiful Adirondack town as charming as Inlet or Eagle Bay but not as touristy as Lake George. And the people here have been nothing but accommodating and pleasant. Word of the new Sheriff in town (also new widower with an only daughter) has paved the way for fruit baskets, pies, homemade bread, frozen venison and casseroles galore, all this past year.

But as time has passed and the town's strangeness has bloomed, it's dawned upon me that maybe this town is *too* accommodating, because someone should've petitioned the Town Board for my immediate resignation a long time ago, especially considering all the odd cases I haven't been able to solve.

But there've been no petitions.

No complaints.

No outraged demands for my dismissal. Just encouraging pats on the shoulder and the occasional: "It's all right, Sheriff. Did your best. Sometimes there's no answer."

Sometimes?

Hell, in this town, never.

But maybe that's all about to change.

Maybe.

Gavin slides into the booth across from me, handing over the folder I'd tossed at Fitzy. His other hand lays a thick, black, leather-bound journal on the table between us, and he handles it reverently, as if in awe, or maybe even . . .

Fear.

I open my mouth but Gavin beats me. "Have I ever told you what I did before teaching?"

I think about it for a moment, realizing it'd never occurred to me. A little embarrassed, I admit, "Honestly? I figured you'd always been a teacher."

He smiles and shakes his head. "No. Only been teaching for about four years, now. I was a writer before that. Science Fiction and Thrillers. And I doubt you've read me."

I shrug, feeling a little embarrassed. "Yeah, but that doesn't mean much. Outside a few Louis L'Amour westerns, I'm not much of a reader. Meg is, though. And so was Liz. So I try . . . "

Despite all this time, my voice hitches. I push on, however. "I read to Meg as often as I can, even though she can read herself, now. It's what Liz would've wanted, I think . . . for Meg to love books and stories, just like she did."

Gavin nods. "I wrote a few novels several years ago, one hardcover and several paperbacks, the kind you find in grocery stores and airport gift centers. Won a few small awards, nothing big, really. Problem was, *I* thought I was big. And things . . . "

He winces and looks away, visibly struggling to compose himself. Several seconds pass, he swallows and says, "I started drinking. Became very troubled. My exit from publishing was . . . unpleasant. And I doubt I'll ever write for publication again. Not sure anyone would have me. But, writers never stop writing. Not really."

Gavin meets my gaze with a deep, probing one of his own. "You want to know the truth about this town. About the things that happen here."

"Yes. I'm the Sheriff. I need to know these things if I'm going to do my job."

His voice hovers just above a whisper. "Even if it's nothing you can change? Nothing you can investigate, arrest, or put into a cell? Nothing you can solve?"

My response is immediate. "Yes. I'm the Sheriff. I *need* to know."

Gavin nods briskly, like this is a clean-cut business transaction, and I suppose that's the way it needs to be because some things are simply too horrible and strange and must be held at a safe, dispassionate distance.

Well, *hell.*

I'm already thinking like everyone else in this town, aren't I?

Gavin looks down at that large, black leather-bound book and pats it. "I really don't know how much I can tell you, but I do know that everything changed about a year ago when we first met. I'd still been drinking pretty heavily, when . . . "

He sighs and pushes the book toward me. "Go ahead," he whispers.

"Read it yourself."

LAMENT

SHE SWINGS THE hammer down again and again. Bone crunches, blood splatters. Her stomach churns as she raises the hammer to swing it down once more . . .

But she stops and squeezes the hammer's slick rubber grip. Blood oozes between her fingers. The hammer shakes in her hand.

And then she drops it to the pavement where it hits with a dull ring and she looks at what she's done to his face, and realizes . . . she *likes* it.

And wants to do it some more.

She kneels and sobs.

Then vomits.

MONDAY

Gavin Patchett glared at the stack of essays sitting on his desk, then glanced at the first one before him. He tapped it with his red pen, leaving clusters of smeary crimson dots near its heading. He read the first paragraph, squinted and read it again, hoping it would make more sense the second time.

It didn't. Just made him feel tired was all.

He closed his eyes, sighed and rubbed his warm forehead. Maybe he'd call in sick tomorrow, stay home and do a little writing of his own for a change. If he could just get a whole day to himself, maybe . . .

His classroom door opened.

And Emma Pital entered, scowling, which made him feel even more tired.

He fake-smiled. "Emma. You okay?"

Emma said nothing, just hugged herself and approached the window overlooking the school parking lot. He looked back down at the essay before him. He didn't want to be rude but this was his only free period today and he didn't have time to . . .

"Fucking *animals*."

"Excuse me?"

He glanced up at her; saw her stiff posture, her neck muscles twisting beneath russet-brown skin.

"Fucking animals don't deserve to live."

His scalp tingled as he glanced at his open door. He stood, unsure what he should do. "Emma. Is something wrong? Maybe you should go to Guidance and . . . "

She snorted. "Yeah, Guidance. That's fucking hilarious."

"Emma . . . "

"Heard the latest? Sure you have. You all have. You just won't do anything about it."

He stepped toward the door . . .

"*Sand nigger*."

. . . but stopped as the word jerked him around.

"Soaped on my brother's truck windows, this morning." Her eyes glittered.

"Emma, listen . . . "

She offered a rigid smile. "I know. It didn't happen on school grounds, so it didn't happen. Police'll say it's harmless. Harmless? No fucking way." Her eyes narrowed. "And you know. Of all people, you *know* it's not harmless."

"Emma, please . . . "

"No." She turned away. "No more talk."

The door slammed.

He stood for a few minutes, then sat to continue grading, because there really wasn't anything else for him to do.

***

"I swear, Emma . . . not a word. Not. A. Word."

"You must tell someone about this, Daniel." She lowered her voice as they walked. "Your truck. The one Father . . . "

Daniel scowled but she persisted. "Please. Say something, to *someone*. To the police this time. They'll listen. They'll have to."

Daniel shook his head as they ascended the school's front steps, empty this early Monday morning. "They won't listen and you know it. A prank, they'll say. Why bother?"

She grabbed his elbow. "Then do something about it! We know who did it. Find them, and . . . "

Daniel pulled away. "What? What would you have me do?"

He stopped and readjusted his backpack's straps, looking exactly like every American high school senior should . . . except for the color of his skin, of course.

Always the skin.

"Soon we'll graduate and then we'll leave here with our heads held high. How Father would've wanted."

"But this is wrong. We shouldn't be treated this way. We're American, as much as anyone else. Or we were, before . . . " She shook her head. "But not now. Not ever again."

Daniel sighed. "Emma, it's Ramadan. A time to pray and ask for guidance, not a time for vengeance. Pray, Emma. Perhaps Allah will take this from us." He looked at her. "Besides. They won't touch us. They won't go that far."

"How can you be sure? And since when do you observe Ramadan, Mr. Hilfiger?"

Daniel's brown pupils swam. "After Father died. When did you *stop*?"

He walked away.

Emma squeezed herself. "Same time."

***

"Fuckin brilliant!"

Connor Finch looked up as Brian Cavanaugh scrambled into the back of John's pickup. He frowned. "What's brilliant?"

They ignored him and slapped high-fives, laughing. Connor often tried to laugh with them just to fit in, to hopefully avoid their abuse, but not today.

Not at this.

Brian squatted next to John and punched his shoulder. "Awesome, man. I woulda used paint, but soap on the windows? *Great* idea. It washes off, doesn't really mess anything up, so he's got nothin to say, an no one cares!"

John grinned. "Except him, that fuckin raghead."

Connor looked down, because he knew this story, and he also knew they were right.

No one cared.

But he surprised himself, daring to look up and say, "Maybe you oughta stop, Johnny, before . . . "

They stared at him, their faces mean and ugly. "Wait a fuckin minute. Are you defendin those ragheads? 9-Fuckin-Eleven, dipshit!"

Connor's heart skipped a beat. He'd pushed too far. Stop now and he'd be fine. Push John any further, though . . .

Again, he did the unthinkable. "S'not like *they* did it, Johnny. Emma an Danny are jus like you an me . . . "

"SHUT YER FUCKIN MOUTH!"

John stood and the truck's bed shivered. Connor stared down at John's combat boots, the ones he'd gotten from Dad . . . before he'd died.

"C'mon, Johnny," Brian sneered. "He don't know no better."

Silence. Nothing but John's breath, until: "Yeah. Fuck it. 'Sides . . . I know how he can make up for it."

Something metallic clicked.

Connor looked up and instantly wished he hadn't. Brian and John towered above him, their eyes shining, John holding a gun he must've pulled out from under his belt. A Berretta 92.

Dad's service pistol.

Brian grinned at John. "You got somethin else in mind?"

"Hell yes. An seein as how Conner here's got such a hard-on for the A-rab, he can help this time, or . . . "

John aimed at him and mimed pulling the trigger.

"Blammo. Cause that's what we do to traitors during wartime. Right, dipshit?"

Connor said nothing, just looked away and shivered.

***

And now she stands on wobbly legs, leans against the Ford, her thighs trembling. Her stomach spasms and she thinks she might vomit again so she presses her forehead against the tailgate's cool metal and closes her eyes and breathes through her nose.

Her legs steady. The nausea fades, replaced by a hard, cold burning in her guts. She swallows bile, straightens and fiddles with her torn windbreaker. Her hands brush her skin and she remembers HIS hands as they pushed her down onto the truck's cold leather seats, remembers his rough, calloused, twisting fingers.

Animals.

Fucking animals don't deserve to live.

She looks at her mother's tiny Miata, still parked and running in the lumber mill entrance. Then she turns and stoops next to his body, ignoring what she's done to his face as she digs through his pockets for keys.

***

TUESDAY

Connor fidgeted against the football field's chain link fence. He didn't want to do this but he had no choice. Maybe if Dad hadn't died and he was still around to hold John's leash, this wouldn't be happening.

Well, maybe the pranks. John had been real pissed when Dan replaced him in the backfield two years ago, and he'd stayed pissed. He quit football and school, started drinking, ranting about getting even, and Dad had ranted right along with him, cursing at Coach Pandich and Dan Pital whenever he could, so Dad might've dug the pranks.

Then Dad's reserve unit got activated and shipped out to Iraq.

And not three weeks in-country a suicide bomber with explosives strapped to his chest charged Dad's Humvee.

No one survived.

With Dad gone John took over the lumber mill, which turned out to be a small blessing. It kept him busy for a while.

But not long enough.

Because Connor supposed there wasn't enough busy in the world to cover John's anger. The pranks had started small a year ago, graffiti on Pital's locker, trash cans knocked into the Pital's front yard, prank phone calls and threatening texts.

But now this. Maybe Dad would've stopped *this* crazy shit.

Connor bent his head, closed his eyes and sighed. But maybe not. John was just like Dad, after all. And him? He was more like Mom, quiet and weak. She didn't care about the color of a person's skin, but she'd always done whatever Dad wanted.

Just like he'd always do whatever John wanted.

Shouts came from the football field. Connor looked up, saw players jogging past him on the other side of the fence toward the school. He pushed off and followed a player lagging behind, one whose brown face shined with sweat.

"Hey! Dan . . . hey!"

Daniel Pital slowed, turned and frowned. "Don't want to talk to you, Finch."

Daniel's tone cut him. Not for the first time, Connor realized he hated his brother John.

"Listen. I didn't have anything to do with . . . You know John. He's an asshole."

At least *that* was true.

Daniel's rigid posture spoke volumes. "Don't care, Finch. You're just like everyone else. You let it happen. Far as I'm concerned, you're just as bad, so I'm done with you. All of you."

He walked away.

Connor almost let him go.

But he knew what waited for him if he did, knew Mom couldn't stop John from punishing him if he didn't do what he was supposed to.

"Dan! It's important. It's . . . "

The lie trembled on his tongue. "It's about . . . Emma."

Dan stiffened, clutching his helmet's face-mask. An image flickered in Connor's mind, of Dan smashing the helmet against his face. The chain link fence still separated them, but a chill crawled along his skin regardless, and he stepped back several feet.

"What *about* Emma?"

The lie stuck in his throat and he coughed. "I think I know what they're gonna do next. You gotta believe me . . . "

oh god please don't

" . . . I'm just tryin to help."

Dan's eyes narrowed into slits. "Tell me."

Connor looked around. He wasn't faking, because John *was* out there, somewhere, watching, making sure he obeyed. "N-not here. If John catches me . . . "

"Fine. Where?"

Here it was. Lie like he was supposed to or tell the truth and get his ass kicked or worse, because he *knew*, too well, what John was really capable of.

"At Old Bassler House. Outside town? Get showered and . . . " he glanced at his watch. "Meet me there . . . thirty minutes?"

***

Gavin rubbed his forehead, thinking he should've called in sick like he'd wanted to yesterday. Seemed like he hadn't made any progress on these essays. Of course, that's the way it always was these days. He never really cleared his desk, just dented the piles was all.

His door opened and Emma walked in.

Good. He wanted to apologize for being so dismissive yesterday. Maybe it was a pointless gesture but it made him feel better about himself. A little, anyway.

He shuffled some papers. "Emma, about yesterday. I'm sorry . . . "

He looked up. Emma's large eyes—red from crying—stopped him. She sniffed, swallowed then spoke softly. "No. *I* am sorry. I should not have said those things. You've always listened to me, more than anyone. I was wrong to blame you."

Shame filled him because really, he *wanted* Emma to blame him, for doing nothing, for hiding behind his desk like everyone else, for staying *safe*.

He cleared his throat and managed the only thing he could think of, a vague and empty platitude that was also safe.

"It'll get better, Emma. Someday."

A comfortable lie. And as he met Emma's gaze, he knew she didn't believe him. But she nodded, turning for the door, stopping with her hand on the knob. "It's very strange. Daniel told me to pray about this, to ask

Allah for guidance. It's Ramadan, you know. Ends Thursday, at sundown."

She smiled sadly. "So odd, Daniel talking about Ramadan. He never used to. And me? Not since . . . well. Not for a while. Strange that something like this should . . . "

He said nothing, just nodded because of course, it was safe.

"Well. Good luck with your writing, Mr. Patchett. I hope you'll publish another book someday."

She left and closed the door softly behind her. He shook his head and kept grading papers, though he had a hard time understanding what any of them said.

***

She speeds down Haverton Road toward its intersection with Lillington, tires humming over cracked asphalt, the engine throbbing as pain roars in her chest.

Pain.

A burning knot where her heart should be. Everything else fades as pain blazes through her. She's an engine of pain, running hot on grief.

She wants to scream.

Instead she bites her tongue, holds the gas near the floor, realizing if a dog or deer jumps from the woods into her path she's dead, but Dan's class ring rattling around her index finger has numbed her, killed her inside.

Red flashes through the intersection ahead, heading south . . . away from town.

Dan's truck.

But it isn't Dan's anymore.

Is it?

Now she screams and slams the pedal down. The truck lurches forward, engine shuddering. She hits the intersection, shifts, jerks the wheel left. A stray thought: good thing Dan taught her to drive Stick last summer, and good thing she's always been a quick learner.

Because now she's learned something *new*.

The truck fishtails. She eases off the gas, taps the brakes, rights the truck and stomps the gas back down.

Screaming.

She's still screaming.

And then a tailgate reading CHEVY fills her vision. There's a spine-ratcheting jerk, and a loud BANG.

Tires squeal.

Metal screeches.

And then darkness.

WEDNESDAY

"Don't know what yer talkin about, Queen Sheba. No idea where Danny-boy is."

Emma glared at John Finch as he leaned against his truck's tailgate. This was insane. The police told her to stay home while they investigated Dan's disappearance, and that's where she should be, anywhere but here at Finch's family lumber mill, outside town after work hours, alone with John Finch.

Still, she couldn't sit at home and wait, listening to Mom rationalize about why Dan never came home last night. He'd been missing for almost twenty-four hours. Of course, the cops doubted foul play, because they were just like everyone else. Blind. Ignorant.

Afraid.

But one of Dan's teammates had called her and said he'd seen Dan talking to Connor Finch—John Finch's younger brother—after practice last night, so here she was, though she'd much rather be anywhere else.

She forced herself to speak calmly. "I don't believe you. Someone saw him with Connor last night, and he never came home after. He *always* comes home, even when he studies late. You did something to him. Just like always . . . "

John's eyes glittered. "Can't prove nothin. Know why? Nobody. Fuckin. Cares."

He relaxed, inspecting his fingernails. "Maybe he got wise an left town. Maybe you an your curry-assed Mom oughta do the same."

Her stomach twisted. "Where is he?"

John looked up and smiled, slow and lazy. "Gotta admit. Pretty brave, you comin out here after closing, when you'n me are all alone. Must love Danny-boy an awful lot."

He leered at her. She felt sick and violated.

"Question is: how *much* do you love him?"

She swallowed her disgust. "Last time. Where is he? Or should I call the cops, tell them you took Daniel, hurt him somehow. Even if there's no proof, it should make things interesting for—"

John's face hardened and Emma *knew*. Dan was dead and John Finch had killed him. But the look on John's face passed and he raised his hands in mock surrender. "Okay. You got me. Dan an I met last night an chatted for a while. Then he was gone. Maybe I scared him off, or somethin."

"Bullshit!" Anger burned her cheeks. "Dan's not afraid of anything. Especially not common trash like you."

John's smile faded. "Oh, I promise you, sweetie. He was all to *pieces* when I finished. Don't know where he is, now, but I'll help you some." He dug into his jeans pocket and pulled out a small, glittering object. "Found it this morning."

He tossed it to her. She snatched the cold, metal thing out of the air, spread her fingers . . .

And stopped breathing.

Dan's class ring.

She opened her mouth.

Closed it.

Looked up at John and finally managed. "Whe . . . where . . . ?"

John jerked his thumb over his shoulder at the slim metal tower behind the lumber mill. Smoke curled upwards from its tapered mouth. "By the wood chippers, after I loaded all the day's chippin's into the sawdust burner. Been burnin hot, all day. Like I said. Don' rightly know *where* Danny-boy is now. Could be anywhere. All *over*, even."

He turned away. "Got work to do. Have a good one."

Emma stared at the ring. Brownish-red streaks marred its gem. Topaz. For November.

Dan's birthday.

She swallowed, slipped the ring over her index finger and made a fist as everything in her head went away.

She screamed and ran after John.

But he was ready.

He turned and slapped her open handed across the

jaw, all of his weight behind the blow, which rattled her teeth and threw her against the truck's cab. Grabbing her shoulders, he slammed the back of her head against the passenger window and pressed himself against her, grabbing, squeezing . . .

He ground his pelvis against her. He was excited; she could feel it through his jeans. He bent close and whispered into her ear, his breath washing over her face and smelling of garlic and cloves, "So ya wanna be an All-American girl, jus like everyone else?"

Her windbreaker's fabric tore.

And she gasped in terror as his cold, calloused fingers brushed her skin.

"Well, here's your chance, Sheba."

He opened the passenger door with his free hand, grabbed her biceps and heaved her into the cab onto the cold, leather seat. Filling the doorway, he yanked something silver from his belt, waggled it and leered, "This'll make you behave."

A gun.

He clambered into the truck onto her. She screamed and flailed, reaching to the floor, under the seat, groping for something, anything to swing . . .

Her fingers brushed a rubber handle under the driver's seat. She grabbed hold, pulled and swung, screaming louder. A hammer's claw-end slammed into John's temple, tearing skin, splattering blood. He grunted, and she swung again.

And *again*.

John jerked with each blow, his eyes glazing over. He went limp, dropping the gun to the cab's floor and sagging against her but she didn't dare stop. She pressed a knee into his chest, lifted him back up . . .

And swung again. Blood splattered onto her lips and tasted like warm, salty broth. She cranked the hammer back once more . . .

But stopped. There was no movement, now. No jerking or twitching. His eyes stared blankly at nothing. It was over. He was gone.

But she wasn't done.

Not *yet*.

She pushed him off her with her knee and he tumbled backwards out of the cab, falling and hitting the pavement with a wet, meaty smack.

She scrambled after, hammer raised, screaming.

***

Gavin fidgeted on the lumpy couch outside Principal Stedman's office. He knew what this was about and that it was serious, but with the school day just over and those essays nearly graded, he was so close to going home and writing, he could taste it.

Which only deepened his guilt.

Principal Stedman opened his door and peered out, blinking owlishly like a burrowing animal reluctant to leave its underground den, where it was warm and safe. "Mr. Patchett? We're ready for you."

Gavin rose and entered. Mr. Stedman, a bald, pear-shaped man looking mildly oafish in a three-piece suit, closed the door and waddled around him, nodding at the only free chair before Stedman's polished and gleaming mahogany desk. "Have a seat. Sheriff Baker has a few questions for you."

Gavin sat down slowly as Stedman seated himself in the big, red plush chair behind his desk. Sheriff Baker sat next to Gavin, lean and tall and all khaki. He held a small notepad, an apologetic look on his face.

"Sorry to bother you, Mr. Patchett. Imagine you're pretty busy this time of day. A few questions and I'll be on my way."

Gavin nodded, feeling numb, disconnected, and slightly nauseous. "No problem. Happy to help. Is this about . . . "

Baker nodded slowly. "Yes, the Pitals. I'm sure you've heard by now. Daniel Pital, a senior, was supposed to study at the library last night. 6:00 AM today, his mother called us because he'd never come home. We called the library, had them put us in touch with those who worked last night. According to them, he never showed. They never saw Daniel Pital, not once the whole night. Far as we can tell, *no one* has seen him since last night's football practice, which ended at 5:00 PM."

Baker paused, consulting his notebook as he continued. "We've taken statements from Mrs. Pital and her daughter about escalating ethnic persecution over the past few years, relating to 9/11. Mr. Pital was an actuary and had business at the Twin Towers that day. His body was never recovered."

Gavin nodded. He knew this from Emma's essays and journals and from the little bits and pieces she'd shared with him the times she'd visited his classroom at lunch to talk.

"Emma Pital was one of your students, and also your editor for two years on the school's literary journal. Did she ever mention anything about harassment or persecution to you?"

Gavin's stomach twisted and clenched, but he forced himself to maintain what he hoped was a neutral expression. "She occasionally hinted at some difficulties in her essays and journal entries," he lied, "but she never really told me directly that . . . "

"I see." Baker's pen scratched paper. "Mrs. Pital is making charges of vandalism, intimidation, harassment . . . and apparently, yesterday morning, an ethnic slur soaped on Daniel's truck windows."

Stedman's bland voice intruded. "Minor cases of school vandalism, involving mostly lockers and books. We've never had any suspects, really. And the incident with the truck occurred off campus, so . . . "

Gavin looked at Stedman but said nothing. He knew the score. Stedman wanted to avoid as much responsibility in this as possible, and God help him . . . Gavin would toe the line. But that didn't stop him from hating Stedman, and himself.

"I see." More pen scratching paper. "Last question Mr. Patchett, and then you're free to go. Emma Pital stayed home from school today. At 2:30 PM, Mrs. Pital called us, reporting that after waking from a nap, she'd discovered Emma and her car gone, Emma's cell phone left on the kitchen table. Mrs. Pital is afraid that . . . "

And suddenly Gavin felt cold.

Good luck with your writing . . .

"Mr. Patchett?"

fucking animals don't deserve to live

He swallowed. "Sorry. Fuzzed out there."

Baker nodded. "Understandable. Anyway. Where could Emma be? Did she ever share her suspicions of whom she thought was behind their harassment? Did you ever ask?"

Gavin opened his mouth.

But he had nothing to say.

***

Conner sat on the crumbling front steps of Old Bassler House, shivering in the cool dawn air. He'd already puked twice and he thought he might puke again, though all he probably had left to throw up was mucus and blood.

His guts twisted. He ground his teeth, somehow keeping it down, but it didn't matter, really. It wouldn't be long before John cleaned up and then Connor would have to see it all over again . . . the blood . . . and cuts . . .

Connor's stomach roiled. He swallowed, burped, then lurched sideways and dry-heaved into the bushes next to the front porch. Behind him, Bassler House's front door creaked open and heavy steps thumped out. "Damn. You still sick? Fuckin lightweight."

Connor heaved once more and wiped his mouth, shivering. John nudged him with one of his Timberlands. "Fag." A pause. "But so's Brian. Who woulda thought?"

Connor shivered, unwillingly thinking about last night. In a way, Brian was lucky. When he'd showed up and had seen Pital gagged and tied to a chair, he'd told John, "No way, man. This shit's over the edge." John had lost it, lit into Brian and beat the shit out of him. When he was through, he'd let Brian crawl away, threatening to "deal with him later."

But Brian was probably long gone by now. His mom was drunk most the time and his dad had split years ago. Who'd miss him? Brian had always hated this town, was always talking about loading up his Pinto and leaving. Usually he was all bluff. After last night, though . . .

John grunted. "Gonna be a good day."

Connor didn't want to, but he couldn't help it. He glanced up. John stood there smoking, looking blissfully calm and relaxed, clutching their father's service Beretta by its barrel. Thick gore coated its grip.

Connor looked away, staring into the trees along Bassler Road. When John pulled off his paper-bag mask last night, letting Pital see his face . . . then Connor knew, without a doubt, that Dan Pital was going to die.

Connor hadn't watched and he certainly hadn't helped. But he hadn't run, either, just stood staring into a corner, flinching with every wet thud of metal against flesh. And then, when John paused for a breath, he'd taunted, "Where's your daddy? Huh? Bet he's hidin out with Osama right now. Suckin him off. Bein a good little Taliban whore. That it? That what your daddy's doin?"

Pital wheezed, spat, then sneered, "If he is . . . then I pray to Allah that he's the one who killed your inbred, no good fucking white trash . . . "

John swore.

Metal cracked against bone, and Daniel Pital stopped speaking, forever.

Connor coughed, clearing his throat. "What now?"

"I'll wrap it up in some plastic, toss it in my truck. Burn it with this morning's sawdust an chippings at the mill before Cliff an Bobby Lee show. Maybe run it through the chipper first. Bury all the pieces deep, stoke the burner high . . . it'll be white hot by noon. There'll be nothin left by the time anyone comes lookin."

Connor sat there and hugged himself, squeezing tightly, rubbing his upper arms in an effort to warm himself against the cold, damp morning chill. It didn't work, though, and somehow deep inside he knew a part of him would never feel warm, ever again.

"What about his truck?"

"Take the plates off, skip school an take it to that salvage place in Boonville, pronto. I'll call Cletus; get somethin arranged for this afternoon. Get some good cash for it, I bet." John turned and glared at him. "Take the back roads, dipshit. Don' get caught."

With that, he spun and thumped back inside Bassler House. Connor sat there and shivered, knowing he had to leave soon, because he didn't want to be here when John loaded up his truck.

***

And now Emma blinks, her temples throbbing. She touches her forehead, hand shaking, and finds a sticky wetness at the hairline. She blinks again and opens her eyes.

More pain.

Her brain pounds, swollen too big for her skull. She tries to cry out but only dry, shuddering gasps come.

She looks out the truck's window, wondering where she is, what's happened . . . but then she sees the wrinkled CHEVY on the crumpled tailgate of a truck plowed into a telephone pole . . .

Dan's truck.

The one she rammed from behind.

She glances down at the loose ring on her finger and anger washes away her pain. She looks around for a weapon. The hammer's not good enough now, she needs . . .

There. On the cab floor, where John dropped it.

The gun.

She reaches down, ignoring the hot pain stabbing

her side and grabs the gun off the floor. She straightens and slams the door with her throbbing shoulder while she clicks the handle.

Stuck.

Warped by the crash.

She jerks the handle and slams the door again. With a screech it pops open, spilling her out onto the asphalt, face-first. She barely catches herself before cracking her chin against the pavement.

And she lays there for a minute, shuddering, her arms and legs rubbery and weak, twitching. At first nothing seems to work, but then she hears it: sirens. They're far away but nearing fast. Someone called the police. Mom or someone else, but they're too late because she's going to finish this, *now*.

Life shoots through her.

Her calves twitch and she crawls forward onto her knees, staggers upright and lurches forward, gun clenched tight.

The truck's driver door . . .

Dan's truck

. . . hangs open. There's spastic movement inside, hands flailing. Sirens howl closer, now. She has to move faster. And somehow she makes it to the truck . . .

Dan's truck

. . . before the driver can get out.

She switches the gun to her other hand. It doesn't matter which she uses, or that she's never fired a gun before. She'll be too close to miss. She steadies herself with a hand flat on the truck's cab . . .

Dan's truck

. . . and leans inside the open window.

There he is.

Blinking slowly.

Hands weakly tugging at his seat belt, mouth opening and closing silently, blood streaming from both nostrils. His chest looks wrong, rumpled beneath his seat belt. His legs, twisted at odd angles, lie still.

The sirens come closer.

She stares into his white eyes. He blinks and grimaces, tries to speak but says nothing.

Everything inside her goes away. She raises the Beretta and plants its muzzle to his forehead. His eyes widen and with the faintest movement . . .

He nods.

She pulls the trigger.

The blast echoes in the cab.

His head jerks away, which is good, because all she can see is the small, ragged entry wound on his temple.

She steps back and realizes the pain's gone. There's nothing left inside her, now.

She drops the pistol.

Sirens roar up with squealing tires.

She kneels and bends her face to the ground. She doesn't know if she's facing east or not, but that doesn't matter anymore.

Because Ramadan is over.

THURSDAY EVENING

Gavin sipped from his whiskey. Its ice had long since melted, leaving it lukewarm, tasting thin and flat. No matter, it did the job, all the same.

He had some leave time coming. He thought it

would be a good idea to spend most of it drunk. Better than thinking about . . .

He took another swig.

Well.

Better than thinking about anything, really.

His plan wasn't working very well, however. Sure, he was shitfaced. But he hadn't stopped thinking yet, *couldn't* stop thinking, of what he could've done, or said.

And hadn't.

Also, he felt like something was missing, felt like he had something he should do, but he just couldn't seem to figure out what . . .

His burning and tired eyes focused on the small digital numbers on his DVR, atop his black and mute television, which read 6:00 PM.

His mind churned. What day was it?

End of the month.

Ramadan.

He tipped his head back, emptied his glass, then pushed himself standing. He weaved a bit until he steadied, then walked with careful, drunken steps to the middle of his apartment. Best as he could, he faced east.

Then knelt.

It was sundown.

So he prayed. To what he didn't know. And it was a pitiful gesture, but it was all he had.

3.

I LEAN BACK against the booth's thin leather cushions and pull my hands away from the journal, staring for a moment at Gavin's elegant script. The words themselves seem to shiver and twitch across the page.

I look up at Gavin, who's nonchalantly devouring the stack of blueberry pancakes he ordered while I was reading.

My mouth opens, but nothing comes out.

Fortunately, Gavin speaks for both of us, after swallowing a forkful of syrup-drenched pancakes. "That whole thing was horrible, and I feel awful that it took a tragedy like that to sober me up. But after everything died down, when I finally dried out . . . I knew things had to change. I haven't had a drink since."

I reach toward the journal but don't touch its pages. It's as if I'm afraid of something happening to me if I touch it, which is ridiculous. It's only a journal. Paper bound by a leather cover.

That's all.

"You wrote this. After it happened?"

He reaches for his glass of orange juice,

compliments of the waitress, takes a sip and says, "A week after I threw my booze out, I knew I had to write it. So I did."

My throat feels dry and tight, my forehead warm for some reason. "Why? For self-therapy? Closure? You turned what happened into a story so you could . . . deal with it? Get it out of your system?"

Gavin lays his fork and knife down and folds his hands. "What do you think? Better yet, what do you *believe*?"

I look into his eyes, a faint sense of vertigo stealing over me. "That you made most of this up. Gleaned it from whatever you knew about Emma's situation before the incident and from whatever you learned from the news and Fitzy and Father Ward afterward. Except . . . "

He raises an eyebrow. "Except?"

I release a breath I didn't know I'd been holding. "Except a lot of those details—Bassler House, Dan Pital's class ring, how John tried to rape Emma—we *didn't* release to the press, to *anyone*. I'd only been Sheriff for a few months. County Sheriff Mitch Rhodes took point, handled the PR, keeping a tight lid on everything, especially the more shocking details, the details in *your* story. And . . . "

"And?"

"The body. Daniel Pital's body." I comb my hair with my fingers. "Holy Mother of God, Gavin. Emma literally hasn't said ONE word about what happened to Dan's body. Is . . . is this . . . *can* it be true?"

Gavin sighs deeply, picks up his knife and fork but doesn't begin eating right away. "Something happened to me about five years ago. It ended my writing career but it changed me, too. Changed me inside, *in* my head. And that's why I started drinking so much, even as I somehow managed to earn my teaching certificate and land a job back here. Somehow, deep inside, I knew if I sobered up, started *writing* sober . . . "

He points at the journal with his knife. "Somehow, I knew I'd eventually start writing stories like *that*. Stories with truth in them."

Feeling a little dizzy, maybe even feverish, I shake my head. "I don't understand. The truth of *what*?"

"Things." He shrugs and says, "Read the next story, about what happened to me five years ago, because when I finished Emma's story and realized what was happening to me, I wrote about that too, trying to sort things out."

I stare at the book, a chill creeping down my spine. "You mean . . . there are more stories in here? Written by you?"

Cutting a hunk out of his pancakes, he says, "More stories, yes. Written by me?"

He stuffs a forkful into his mouth, chews thoughtfully, then whispers, "Honestly? I'm not sure . . . "

WAY STATION

IT WAS QUESTCON, New Hampshire's largest
SpecFic convention. Attendees packed the main
lounge of Portsmouth's Holiday Inn, bunching up in
clots around tables and chairs and the bar, chatting
with old friends, hitting up new ones. Con veterans
worked the scene, happy to be among colleagues and
friends. Younger, more inexperienced folks bounced
nervously about, balancing between worshipful awe
and their overwhelming desire to be "noticed" by peers
and role models, and amongst them drifted fans asking
for signatures, wondering respectfully (most of the
time) when their next book or comic book would hit
the stores.

It was a full house, everyone busily engaged and
enjoying themselves and, Jim Goersky couldn't help
but feel, glancing at him and Gavin Patchett from the
corner of their eyes.

"Listen, Franklin," Gavin snapped into his cell
phone, "the distribution sucks and you know it. Why
the *hell* weren't there more copies of *Forever War* at
the Barnes & Noble here in Portsmouth? They only
had five in stock!"

"Careful Gav," Jim muttered as they navigated

through the crowded lounge. "Don't go poking a tiger with a stick, okay?"

Gavin ignored him and continued. "Hell, Franklin, the answer's simple. My sales are down because there are NO COPIES OF MY BOOKS, ANYWHERE."

Jim glanced around as he and Gavin approached the sliding glass doors at the rear of the lounge, which lead to a mezzanine overlooking the hotel's front parking lot. An embarrassed flush rose past his collar. He nodded and smiled weakly at an acquisitions editor he knew standing at the bar. She gave them a look, and it wasn't a *good* look, at all; more like a pitying, *you sorry bastard* kind of look.

"Gav," Jim whispered as they weaved past tables and chairs, "remember that joke of yours? That my main job is making sure you don't act like an ass? You're kinda not letting me do it."

Gavin frowned and waved him off. Still complaining, he tugged the sliding glass door open and they stepped out into the biting winter air on the thankfully empty mezzanine.

Brittle wind nipped at Jim's skin. He turned up his blazer's collar, stuffed his hands into his pockets and hunched his shoulders against the cold.

"Listen," Gavin continued, his tone cutting, "that's shit and you know it. I *never* had this distribution problem with the first three books. I showed up at that Barnes & Noble this afternoon and looked like an idiot. My table was almost empty. *No*, it doesn't matter how many people actually showed up, it's the *principle* of the thing. I'm one of your bestsellers. That's *not* how you treat a bestseller."

They stopped at the mezzanine's railing. The

Holiday Inn sat on a slight hill above the surrounding area and Jim gazed out over the parking lot, past the interstate to the city streets: luminous rivers of headlights, neon signs, and streetlights. The distance muffled the city's sounds and with just a little effort, Jim could imagine he was looking upon a far off, ethereal world.

"What the hell is that supposed to mean? I'm not as *focused*? What the hell do you mean by that?"

Jim looked at Gavin, who leaned against the mezzanine's railing, cell phone in one hand, a glass of whiskey in the other. Jim tried to remember just how many drinks Gavin had consumed so far and realized he'd lost count hours ago.

"That's bullshit. You've published plenty of science fiction, so marketing mine shouldn't be . . . not as good as the first two? What the hell? Then why'd you publish it and offer me a contract for two more, you pompous son of a bitch?"

Jim winced. Gavin only acted this way when drinking, and he'd been drinking a lot the past few months. A few more beers than usual with dinner. A glass of whiskey next to his iBook when writing. Gavin's fully stocked liquor cabinet had seen quite an upswing in use, recently.

Jim shook his head. Truth was, Gavin had reached a critical mass and was barreling toward a threshold. And, like many authors Jim had worked with over the years this meant only one thing: *trouble*. A train was roaring down the tracks and Gavin seemed pretty content to stand in its path and stare it down like the stubborn son of a bitch that he was.

"*Yes* I've got a Myspace. And a Facebook Fan Page

and a Facebook personal page. I'm Linked In, Foursquared and Twittered to hell. Set that all up myself thanks very much, with no help from you."

"I did that," Jim whispered, tapping his chest, "me."

Gavin waved a preoccupied *I know, hold on a minute* at Jim, scowling. "You're right. We *do* need to meet. Jim'll put together some numbers on how much money I've made you the past few years . . . "

Jim clapped a hand to his forehead and groaned. *Dammit, Gavin. What the hell?*

" . . . and we can discuss how much you want this next book . . . "

Which you haven't even started yet, you fucking idiot.

" . . . and whether or not I'm even going to give it to Hammer-Fiske, or instead maybe approach Titan or TOR, take them up on the deals they've been offering for *years*. See you Tuesday."

With that, he flipped his phone shut, stuffed it into his jeans pocket and took a deep swig of whiskey. He emptied the glass and met Jim's gaze defiantly. "What?"

Jim struggled to keep his tone light. "Well. *That* went well. Hey listen, remember our conversation on the drive up here, about being subtle with Franklin? Just wondering . . . what does the word 'subtle' mean to *you*, exactly?"

Gavin's face stiffened. "Don't start, Jim."

"Hey, hey." Jim raised his hands. "I'm on your side. You know that. I agree with you, Hammer-Fiske *is* mishandling this project. But," he folded his arms, leaning back against the mezzanine's cold railing, "if you'll remember, I told you three years ago you'd be better off sending *Forever War* to either TOR, Titan, Baen or Pocket Books, someone with an established name in science fiction."

Gavin shook his glass and looked into it, as if searching for answers there. "Hammer-Fiske has published four science fiction novels in the past five years. They should know how the hell to market *my* science fiction novel."

Jim sighed.

Seemed he'd been doing that a lot lately because Gavin had done nothing but ignore him. "Those other novels were commercial techno-thrillers, video game and television series tie-ins. Not classic, epic space operas . . . which *Forever War* is. It's a great novel. You'll get no argument from me. But they don't really know what to do with it, which I warned you about *three years ago.*"

"Fine. We'll solve that Tuesday morning, or we'll bid Franklin and Hammer-Fiske sayonara."

Jim clucked his teeth with his tongue and looked away into the snow-speckled night, debating what to say next. Apparently, Gavin wasn't *that* drunk, because he asked in a tight voice, "Hey. You're not telling me something. What is it?"

Jim fought with himself for several more seconds, then said regretfully, "Listen. Before you march into the Pinnacle Building Tuesday morning ready to kick ass, you gotta know about the rumors floating around the office."

Gavin's eyes narrowed.

And even though Jim knew Gavin wasn't *really* dangerous or violent, he couldn't help but feel a little threatened. "And?"

Jim took a deep breath, released it slowly and said, "Word is Franklin's pissed about your public bitching."

"*Bitching?*" Gavin's face reddened in the pale glow of the mezzanine's halogen lights. "But you agreed with me!"

Jim shot Gavin a look, deciding it was time to show some claws of his own. "I do. But you *have* been bitching, for a long time and very loudly." He raised an eyebrow. "How about all your blogs, Gavin? All sorts of folks read them. Your fans, casual readers, genre fans, industry-people. My personal favorite? The one entitled, 'Hammer-Fiske Hammer-Heads and Other Publishing Assholes.'"

Gavin smiled weakly. "Oh, come on. Every author's gotta complain about his publisher now and then. It's how we maintain our street cred."

Jim shrugged. "Well, Franklin's been reading up and I can't say he agrees."

Gavin smirked and patted Jim's shoulder good-naturedly. "Like I'm really worried. They'll slap me on the wrist, and then . . . "

All right, Jim thought. *Enough screwing around. Time to drop the bomb.*

"They're *done* with you, Gav. They're calling your bluff before you can even make it. They want to terminate *this* contract, all your other contracts and sue for breach of contract because they *know* you haven't even started the next book you owe them, the next book that's *three months late.* They want to wash their hands of you, completely."

Gavin gaped at him for several wordless seconds until he finally managed, "That's *crazy.* I'm one of their bestsellers!"

"But you're not Stephen King. Or Peter Straub or

Dean Koontz or someone with a rabid fan base, like Brian Keene. Not a flashy newcomer, either. You're a burned-out mid-list author with a big fat drinking problem to boot."

Gavin's eyes flashed. "Hey. That's not *fair*. You've got no right to dig me because I enjoy an occasional drink now and then."

Jim snorted. He was dangerously close to tripping Gavin's hot-wire but he didn't care. "Sure, you enjoy an occasional drink. Occasionally at lunch and dinner. At parties and conventions. While you write. Before and after you write. Before going to bed. Occasionally. At all these occasions, all the time."

"You're not my mother, Jim, so stop bitching at me like I'm some snot-nosed–"

"Gavin. *Listen*."

Jim's urgent tone brought Gavin up short. Thinking this could very well be his last chance, Jim plunged ahead. "You're right. I'm not your mother. I'm your friend and your agent. So not only do I care about you as a person, I care about you as a professional. I don't want you to throw away your career, and you're *this* close," he held up his thumb and forefinger, spread an inch, "this close."

He paused, folded his arms and said with as much concern as he could muster, "I want to help, Gav. *Let* me help. Please."

A shadow passed over Gavin's face.

And Jim saw an emotion he'd never seen in Gavin's eyes before: *fear*.

Gavin looked away into the night, clenching his glass so tightly his knuckles whitened. "You can't help, Jim," he rasped, "no one can."

Jim sighed. "You're destroying yourself. You know that, right? You walk into Franklin's office Tuesday morning with a list of demands, you're done."

Still not looking at him, Gavin murmured, "You won't be there?"

Jim shook his head. He felt sorry in a way, but he was also out of patience. "If I back you on this, I can kiss a lot of *my* street-cred good-bye."

"If you were my friend," Gavin whispered, "you would."

"I'm sorry, Gav. This is one grenade I'm not jumping on." He patted Gavin's shoulder lightly. "Go up to the room and sleep it off. We'll hash this thing out tomorrow on the ride home. Okay?"

He paused, letting the silence draw out between them, but when Gavin said nothing, he said, "Night, Gav," turned and walked away.

***

Gavin's Prius flew along North Portsmouth I-95, far too fast for the icy conditions and his altered state. His eyes itched and the dark road swam before his eyes. His stomach glowed with warm liquor. More than once, he'd caught himself nodding off before lurching awake, heart pounding after he'd almost veered into the median.

This is stupid. Get off the road before you kill yourself or someone else. Go back to the hotel and sleep it off.

This is crazy . . . it's fucking suicide.

The steering wheel jerked as the right front tire hit a patch of ice. For a second, he felt the vehicle fishtail. Cursing, he lifted his foot off the gas, lightly tapped the brake and brought the car back under control. He sighed and wiped his tired eyes with the heel of his palm.

After Jim had left him on the Holiday Inn's cold, wind-blown mezzanine, a crippling sense of loathing had overwhelmed him. He *was* destroying himself, ruining everything he loved about writing. Deep inside, he knew Jim was right. He'd treated everyone miserably, biting the hands that had fed him, stomping on the feet of those who'd helped him into the writing world. However, he'd stumbled on. Drinking, back-biting and burning every single bridge behind him, seemingly hell-bent on self-destruction. It had been that way for so long that he could hardly remember how it was before.

Confronted with this stark truth he'd fled the Con, not speaking to anyone. He'd gotten into his Prius, squealed out of the parking lot, roaring onto the highway, driving . . . nowhere.

Nowhere.

"Screw this," he mumbled, "I need some music." He fumbled with the radio, jerking the wheel in the process, causing the Prius to jink back and forth. After several shaky attempts, he finally punched the music on.

Instantly, the loud twang of country music filled the car.

"Oh, *hell* no."

He pressed 'search' for several seconds until he found some loud but at least tolerable techno. "There," he grunted, tapping the steering wheel, "that's a beat you can drive to."

With the bass pounding he fled down the ice-slicked highway, his ego taking over and pushing aside his self-loathing as he hummed to the music. Twenty minutes away from the Holiday Inn had put distance between him and his fears; making them vague, indistinct.

"When I get back to New York, I'll cut down the booze," he chattered as he drove, "get my shit together. I'll sleep it off, call Franklin, sort him out, or I'll take my act elsewhere."

Yeah.

Right.

And where exactly will you take it, dumbass? You heard Jim. He's not going to back your play and if you hit Franklin with this you're just gonna get your ass handed to you.

You're destroying yourself.

And you don't even care.

"No I'm not," he muttered, reaching to turn the music up louder, "I'm doing *just fine.*"

It happened in a heartbeat.

He missed the radio's volume button.

Leaned forward to try again, his grip on the steering wheel loosening as he rounded a curve to the left that banked slightly, and the car's front wheels hit a patch of ice. The steering wheel jerked out of Gavin's numb grip. He grabbed the wheel with both hands, but it was too late.

Panic filled him as the Prius swished back and forth, and in his frenzy he slammed on the brakes. The car shuddered and slowed just for a moment, then the steering wheel jerked to the right, the guardrail looming in the car's headlights. Gavin twisted the wheel one last time . . .

a heartbeat

a breath
impact
screeching metal, roaring engine, him screaming

His forehead slammed into the air bag exploding from the steering wheel. The world spun away into darkness and as he struggled on the edge of unconsciousness, he realized dimly he'd ricocheted off the guardrail and was now spinning across the highway toward the median.

Tires skidded and gravel crunched on the highway's shoulder. The engine revved, the car thumped off-road and for a moment, he flew.

A final jerk, a rending of metal.

Then . . .

***

. . . darkness. Cloying, suffocating darkness everywhere, so perfect and total that even though he felt his muscles and tendons work and flex, he couldn't be sure they were really there. The dark felt alive, liquid, pressing against him . . .

swallowing him

And in the distance, whispers uttered secret, unknowable things. He turned but saw nothing, only more darkness. His throat constricted, panic swelling, and his teeth grinding as the whispers came and went, came and went . . .

mene, mene
tekel upharsin
There.
A light.

Flaring in the distance, piercing the darkness

around him. He glimpsed only lurching shadows in the flares but as each grew brighter, fragile hope blossomed in his heart.

And then he heard it.

A sliding beyond the dark.

Some awful thing waited for him out there, a beast hungering to tear the skin and muscle off his bones. He shuddered and crossed his arms over his chest, suddenly feeling cold.

A squelching behind him.

He whirled and scanned the dark but saw nothing, his mind struggling like an animal caught in a snare. Unreasoning terror filled him as he imagined some creature circling in the dark, primal fears painting an image of gleaming claws hungry for flesh . . .

Obsidian eyes.

Thick, mucus-slicked hide bristling with tiny hairs.

Soul-plundering teeth clicking in anticipation.

A voice screamed, shattering the silence with syllables that blasted his mind. Gavin clapped his hands over his ears but the booming voice set fire to his thoughts and as he collapsed to his knees, screaming, the words burned themselves onto his brain . . .

MENE, MENE!
TEKEL UPHARSIN!

Everything convulsed: himself, the darkness around him, his insides. He jerked and seized. The light exploded, the voices exploding into a wailing crescendo . . .

MENE!
TEKEL UPHARSIN!

And Gavin collapsed to his knees alongside Route 95, North Portsmouth.

***

He looked up. Intermittent highway lights blazed in the darkness. For several seconds he remained there along the highway, kneeling, disoriented. Memories of that dark place and the thing in the darkness with the screaming voice faded quickly. He'd gotten into an accident, had hit his head—on the damn airbag, of all things—and must have hallucinated it all.

He struggled to breathe, the cold air burning his throat. Gradually, he managed to slow his gasps, taking deep, controlled breaths, and an uneasy calm settled over him.

He looked up and down the highway and saw nothing. Both I-95 North and South faded into snow-speckled darkness. The roads were empty. Not a vehicle in sight.

He looked over his shoulder and saw his wrecked Prius, its front fender crumpled, the driver's side door hanging open. A pair of crooked, stumbling footprints led to where he knelt at the highway's shoulder.

He closed his eyes.

And for a moment, he remembered.

Steel shrieking, tires squealing, the steering wheel spinning in his hands, the guardrail jumping out in the car's headlights, his forehead slamming into the expanding airbag . . .

He shivered, opened his eyes and touched his forehead, feeling a warm bump near the hairline. He winced as he remembered again his head striking the airbag, realizing with a deep chill he was fortunate not to be lying unconscious inside his wrecked Prius, in this cold.

I remember the accident. I remember spinning across the highway into the median. I can't believe someone coming behind me didn't hit me . . . but somehow . . . somehow, I got out of the car and stumbled here . . .

A thought struck him. With renewed vigor he stuck his hand into his front jeans pocket, grasping for his cell phone. Relief filled him at the touch of cool plastic . . . a relief that faded when he opened the cell and was greeted with a red X instead of service bars.

No service.

Why the hell not? You can get service everywhere these days.

But there it was, nonetheless. Didn't matter how high he held it up, waved it, walking back and forth along the snowy highway that red X remained, mocking him and his efforts to find a signal. After about ten minutes more he cursed, snapped the phone shut and stuffed it into his pocket, wondering what the hell he was going to do next.

He looked up to scan the highway again and this time saw what looked like an old, run-down diner on the other side: a vintage roadside joint, a trailer mounted on a cinderblock foundation. Above the diner, an old florescent light flickered *Al's Eats*. The place blazed hospitable light; offering him a sliver of hope, but also the slightest touch of dread.

Because he saw no one inside.

Nor did he see any vehicles parked outside. He

supposed some could be parked out back, but even so . . . despite the light streaming from its windows, the place seemed empty, dead still.

And an idea tickled the back of his mind that he didn't remember seeing signs for a diner anywhere along the highway he'd just traveled.

Of course not, dumbass. You were half-drunk and you don't know the area.

A reasonable explanation, one that didn't make him feel any better. However, if the place *was* inexplicably abandoned, light meant electricity, which at least meant warmth and maybe a working phone. Best case scenario the phone worked, the diner's owner was out back cleaning, and he'd not only call Jim (who'd hopefully forgive him for his behavior and come get him) but he'd also get a burger and fries and a Pepsi. Worst case scenario, if it was empty—which didn't make sense with the lights on—at least he'd have shelter against the frigid wind.

With that in mind, he moved toward the diner. But as he stepped onto the road, a familiar sensation pulsed through him. He wavered there, on the highway's edge, staring at the diner, a harsh, guttural voice echoing in his ears . . .

mene, mene
tekel upharsin

He stood there, foot suspended ridiculously like a marionette, cocking his head, listening intently. Part of him strained to hear the dread whisper, convinced it was important that he understood its meaning.

mene . . .

But the voice faded, as well as the strange, dreadful urging. Now he heard nothing, save the empty sighing of a winter's wind.

A little disgusted at his dread fancy, he snorted and trotted across the highway toward the empty diner.

***

For several seconds after the wooden door screeched shut behind him, Gavin stood in the middle of the diner's thick, oppressive silence. All the lights blazed with homely warmth, but no one stood behind the counter and no one bused the tables or swept the floors.

"Hello? Anyone home?" He winced at his squeaking voice and swallowed, injecting a heartier tone as he bellowed, "Got a paying customer out here, *Al.*"

Nothing but silence, and perhaps most disturbing was its quality. There was no echo, as if he'd spoken into a hungry vacuum that swallowed his voice.

He passed a cursory glance around, seeing nothing unusual. A chipped Formica counter ran the diner's length on one side. Booths with dull, faded red leather cushions lined the other. Along the counter stood evenly spaced stools with red, round cushions that looked like gigantic push-buttons on a toy radio. Behind the counter gaped a rectangular window peering into the kitchen beyond, through which a short order cook could slide plates and trays, presumably ringing a bell and barking out orders in a clichéd, gravelly voice.

He stood on his tiptoes and peered through the

rectangular window for a glimpse of the kitchen, but he couldn't make out much past a row of what looked like silver heavy-duty refrigerators. He gave up and turned toward the entrance, spying an old cash register sitting on a podium next to the door. But when he craned his neck, looking closer, he saw the empty cash drawer hanging out.

He sighed and took a few circular steps, eyeing the place some more. He'd dined in plenty of these joints over the years. He remembered college road trips and more vividly, two years' worth of weekends in similar establishments as he chased stories all over the Adirondacks for The Utica Times-Herald, covering everything from human interest stories, fall festivals, school board meetings, court cases, and local high school sporting events. He'd been paid a meager freelancer's rate but he'd been young, fresh from college and working as a sorter at the local can and bottle recycling center, and his weekend reporting trips had been necessary breaths of fresh air. He'd been writing and getting paid for it, which had felt like a small slice of Heaven at the time.

Also, he'd eaten in plenty of these places during his book tour for his first hardcover, *Shades of Darkness*. He especially remembered one diner just outside Philadelphia, the tour's last stop. He and Jim (Gavin was one of his first clients) had sat at the counter, eating burgers and fries. The book tour had been a moderate success. He'd hawked considerable copies of his first novel, made some good contacts, and had a good time.

He remembered sitting at the counter of this Philadelphian diner, chatting with Jim, when the diner's owner—a large, forty-something, barrel-chested man named Hank—approached them and rumbled, "Get ya dessert?"

Jim smiled, shaking his head, Gavin saying, "No, thanks. It was fantastic. Not sure I could fit dessert in, honestly."

Hank accepted the compliment with a brisk nod. Instead of drifting back to check on other customers, he asked gruffly, "Couldn't help over-hearin you fellas talkin." He nodded at Gavin. "You a writer?"

Gavin smiled like a mindless idiot. *Damn*, he thought to himself, *I guess so*. Aloud, he'd replied, "I am. Just finished my first book tour, and I'm heading to my hometown to speak at my alma mater's graduation."

Hank grunted. "Where'dja grow up?"

"Clifton Heights, New York. In the Adirondacks, north of Utica."

"Huh. You usta be country folk?"

Gavin smiled at memories of running through the forest causing mischief, diving off his best friend's lakeside dock and lazy afternoons fishing, catching nothing but sunburns, bug bites and a few puny blue gills for their troubles. "Yes sir, I was."

"Well now. I heard you boys talkin about novels an all when ya first sat down. I expected ya to be pains in my ass." He paused, swiped the counter with his dingy towel and pronounced confidently, "Yer not, though. Seem like stand-up guys."

"*Not* a pain in the ass," Gavin remarked, grinning, "I think that's the nicest thing anyone's ever said about me."

Jim chuckled. "Don't look at me. You've *always* been a pain in my ass."

Gavin popped him lightly on the shoulder. To Hank, he said, "You read much?"

The big man shrugged. "Some. I talk rough, but that's just my way. I read, yeah."

Gavin grabbed the satchel sitting on the stool next to him, unzipped it and rummaged through its contents. "What do you read, Hank?"

Hank smiled. "Favor Robert E. Howard an Dashall Hammit myself."

From his bag Gavin pulled a black and white hardcover book, a picture of an adolescent's shadowed profile on the cover. "Hank, this was one of the best meals I've ever eaten, and you're a pretty stand-up guy yourself . . . " he held out the novel to the short-order cook, "I'd like you to have this. It's my last copy, and though it's not Howard or Hammit, I think you'll find enough action in here to suit you."

Hank accepted the book with an air of rustic grace. "That's good of ya. I'm sure I'll enjoy it." He laid the book on the counter. "Mind signin it?"

"No problem." Gavin snagged a pen from his shirt pocket, opened the book to its first page and dictated while he wrote, "'To Hank—best cook in Pennsylvania, who called me 'not a pain in the ass.'" He signed his name with a flourish and returned the book to the cook.

Hank accepted it almost reverently. "That's *awfully* good of ya, sir." He looked at the book with a grin and then said, "You come back through anytime ya want. Dinner's on the house." He nodded, tucked the book under his arm and moved toward his other guests.

And in that abandoned diner, Gavin was still

reminiscing on the memory when his eyes fell on the hardcover book sitting on the empty front counter.

***

His heart stuttered.

It wasn't really a book. It only *looked* like one in the dark, and . . .

He frowned. It *was* getting dark. Odd, because moments ago the diner blazed with light. As he looked around he realized with cold shock that it had gotten much darker than it had been minutes before, the diner's lights dimming, as if on the verge of blacking out entirely.

He looked back at the book on the counter.

No, that's stupid. It's not *a book. It's an account register; a ledger . . . but it's not a book, no way.*

But as he eased closer to the counter he couldn't deny what he saw. The object looked just the right size for a hardcover novel. He squinted, trying to make out the author's name or the book's title . . .

No.

No, his stubborn mind protested, *it can't be.* But as he moved closer, his unbelieving eyes discerned an adolescent boy's gray profile, features shrouded by darkness, and printed across the bottom was: *Gavin Patchett.*

One of the story's main protagonists, Michael Lockenstein, was an autistic savant whose prophetic visions had become entangled in a serial murder case. Hence the book's title—*Shades of Darkness*—because it described the different shades of darkness the boy had endured his entire life.

His first novel.

And deeply personal, based in part on an autistic

boy he'd known growing up. While he'd written it, he'd truly felt alive, as though he'd been accomplishing something important, something *real*. He'd enjoyed writing all his novels well enough but he hadn't felt the same since that first one, like his writing was making a difference.

He lifted a trembling hand.

And with an odd combination of loathing and need he flicked open the book's cover, revealing the inscription: *To Hank—best cook in Pennsylvania, who called me 'not a pain in the ass'.*

He jerked back. "What the *hell*?"

Something scraped the floor behind him.

A footstep, approaching.

Gavin spun and saw a fifteen-year-old boy standing about ten feet away, dressed in jeans and a white T-shirt with a checkered red and black flannel over it. He wore an open winter jacket and his feet sported ragged, mud-splattered Nikes. The boy's hands were jammed into his pockets. Unruly brown hair spilled across his forehead and clear blue eyes pierced Gavin with a disconcerting stare.

"All right," Gavin rasped, "who the hell are you?"

The boy remained silent for several seconds, staring at him with those burning blue eyes until he finally said, "You *know* who I am."

Gavin stared, speechless, a dread kind of understanding tickling the back of his mind . . . but he pushed it away. He didn't believe it. He *wouldn't* believe it.

There was just no way.

"Hell I do. Maybe you look a little like . . . but no. *Fuck* no. I don't care *what* you say, you're NOT him."

The boy shrugged, as if his disbelief meant nothing. "But I AM a messenger, here to remind you of things. *Important* things."

Suddenly, the situation was too bizarre for Gavin to swallow anymore: an empty diner on an empty highway, a book that couldn't be here, this boy (who couldn't be who he looked like, couldn't be) glaring at him like *he* was the child, those voices lingering at the edge of his mind . . .

mene, mene
tekel, upharsin

He shook his head. "What the hell are you talking about? Never mind. I don't *care*. What I want is to get out of here, flag down a cop or a trucker or someone and . . . "

He took a step forward.

And *pain* twisted in his chest, cut by a phantom, burning knife. He doubled over and convulsed as a terrible vibration pulsed through him, jolting him to the bone.

The sensation passed.

He collapsed to his knees, gagging, drooling through clenched teeth.

"You don't understand," the boy remarked calmly. "There are no police, no cars to flag down here. There's only you, I and the *Other*."

An instinctual kind of panic crept along the edge of Gavin's thoughts. He looked up at the strange boy and croaked, "What do you mean? Where are we?"

The boy tilted his head, his face blank, his eyes unfeeling. "An in-between place. A crack between worlds. A way station, of sorts."

Gavin loathed his next words but that hysterical panic was crawling ever closer. "What are you saying? Is this . . . "

"Hell?" The boy's eyes hardened, looking inexplicably old and ancient. "A place you couldn't *possibly* begin to fathom. Especially considering you don't believe it exists."

It was desperately sad, some part of Gavin realized, that his only defense was petulant sarcasm. "C'mon. I'm a midlist genre author. Pretty sure I know what hell is."

Almost instantly another burning seizure slammed him against the floor, jerking his arms and legs as he kicked and flailed in agony. It passed as quickly as before, and he collapsed face-first, hacking and coughing. His arms weak and rubbery, somehow he crawled onto his knees and elbows, and in between ragged gasps he croaked, "So. Am . . . am I dead? Is . . . is that it?"

The boy drew himself up and clasped his hands behind him, as a lecturing professor might. "No. Not *yet.*"

Gavin's response was cut off as he shrieked to another muscle-shaking jolt that throttled his spine while he flopped and kicked and jerked.

"You're here because you need to *choose.*"

The seizure released him. Pressing his forehead into the diner's cool floor, he mumbled, "Choose? Choose *what*? What the *hell* are you talking about?"

He breathed.

And amazingly enough, the shock didn't return, so he lurched upright, sat back on his haunches and wiped his mouth on his forearm. "What is this? Some shitty, low budget version of *A Christmas Carol?*"

A burning look from the boy and all his sarcasm died. "You're here to decide your destiny, Gavin Patchett."

Gavin scowled despite the lingering pain in his guts. "Destiny? I don't *have* a destiny. I'm a writer. A *genre* writer." He wiped his mouth on his arm again. "No destiny here. Sorry."

The boy remained still, his blue eyes boring into Gavin's. "You will choose today, Gavin Patchett, what you will serve: Order or Chaos. Light or Dark. Purpose . . . or the Other."

Gavin shook his head. "Other? What 'Other?'" He staggered to his feet, but even though he towered over the kid, he felt dwarfed by an incomprehensible presence and regarded the boy warily.

The boy's eyes pulsed. "You know the Other. You've served It most of your adult life. But now It wants more. It wants you as Its Herald."

Ludicrous. The stuff of cheap horror flicks or badly written End Times novels. However, the boy's words struck a curious resonance in him, and a memory surfaced, of a massive and inhuman *thing* slithering in the dark . . .

mene, mene
tekel upharsin

And that's when he heard it.

A liquid flopping. He whirled, eyes searching the dimness . . . as *something* squelched wetly behind the counter. He leapt back, fearing It would come after him, even though he had no idea what It was.

The slithering sounds swelled, accompanied once

more by that throbbing voice, which evoked primordial fears as each unintelligible syllable pounded against Gavin's brain, over and over . . .

mene, mene, tekel upsahrin, mene, mene . . .

"What *is* that?"

The words slammed into him, turning his insides to jelly. He whirled on the boy, desperately shouting, "*What is that?*"

The boy stood calm and still, and somehow his voice echoed above the chanting. "That's the Other. It has many names. The Destroyer of Worlds. Eater of Light. Crawling Chaos."

Ice-cold fear filled his belly and his bladder twitched. "What does it want?"

"It wants to *use* you. You have a gift It desires above all else and It wants to make you Its Herald."

Still holding his hands over his ears—which didn't matter, because that voice kept echoing over and over, inside his head—Gavin shouted, "Herald for *what*?"

The boy's eyes glowed with blue fire, his countenance transformed into something unearthly. "The coming destruction of all there is."

"Why? Why *me*?"

The boy cocked his head, frowning. "You're a writer. One who turns life into fiction, and fiction into life. What's spawned through your pen becomes life, comes *from* life. But you've forsaken your destiny, leaving yourself open to the Other's designs."

"*What* are you talking about? What destiny?"

The boy lifted his chin and gazed at him, daring a refutation of his claims. "To be a Witness. A Seer. An Oracle of things to come. You must chronicle these things for the Guardian, *not* the Other, so the

Guardian can protect the Threshold, so he will know how."

"The Threshold? The Guardian? Who the hell is . . . this is crazy! I'm a writer. I write fiction! I make shit up! None of it's real! *None* of it!"

The boy's voice dropped into a whisper that shook Gavin's insides. "It *is* real. All of it. So is everything else you are meant to write . . . if you *choose* to."

No.

It wasn't possible. Couldn't be.

A terrible understanding inside of him, however, told him *it was.*

"No," he whispered, not sure where his words came from, "please. I can't. I *just can't.* It's too hard. I'm too *afraid.* I tried to write about you once before, and I just can't . . . I *can't.*"

The boy shook his head. "It doesn't matter, Gavin Patchett. Because it's time.

"You must choose."

A sharp lashing cut the air.

Something thick and fleshy snagged Gavin's ankle and yanked his feet out from underneath him. He slammed down head-first, chin and chest hitting the floor. Salty blood filled his mouth as his teeth dug into his tongue.

And that voice chanted over and over . . .

mene, mene
tekel, upharsin

Close to screaming, Gavin looked over his shoulder at the thing, the tentacle wrapped around his ankle. A vision borne of nightmares, it throbbed and writhed with a muscular pulse. A dark, mottled green-brown, its hide bristled with thousands of tiny hairs, and as the tentacle tightened around his ankle, those hairs unbelievably pierced his pants and dug into his skin.

And at the tentacle's end, he saw curved hulks defying description, lined with rows of mad, glittering alien eyes. Its form continuously shifted as tentacles coiled and writhed above It in a serpentine halo.

Another tentacle whipped at him and Gavin cried out as it wrapped around his knee, hairs digging into his skin like rows of needle-sharp teeth, and like a fisherman tired of playing with its catch, It heaved and yanked Gavin toward It. He screamed, high and shrill, hands flailing along the floor, reaching, grabbing for anything . . .

. . . and he snagged the base of the cash register's stand. Even as the strain in his knees and hips intensified, somehow he wrapped his arms around the stand's base, anchoring himself.

Desperately he looked up and there was the boy, standing only a few feet from him, hands shoved into his pockets, his blue gaze cold and remote.

"Please! Please . . . *help me!*"

The boy raised an eyebrow. "Will you write what you *see*? Will you be a Witness for The Guardian, so he may protect The Threshold?"

He heard a rustling, dry sound, like a snake sliding through autumn leaves, and Gavin realized yet another fleshy arm was hurtling toward him. He kicked out with mad fright, his heart throbbing with both glee and disgust as his foot knocked away something hard and leathery. "Whatever! Just take me away . . . please!"

The boy squatted face to face with him, blue eyes

pulsing. "Have a care," he warned, "pledging your fealty will save you from ruination; but it won't save you from death or suffering. There is no 'safe path' to choose."

"I don't *understand*," Gavin whimpered. He heard more wriggling and squirming but another kick met only air as a third tentacle wrapped around his thigh. His shoulders creaked with the increasing strain and he reached deep inside, willing himself to hold on . . .

But he couldn't.

Arms shaking, he looked at the boy, his vision fading, dimming at the edges. "What do you want me to do?"

The boy gazed at him, his blue eyes filling Gavin with warmth. "Your gift is your writing. Your tool. Your *power*."

mene, mene! tekel upharsin!

And those horrible tentacles pulled harder. Terror suffused him as his fingers slipped on the worn edges of the podium. "What if I can't?"

The boy sat back on his heels, the warmth fading from his eyes. "Others will write," he responded tonelessly, "and you'll be lost.

"You *must* choose."

Gavin opened his mouth but before he could speak or even breathe It tore him loose with a mighty jerk. Pain blazed up his legs, through his joints, his muscles on fire, but none of that mattered as he flew forever backward while the pain rose in his chest and exploded there, radiating outward through him as the darkness swallowed him whole . . .

***

"Clear!"

Pain.

Pain blazing through his body, exploding in his chest, radiating outward, jerking him in spasms like before, back there, only different somehow . . .

"We've got him! Heartbeat, very weak . . . "

And the voices faded into an indecipherable hiss as his head lolled on a rubbery neck. He lay flat on his back, was rushing forward . . .

ambulance

. . . a droning, shrill cry waxing and waning, coming and going . . .

siren

. . . and before everything faded away to a blessedly empty, weightless black he saw an EMT lean over him, a man whose blue eyes blazed with power and strength and warmth . . .

***

" . . . I *said*, you're pretty damn lucky, y'know?"

Gavin blinked rapidly.

Swallowing, feeling lightheaded and weak. He tried to move his legs and fear spiked his heart when he felt them restricted, bound . . .

he cried out as it wrapped around his knee

. . . and the world slowly coalesced around him. He was reclining in a hospital bed, staring out the window as snowflakes fell endlessly from a whitish-gray sky.

He swallowed again.

His abdomen ached dully, the pain blunted by meds but still throbbing insistently. Small cuts and abrasions on his cheeks and forehead stung. His head pounded, echoing his heartbeat, and though he knew it to be fancy, he thought he felt two ghostly, burning patches on his chest.

clear!

"Hey. Gavin. You with me?"

That was Jim. He'd been talking for a while, but the fatigue and the drugs had left Gavin fuzzy. Reluctantly, he turned his attention from the snow's mesmerizing descent to his agent's worried face. "Sorry? I spaced out for a bit."

"I *said* you're pretty lucky that old guy in the truck showed up when he did. You were only out there for about ten minutes. Any longer, you probably would've bled to death."

Gavin shook his head and looked away, his eyes drawn back to the wintry scene outside. "Ten minutes," he whispered, seeing fragmented images of an elderly man with amazingly blue, compassionate eyes and an EMT on the ambulance with the same blue eyes, interwoven with other, nightmarish images he had no words for. "Felt like a lifetime."

Jim nodded as he leaned against the wall. "Very well could've been. They lost you on the way here, you know. Heart just quit for some reason. Stopped, total flat line. Had to shock you a few times before they got you back, I guess."

clear!

Blazing, blinding pain, jerking through him.

"And you're lucky your kidneys were only bruised. At first, the doctors thought they'd both been lacerated, and they thought you'd be on dialysis for life." Jim smiled wryly. "Can you imagine that? Carrying around a piss bag for the next twenty years?"

Gavin snorted, still looking outside. "Only bruised, huh?"

"Yeah. Someone must have read the CT scans wrong because when they did a laparoscopy for a closer look, everything checked out." Jim shrugged. "Like I said, pretty lucky."

"Yeah."

They remained silent for several moments, until Jim finally stirred and said, "Listen, I talked to Franklin, and he says not to worry about–"

"I'm an ass," Gavin said.

"What's that?"

Gavin turned and met Jim's gaze, marshaling what little courage he had left. "I've acted pretty miserably lately, haven't I? Drinking too much. Bitching like an ungrateful bastard."

Jim shrugged, his expression neutral. "Everyone hits a bad patch now and then."

Gavin swallowed and forced himself not to turn away. "Call Franklin. Tell him I screwed up. Tell him I'll stop my complaining, that I'll try to make it right, no matter what."

Jim smiled faintly. "I'll tell him, Gav. He'll be glad to hear it." He paused, then added, "We'll work it out. Promise."

He glanced at his watch. "Woa. I've gotta run back to the hotel, shoot off about a dozen emails." He looked back at him with such concern, Gavin instantly felt horrible for the way he'd treated Jim the night before. "You'll be all right for a bit?"

Gavin waved limply. "I'm fine."

Jim moved past the foot of the bed and then abruptly checked himself, remembering something.

"Almost forgot. When the EMTs brought you into the OR you were clutching these as if your life depended on it. They had to pry them from your fingers, so I figured they were important and you'd want them."

He withdrew the objects from under his arm and handed them to Gavin, who accepted them wordlessly; afraid his pounding heart might trigger the nurse-call alarm. "Hang tight until I get back." He flipped Gavin a jaunty salute and left the room.

Gavin stared for several seconds at what he held. The topmost object was a marble black and white composition book. He'd written the bulk of *Shades of Darkness* in notebooks like it; had even started writing its sequel in one before pitching it and moving on to other stories he'd thought more marketable at the time.

Carefully, his hand trembling, he shifted the objects, and when he saw the other thing—a hardcover novel—his heart stuttered, because in his hands he held a slightly soiled, faded copy of *Shades of Darkness*. His mind rebelled against the implications, because he knew without a shadow of a doubt the only copy he owned was at home in his office, but here it was, nonetheless.

He breathed once.

Waited for an interminable moment, then flipped the cover open to find the following: *To Hank . . .*

Gavin slammed it shut.

Tossed the book onto the table next to him like it was a ticking bomb. Sucking in deep gulps of air, he mumbled, "No way. It's not possible. There's no way."

And yet, two opposing refrains echoed in his mind . . .

mene, mene, tekel upharsin

you're here to decide your destiny

Gavin reached out and grabbed the standard hospital pen that all rooms came amply supplied with. He picked up the notebook he'd dropped into his lap and opened it to the sight of a white, pure, empty page. He clicked the pen, waited for a moment . . .

And began to write.

And he wrote into the night, as the bitter wind howled and beat against his hospital room window.

4.

GAVIN HAS FINISHED his pancakes and is now sipping from his coffee, watching me with a neutral expression. I again push the book away from me, as if prolonged contact with it could hurt me, somehow.

Which is ridiculous.

It's just a journal full of stories, that's all. So what if Gavin's story about the Pital girl was eerily accurate? Gavin wrote fiction for a living, he made stuff up. That's what writers do, right? Make stuff up.

Right?

I meet Gavin's calm gaze and speak carefully. "So. This story's . . . a . . . what do you call it? A metaphor. Symbolic. Of how you realized there was more to life than your writing career."

Gavin raises his eyebrows and says, "Is that what you think it is?"

I clasp my hands together on the booth's tabletop so hard my knuckles ache. "I don't really know *what* to think, Gavin. You brought me here with cryptic allusions to a Truth, then have me read these stories . . . "

I wave at the book and I swear Gavin's flowing script wavers and trembles, beckoning me to read on. "These stories can't be true, not literally. Okay, so you had an accident and you re-evaluated your career and your life, then used that experience to tell an entertaining story. Maybe you embellished a little in places, maybe you hallucinated some and used that as material. But . . . "

Gavin sets his coffee cup down gently. "That's what I thought for a long time. I couldn't explain what happened that night, how I also woke up with those books, so I denied it all, pushing the truth away. And after I left the hospital, I started drinking even worse. I stopped fighting with my publisher and agent, but at that point, nothing much mattered anymore. I was through writing professionally."

Silence.

I look outside. It's getting dark, now. The Skylark's parking lot is mostly empty, save a few cars. And it strikes me, suddenly, how much this place resembles the diner in Gavin's story. I tell him so and he nods, a small smile playing on his lips. He says nothing more for a minute or two.

Then he leans back.

Tapping the tabletop with one hand, meeting my gaze with bright eyes. "Let's play 'Pretend' for a moment. Let's pretend everything in that story happened, either in the real world or in some other dimension or reality. Or, on some sort of spiritual plain, as I lay unresponsive in an ambulance speeding toward the hospital."

I nod. "That was a nice touch. Those painful spasms being the shock paddles, trying to re-start your heart."

He tips his head. "Did you know that every year, hundreds of near-death experiences are documented worldwide? I know; I've read quite a few recently. One common element stands out, that people often return from these near-death experiences fundamentally changed. Different. They've 'seen the light.' They've 'ascended,' had their 'eyes opened,' become more 'aware' of the world around them."

Gavin looks out the window into the darkness. "Did all that really happen? Honestly, I don't know. I still have nightmares about that thing in the dark. Or at least I did, until . . . "

"Until you sobered up and started writing again, about a year ago."

He nods. "After the accident I drank more, usually at night, so I could sleep. I didn't write at all, not anything that mattered, anyway, because I was never sober. And that thing in the shadows was always waiting for me in my nightmares, or every time I closed my eyes. That and those damned whispers. You know after a while, I wrote those words down and Googled them. Want to know what they mean?"

I shake my head because suddenly, I want this to be done. Gavin's a great guy but I just want this to be *done*. My gut's been squirming the whole time and even though I know these stories can't be true, I can't deny a feeling of instinctual dread about the *other* stories in this book, and what they'll say.

Because there *are* other stories in this book. This I know without even asking, and that's another thing: this book, its pages, and the words on them, that shift and flow and quiver when looked at from the corner of my eye, that practically command me to read them.

I tap the table next to the book, because I don't want to touch it again, not yet. "What's in the rest of this book? How does it relate to the Timmy Danvers case, Anne Marie Hauer, and everything else? Are you saying . . . that some THING, like in your story took them, that . . . "

Gavin shakes his head. "No, nothing like that."

"Then how the hell are these stories supposed to help me?"

Gavin exhales and stares silently at the book for several seconds before he finally says, "Honestly? I don't know how much it will help you with your case, specifically. But these stories tell about this town, about what happens in its dark corners. And I don't know if there's any explanations for them. They just . . . are."

"Okay. So what did that weird kid mean when he said you were supposed to be a 'Witness' to the end, and that you had to . . . "

" . . . write true things?" He smiles helplessly. "I'm not sure. I did nothing for five years, refusing to write *anything,* and my life only worsened. Drinking, nightmares all the time, until I gave in after what happened with Emma, *gave* myself to it and started writing. And now the nightmares have gone away and I've stopped drinking.

"And they're true? These stories really happened? That's what you're saying?"

He shrugs. "According to that boy . . . it's my gift, or my curse, depending on how you look at it. Or, maybe I hallucinated the whole experience in Portsmouth and maybe coming so close to death flipped a switch in my head so now I'm *receiving* these stories, like I'm an antenna for them, or something. Or maybe it's a little of both. Take your pick. Regardless,

I've written every night since Emma's case and everything," he points at the open book, "is in there."

I look at the book's flowing, trembling script. "And Father Ward and Fitzy have . . . ?"

"Read enough to believe, yes. They chose not to finish it, however. They're afraid, and I believe they have a right to be."

"Because all these stories *are* true."

"I'm not sure I'd say that, exactly. Maybe there's Truth of a kind in them. And to be honest, I wrote them in manic fugues, the words and ideas pouring out of me onto the page. I remember only bits and pieces of each and haven't read them back-to-back like you are now, so I've really no idea what kind of portrait they paint."

I grunt. "And you don't want to know, do you?"

"No. Not really, because I don't believe it's my place to. But as you've said, you're the Sheriff, responsible for all of us in a way we can never understand. If anyone should be privy to this town's darkest secrets, to better serve and protect us . . . it should be you."

A dreadful inspiration blooms then, as words from Gavin's story flash through my head . . .

*you must chronicle these things for the Guardian
so he can protect the Threshold
so he will know how*

That's when I realize it. They've been waiting for this moment all year long. They've known it would come eventually. *That's* why they've so cagily deflected my questions this past year. Not because they wanted to hide things from me, but they're . . .

"Afraid for me," I whisper, meeting Gavin's gaze.

"You're all afraid for me. That's why you've dodged all my questions about this town."

A slight nod and a small smile. "But, as you've said . . . the time has come for full disclosure. If we want to continue as friends, if we want to move forward with our lives, if you really want to . . . "

" . . . protect this town." I stare at him. "Am I The Guardian, then? And is this town . . . The Threshold? Threshold for what? And what does The End, mean?"

Another limp shrug. "Honestly, I don't know."

I look back at that book, so tantalizingly open and so near to my hand. "And you've no idea what answers I'll get from reading these?"

"No. Just an understanding that, for whatever reason, Clifton Heights . . . "

"The Threshold."

" . . . is like, in many ways, that diner in Portsmouth. A crack. A junction point between realities, a confluence of bent cosmic angles, a place where strange, unexplainable . . . often violent things happen."

I stare at that journal for a heartbeat, then whisper, "The boy. Who was the boy, the 'messenger?' You said he looked like someone, but you wouldn't say who, because you didn't want to believe."

A resigned sigh, that of someone letting everything out, finally. "Michael Lockenstein. The autistic savant I grew up with, who I wrote my first novel about. He looked like Michael Lockenstein."

"And what happened to him? Is he dead, or . . . "

"In a coma. Has been for twenty years or so. That's what I was going to write about in the sequel to Shades, about what happened to him . . . but I couldn't do it. Told myself it was because I really wanted to penetrate the market, build up a solid fan base, but now . . . I know why I didn't. It was because I was afraid. Afraid that I was doing *something* I would pay for in the end, so I took the coward's way out and scrapped the sequel."

He pauses. "By the way . . . I never told you what it meant."

"It?"

"'mene, mene, tekel upharsin.'"

"And?"

Gavin rubs his mouth, then says, "It's from a prophecy in the Bible about the fall of Nebuchadnezzar's Kingdom. Loosely translated, it means: 'you have been weighed and measured . . . and found wanting.'"

about the end

"If this town is The Threshold," I whisper, "Gavin . . . *what* is The End?"

He shakes his head wordlessly and looks back out the window.

So I look back at that journal lying there, begging me to read it. And maybe I've swallowed this whole thing hook, line and sinker, become tainted by the obsessions of a fractured mind with a skewed perception of reality, but I suddenly realize how appropriate the translation of those strange words is because I feel, somehow, that I'm about to be weighed and measured, and as I finally reach to turn that page to the next story, I wonder, at the end of this . . .

Will I be found wanting?

THE WATER GOD OF
CLARKE STREET

IT WAS A cold winter day and Carolyn O'Neil was pissed off at her imaginary friend Bob the Water Sprite.

"I hate you Bob," she rasped, trudging through powdery snowdrifts, "I *hate you!* Adam Stillman thinks I'm a freak, and it's all your fault!"

"I hate you."

Her angry footsteps scraped the frozen sidewalk and her ponytail swished against the back of her neck as she recalled today's disaster in sixth period study hall. It had been the most humiliating experience ever and she had Bob to thank for it.

Adam Stillman was the most popular boy her age. Athletic and graceful, with brown hair teased into a skater cut, his bright blue eyes made her knees buckle. She tutored him in Math every sixth period but they might as well live on separate planets. He was a basketball god that all the cheerleaders worshiped. She was the kinda-chubby smart girl everyone ignored. He only tolerated her because she helped him keep his grades up so he was eligible to play ball. Of course, thanks to Bob she probably wouldn't have even *that* anymore.

"Stupid. So stupid. Why'd I ever listen to you?"

With a grunt she kicked a small chunk of ice off the sidewalk and onto the road, where it rolled and tinkled. To be honest, a lot of Bob's promises had fallen flat lately. Why had she expected this one to be any different?

"Dammit." She shivered and hunched deeper into her jacket. She should've never asked Bob for help. If she hadn't, today would've never happened and maybe Adam would still be able to look at her.

Of course, lots of things in life happened that shouldn't. She and Mom shouldn't have to eat dinner alone all the time. Dad shouldn't always have to work late with secretaries Mom called "slutty tramps" when she thought Carolyn wasn't listening. She shouldn't have to walk home from school in weather like this while Dad was "busy at the office" and Mom was throwing one of her Pampered Chef Parties.

And of course, girls her age shouldn't have imaginary friends, either.

She stopped at the corner of Main and Allen and glanced across the street at Chin's Pizza & Wings. Its front window throbbed with a welcoming glow. Though Mr. Chin would probably let her sit there for a few minutes to warm up, she had no money. Smelling the warm, oily odor of crust, sauce, and garlic without eating would only be torture.

She looked closer at the pizza joint, saw a battered yellow Ford truck parked alongside the curb and groaned. "Yuck. Never mind."

It was a good thing she didn't have any money for

pizza, because inside Chin's at a table near the front window sat Jesse Kretch, eating. Jesse had gone to school with Dad. According to Dad, Jesse had never left Clifton Heights; just graduated high school and worked odd jobs around town. During the winter he worked at the lumber mill. In the summer he bailed hay for local farmers and walked up and down Route 79 outside town, collecting cans and bottles and scrap metal.

Jesse always looked dirty and ragged; his clothes rumpled and stained, as if he slept in them and never changed or washed them. Her classmates swore he smelled like sour milk and cow shit. She had no idea if that was true, but she didn't want to find out, so she glanced down Allen to make sure no one was coming and crossed the street, leaving the pizza joint and the awful Jesse Kretch behind, thinking again about Bob and how Adam Stillman would never talk to her again.

She knew Adam wouldn't tell anyone what happened (unless he lied and told everyone *she* had kissed *him*) but that thought wasn't comforting, because of course that meant he didn't want anyone to know he'd kissed someone like her.

She reached the other side of Main Street and continued out of town. "Bob, I swear . . . I ever do conjure you, first thing I'm gonna do is kick your furry blue ass."

She snickered. Out of all of the swears she'd learned over the past few years, 'kicking ass' was her favorite. It made her feel tough, hard, and mean.

Of course, if you'd just take Bob's offer, you could be all those things . . . and more.

She swallowed hard and kept walking. Most girls

her age shopped, drank at house parties, had sleepovers and whispered in heated tones about what they wanted to do with the boys they liked in parked cars up on the bluffs or in dark movie theaters over in Utica. Compared to them, she was a freak, but she didn't care. Mostly. She was different, always had been, always would be, and she didn't plan on changing any time soon. Books and stories were her life, not boys and shopping, and she liked it fine that way.

Of course, if she hadn't loved books so much, maybe she wouldn't have peeked into that big, black leather-bound book her cousin Heather had left behind after her annual summer visit last year. Then she never would've snuck that book into her room and perused its parchment-like pages in hushed anticipation, and never would've flipped to the page with that drawing of a majestic-looking half-man, half-seahorse or mumbled the strange-sounding words printed beneath it.

And then, Bob wouldn't have shown up in her bathroom sink two days later, and he wouldn't have embarrassed her in front of Adam Stillman today.

"Sometimes," she whispered as she spied Clarke Street, which ran parallel to Black Creek and led to the lumber mill, "I wish I'd never met you, Bob."

Are you sure about that? If Bob hadn't come along you would've spent this last year alone, like always. Is that what you want? To be alone all the time?

She pushed the thought away and stalked forward.

Up ahead before Black Creek Bridge in a ditch on the left side of the road ran a long, wide patch of ice that gleamed in the sun. The sight diffused some of her anger. When she was younger, she'd always loved sliding on patches of ice in the winter. What kid didn't?

In fact, she couldn't think of a better way to cheer herself up, so she broke into a jog, forgetting about embarrassments in front of boys she liked; smelly strange men and unreliable imaginary friends.

She spread her arms into wings.

Hopped onto the ice, feet flat, legs flexed for balance.

She closed her eyes and slid, the winter air burning her cheeks. For just a second, her troubles faded. Things were good. Right now, they were good.

"Hey, baby cakes! What's shakin?"

She twisted her feet and came to a slushing stop. Opening her eyes, she glared down at the ice. Under it floated Bob. His long, furry serpentine body coiled and flexed. A patch of wavy tendrils on his head rippled. His silvery, almond-shaped eyes twinkled.

Bob looked like a fuzzy merman. He sported whiskers on either side of his narrow face. His body tapered into a triangular point. Along his back, a spinal ridge glowed a shifting kaleidoscope of colors.

Bob grinned, flashing rows of teeth. "Lookin' good, Carolyn. Betcha kick Michelle Kwan's ass any day."

She scowled. "Piss off, Bob."

Bob spread his hands. "Aw, come on. Don' be mad. The spell worked, didn' it? Got what ya wanted, a big ole' wet one, right on the lips!" A leer stretched his rubbery face. "Didja get any tongue?"

"Bob!" She kicked the ice. "*Not* cool!"

Bob laughed, his mouth opening so wide she could almost see down his throat. Her stomach twitched as she wondered what squirmed down there.

"Stop it! Stop laughing!"

Betrayal twisted her stomach. She clenched her hands and bit her lip, using the pain to keep the tears away. She never knew anymore when Bob's humor would turn on her. Even though he always acted like it was all in good fun, she'd sensed a darker purpose lately.

"I *hate* you, Bob." She remembered Adam's shocked, almost disgusted expression when he'd realized what he'd been doing. "Adam's probably never gonna talk to me ever again and it's *all your fault*."

Bob's laugh trickled off into a chuckle. He wiped his eyes. "Oh kiddo. Yer so precious when ya get mad. Swear I could just eat ya right up."

Carolyn suddenly felt cold, as she always did when Bob said things like that. "Wasn't supposed to be like that, Bob. You said the spell would make him kiss me on the cheek, *not* on the mouth."

Bob shrugged. "Ah, what can I say, kiddo? Boys 'r boys, after all, nothin but walkin balls an hormones."

He glanced at her with the same look she'd seen some of her male classmates give other girls (the pretty ones with big boobs, never her, of course) and said, "Besides . . . it wasn't all that bad . . . was it? Admit it. Ya liked it when his tongue tried to get in yer mouth. Didn't ya?"

Carolyn stood rock-still.

Icy dread swirled in her stomach. She supposed it was dumb to think Bob wouldn't know about that, to think he wouldn't know she *had* liked it a little, seeing as how he'd made Adam do it in the first place. That's what the spell had done, after all. Let Bob inside Adam, even if only for a minute.

There were other spells she'd copied from Heather's book, including one that would free Bob. She didn't know how that worked exactly, but she guessed it was probably like what happened with Adam . . . only for longer.

Like forever.

She stared at Bob, opening her mouth to speak, but found she couldn't. She suddenly felt very afraid.

Bob straightened, threw back his furry shoulders and crossed his arms. His face softened. "You know kiddo, I worry about ya. A lot."

His tone caught her off guard. She blinked, confused. "What?"

Bob sighed and floated back and forth, pacing. "I worry, kiddo, 'cause you ain't got nobody else but me, y'know? Breaks my heart. Don' wantcha to be lonesome forever. That's why I put some extra mojo into the spell. Don' wantcha to be alone."

He stopped and offered her an apologetic glance. "Sorry if the tongue-thing weirded ya out, kiddo. I was hopin the kid would take a shine to ya is all."

Maybe Bob was trying to make her feel better—in his odd, twisted way—but his words cut deeply. It was one thing to know she was alone, quite another to hear it so calmly announced.

She looked at Bob and realized fear wasn't so far from hate.

"Bob . . . "

She stopped and sighed. This was going to hurt, because she loved Bob too, in a way. In a small town where most girls aspired to hook up with the high school quarterback and imitate the most recent spoiled and rich heiress or celebrity, it had been lonely for her.

Bob had been great company. He'd told her the best stories: about goblins, dragons, and knights in shining armor, filling her days with color, warmth, and visions of another world.

But she'd had enough of his games and this time, his apology rang false. Somehow, she sensed he really wasn't worried about her nor did he care about her loneliness, that all he really wanted was . . .

"Hey. C'mon. Turn that frown upside down, yeah? I've got the answer to all yer problems. You've known that for a while now. All ya gotta do is take the plunge. I can make you the most popular kid in town."

He grinned, showing lots of teeth that looked much sharper than moments ago, and leaned closer, pressing his palms against the ice. "You know the words, Carolyn. You've said them to yourself lots, late at night, alone in the dark when you thought no one was watchin or listenin. You know 'em by heart now, I bet." His grin faded. His silvery eyes swelled. "You've no idea what *wonderful* things I can show you. Such wonderful, delightful things. The whole world could be yours. You'd never be lonely again."

She licked her lips and looked away.

Tasting the faint, wintermint of Adam's breath freshener in her mouth. She sucked down an icy, burning breath. "No." She clenched her hands. "I can't."

Bob caressed the ice. "C'mon, sweetie. It ain't so bad, honest. When you finally let me in we'll be pals, forever. We'll have loads of fun. Promise."

He floated back and rubbed his fuzzy hands. "Kiddo, ya can't even imagine what it'll be like. You'll see an hear things like never before, know stuff no one your age knows. Ace school without even tryin, howdya like that? An you'll be stronger, faster, and quicker."

He pierced her with a knowing look. "An that's not the best part, is it sweetie? You'll be able to do whatever you want. *Have* anyone you want, forever. No more bein alone. When I'm inside you, everyone will want a piece of your action, savvy?"

The last two sentences pulled at her heart. She had the faintest ideas of what "being inside" meant. She imagined Bob dangling a 'Carolyn marionette,' which scared her in ways she couldn't describe, but the thought of having lots of friends and not being alone, of tasting Adam's wintermint lips whenever she wanted . . .

She swallowed and looked at Bob, who whispered, "I'm lonely too. I know what it's like, kiddo, to be surrounded by folks an still be alone. Your parents don' give a rat's ass an ya know it. Dad's too busy bangin secretaries at work. Mom's too busy throwin parties for every bored mother-hen in town. Conjure me up an you'll never be alone, ever again."

She wanted to say yes.

More importantly, she needed to.

Want.

Need.

The horrible thing? Truth rang in Bob's words. Somehow, she knew Mom and Dad's love was merely dutiful. If she conjured Bob inside her and she changed, her parents would probably never notice the difference.

"You're the one, kiddo," Bob revered, "the best. I've spent lotsa time searchin for the best, an out of all the others . . . *you're* the one I want."

A light flickered on in Carolyn's head.

"What do you mean?" She regarded Bob with renewed suspicion. "*What* others?"

Bob stared silently.

Then muttered, "*Shit.*"

"What *others*, Bob?"

Bob's gentle expression faded as he cracked an ugly, fanged grin. "C'mon. Seriously? Ya think yer the only one ever to summon me, to beg for someone to listen to your dirty little secrets? I got a whole laundry list of whiney losers like you."

She jerked, Bob's words slapping her. The urge to flee clanged against her frozen legs. She swallowed, throat tight, and wheezed, "No . . . that's not true. You said I was your only friend in the whole world."

Bob's grin widened. "Girlie, I've got tons of friends, an they're all weak, pathetic, an alone. Just. Like. *You.*"

Sudden tears trembled on her eyelashes. She shook her head in jerky sweeps. "No," she sniffed, her anger dampened by a tide of heavy loneliness, "s-stop saying that."

Bob pushed back from the ice, folding his arms. "Come on. It's true. Sorry princess, ya gotta grow up an face the facts sometime, right? First off, there's Timmy Johnson, livin right at the end of South Street? He's a *pain*. All he does is complain that Daddy beats him when he's drunk cause poor Timmy likes to write poetry, which makes Daddy worried he's a fag, so he tries to beat the gay out of him every now an then . . . "

"S-stop it, stop it . . . "

" . . . there's also Jenny Tillman. You know, the senior who wears the purple eye shadow an the short skirts all the boys like? She pretends she's really dumb cause when she shows her smarts, her trailer-trash mommy beats her cause she's worried Jenny is smarter than she is. Then there's Billy Hopkins," Bob counted each child's name off his blue, worm-like fingers, "the fat kid with the black hair an all the pimples? *That* kid watches way too much Internet porn for his own good." Bob smirked, twirling a furry finger next to his ear. "He's a sick puppy, Carolyn. Make sure you don' bend over to pick up nuthin around him cause he'll get an eyeful of yer a . . . "

"SHUT UP!"

Tears flooded her cold cheeks.

Her fingernails cut angry crescents into her palms.

Bob fell quiet for several seconds before whispering, "Yer the only one I ever told them stories to, Carolyn. I promise. Only you. An even with all them others . . . I'm lonely too, cause yer the only one I want."

Carolyn wiped her face with the back of her hand, which of course didn't help much because of her frosted gloves. Grunting, she ripped off one, turned it inside out and wiped her face as best she could. "You're lying," she rasped, her throat burning from the cold wind. "You're not lonely at all. Not with all those others. And why so many, Bob? Why?"

When no answer came right away, she stomped and screeched, "*Why*?"

"I had ta find the best, right?" He shrugged, adding, "I know I lied to ya, but I wanna bond with a sure thing, a power player, an I hadda figure out which one it'd be. But I'm tellin' ya, I know, now. That sure thing is *you*."

She sniffed and wiped her eyes again.

out of all the others

"No," she whispered, "no, no, no, no . . . "

Bob was still smiling, but nervously, now, perhaps sensing he was losing her. "Listen Carolyn, all those others don' mean nothin. I'm pickin you, get it? Yer the one I want!"

"No Bob, you don't want me at all! You just wanna use me to get out . . . "

"Aw, c'mon," Bob snapped, "don't be such a bi–"

She glared at Bob, floating just beneath the ice, his form no longer oddly attractive but strange and disgusting.

Bob stuttered, waving his arms, "No, no, wait . . . I didn' mean that . . . "

New-found resolve burned inside her. "No! I'm not letting you out, Bob. I want you to go away and never come back. Ever."

Silence.

Bob stared.

Hands flexing, whiskers and furry tuft of hair waving. Hate glittered in his silver eyes, and for the first time in her life, Carolyn O'Neil thought she knew what death looked like.

Bob exploded and attacked the ice.

Pounding and howling.

Carolyn shrieked, slipped and fell to the hard, icy ground. Fear gripped her as she saw the ice tremble and even in some places crack. An unearthly green glow flared beneath, spreading into the gray winter evening.

"Stupid bitch!" Bob pounded harder, each blow shaking the ice. "Say the goddamn words an lemme outta here, now!"

With an ear-splitting howl, Bob struck the ice hard enough to convex it outward. "You damn, miserable little *bitch*!"

And then silence, save the sound of Carolyn's heart thudding in her chest and her breath roaring in her ears. The cracked and humped ice lay motionless, but that unearthly green light still spilled into the air.

She could run away.

She could, she could go right now. But if she did, she'd never know for sure if Bob was gone or just waiting for the right moment to spring, maybe when she wasn't looking in the bath or the shower, or in the pool at school . . .

Or in the body of someone she knew.

She had to try and end this, now.

Slowly, on her hands and knees, she crawled to the edge of the cracked patch of ice and peered over . . . nearly sobbing in terror at the sight of Bob still there, hands on his serpentine hips, glaring at her. "Back for more, huh?" he grumbled. "Good, cause there's a bit of the bedtime story I left out, sweetie. Guess what happens to all the others when one finally frees me? After me an the lucky one bond we get to have some fun; an I mean some serious gut-munchin fun. The first thing we'll do is settle with all the folks that've pissed us both off. Know what I mean?"

Somehow Carolyn lurched to her feet on shaking legs. Cold terror shook her and she trembled, teeth clattering.

Bob's silver eyes glittered darkly. "Oooh, that's right, sister. If someone else lets me out I'm comin to your door first, an then I'm eatin you an Mommy an Daddy's guts for dinner."

Maybe Bob was lying, but deep inside she knew if she didn't do something, Bob *would* get out and come looking for her, to do what he promised. If he looked and sounded and even smelled like a human, how would she ever know?

"Let me out," Bob cooed, "an we can have all the fun you want; do whatever you want. I mean, I may ask for a few *small* favors, but what's some people-meat compared to all the power an friends in the world, right?"

And to her horror a small part of her wondered just how bad it really would be.

With a great sob, Carolyn choked back her tears.

"You've really got no choice, do you?" Bob whispered. "You've only got me, babe—and that's it."

A thought sparked.

Choice.

Her choice.

Not his.

And another thought, on top of that. If he could so easily have someone else . . . why would he keep trying so hard for her after she kept saying no?

"Well babe, what's it gonna be? Are you an me gonna party, or am I gonna hafta find some other kid to hook up with?" Bob chuckled. "Gotta be honest, I'm of two minds. Yer the best kid out of the whole lot, buuut . . . " he pressed his hands and face against the ice, "I bet you're also the tastiest, too. Either way, I'm gonna have a bellyful by tomorrow morning, that's for sure."

Balling her fists, she stepped up to the ice's edge and looked down at Bob. She swallowed, rocking on her toes, and squeaked, "No. Go away."

Surprise registered on Bob's face, and Carolyn saw another emotion there, too.

Fear.

If he can get anyone else he wants . . . why does he look so afraid?

"Carolyn," he reasoned as he folded his hands, "it don' quite work like that." He smiled, exposing his teeth. "You can' just make me go away."

And now, she *knew* he was lying.

Because she saw the fear in his eyes.

"No," she said, emboldened by this, "that's not true. I can do whatever I want. I can make you go away, because I don't want you here anymore."

His smile hardened, anger simmering in his eyes. "If that's what you want, sweetie, so I can come eat your eyes out later . . . "

She stomped and to her surprise, Bob flinched. "No! No more lies, Bob! You can't get anybody else because if you could, you woulda left by now! So no more! You can't hurt me, because I said no. You can't touch me!

"Leave! Me. ALONE!"

Bob threw back his triangle-shaped head and roared. He swelled into a rippling mass of nightmarish muscle, a man, lizard, and a snake—something ancient, primal, and evil.

Carolyn went deathly cold at the sight.

"Listen BITCH! I get what I want! ALWAYS! I AIN'T about to be stopped by you! LET! ME! OUT!"

The ice, flooded by great splashes of eldritch green light, shook and heaved. Carolyn closed her eyes, plugged her ears and screamed back.

"GO AWAYYYYYYYYYYY!"

She screamed for her days of loneliness, wondering where her family was, why they left her alone all the time. She screamed from the hole in her heart where 'Daddy' and 'Mommy' should be, screamed for the best friends she didn't have, the sleepovers she'd never had, and the parties she was never invited to.

She screamed for the stories that were her life, and she screamed for herself.

And the frozen puddle exploded, ice and water and snow flying everywhere. Shards of coldness bit her skin. Everything was bathed in a sickly green glow, the air rent by an inhuman screech.

The blast threw her backward.

She stumbled, hands flailing, feet scrambling for purchase and finding none. She wheeled into the street; slipped and turned, slid to a stop at last . . .

As a droning horn filled her ears.

She looked up to see a battered yellow truck rushing toward her, its headlights blazing, filling her vision . . . and something punched her in the chest, shattering her ribs.

She flew backwards, twisting.

For a moment she thought she was sliding on the frozen puddle again and as she skated gracefully across the ice in her mind, the brisk winter air burned her cheeks . . . her eyes . . .

And then she fell, bones snapping, her spine breaking.

She blinked.

Tried to breathe, but couldn't. Her throat only twitched when she tried. She couldn't swallow either, or feel anything below her neck.

She felt no pain, anger, or sadness, and she thought

this strange. Most kids don't think about dying, and she hadn't been much different, but she'd thought about it a bit. Would it hurt? Would she be sad? The basics, of course.

She thought none of those things, now. She felt tired and she wanted to sleep, and that felt fine.

Carolyn.

Her name came from so far away it sounded like the wind. Didn't matter, really, because it was a whisper lost among dying memories.

Carolyn. Hey . . . Carolyn!

One last neuron in her head flared, allowing her to hear while the rest of her blood-soaked brain shut down. Even though she faced away from Bob's puddle and her neck was shattered, she imagined turning toward him, imagined Bob's blue face peering over broken shards of ice.

"B-o-b." Her lips never moved, neither did her tongue, yet somehow the name cracked between her bloodied lips.

Yeah! Holy shit! Lookit you! Damn, I never meant this to happen, Carolyn, honest I . . .

"N-o. N-o m-o-r-e."

Huh?

"N-o. M-o-r-e. L-i-e-s."

Bob sighed. *Yeah, I get it. No more lies.* She imagined him shrugging. *Well, here it is, kiddo. You in or out?*

Time hung.

She wasn't afraid of dying. She wasn't angry or hurting. Oddly enough, Adam Stillman and all the boys in the world no longer meant anything to her.

In fact, there was only one thing she feared losing, really.

Stories.

And she didn't want hers to end.

She closed her eyes and felt herself slide loose inside.

***

Jesse Kretch lurched from his truck's cab into the middle of Clarke Street. Bone-weary from pulling extra shifts at the lumber mill, mind clouded by too little sleep and too many beers, Jesse stared at the fluffy pink mound crumpled atop the embankment alongside Black Creek Bridge. Disjointed puzzle pieces from the last few minutes fell into place. He squinted as he stumbled toward the pile of pink fur . . .

please be a deer please be a deer oh God be a deer please

. . . bright sun glaring off winter hills, distorting his vision. And there was the mound of pink, fluffy fur, ringed with white cotton, heaped on the snow bank.

Jesse's world crumbled.

"Oh shit." He scrambled forward. "Oh shit, oh shit, oh shit!"

He slid to his knees next to the dead girl, sobbing, tears and snot running down his face. His head pounded. He didn't know what to do. He realized with dimwitted horror that now he'd probably get sent to a real jail after all these years where someone would make him a bitch, all because he'd drank too much and hit a kid with his damn truck . . .

The girl spasmed.

He cried out.

She coughed, hacked up clotted blood onto the snow next to her, rolled her crooked neck straight with several audible clicks and looked at him, smiling. "Sweet!"

Mouth hanging open, Jesse Kretch promptly pissed his pants.

And it all happened much too fast.

The girl jerked and twitched, her bones clacking and snapping inside her. Then she leapt to her haunches and lingered there for a moment as hunger flickered in eyes that shone a bright, sterling silver.

"Yeah," she whispered, "now *this* is the shit!"

She jumped and he flung up his arms but she batted them aside and drove him back onto the cold ground. Jesse's head cracked against cold asphalt.

A great pressure filled his head.

He felt sleepy.

Everything spun and blackness rushed in. The last thing he saw was the skin of the girl's face melting away to reveal a scaly, dark blue face underneath. Its serpentine tongue flicked; its teeth snapped.

He shuddered as the nightmarish head shot for his throat, and then Jesse Kretch went away.

***

Brisk winter air burned her cheeks. Arms outstretched, she balanced on one foot. For a moment her troubles faded as the winter air crystallized her breath. Things were good. For the moment, they were good.

Inside her, Bob raged.

WHAT THE HELL? WHAT. THE. HELL?

Carolyn May O'Neil stood on Black Creek Bridge's guardrail, balancing on one foot, feeling the wind blow through her hair. She no longer felt cold or hurt or angry or sad. She felt nothing, she merely felt *there*, and that was good enough. She knew things now. Deep, ancient, primal things and her insides crackled with a fire that burned but didn't hurt.

All was quiet.

Jesse Kretch lay unconscious on the ground several feet in front of his truck, unharmed.

And she felt peaceful.

Bob was anything but as he railed within. *I can't believe it! All this time stuck in the water, no people-meat for AGES, and you won't let me tear into the guy who ran you down in the road like a dog! What the hell?*

Carolyn smiled.

Allowing Bob inside her so freely had produced an unexpected and delightful result.

"*My* body, Bob," she whispered as she fluidly hopped to her other foot on the icy guardrail, "*my* rules."

No way! It's never been that way an it's never gonna to be that way, EVER! She imagined Bob pounding away on a bright pink door inside her. *I'm hungry! No one's gonna miss that beer sloshed dumbass . . . so let's dig in!*

"Bob," she mused as she gazed at the iced-over creek below, "has anyone ever *liked* having you inside them? I mean *really* liked having you inside?"

Again came the mental image of Bob, this time leaning against the pink door, arms folded, pouting. *Not really. Why?*

Carolyn grinned. "Wonder what that would be like? Working together, I mean."

Bob grew thoughtful, his expression softening and slivery eyes twinkling. *Dunno. Might be . . . fun.*

Carolyn nodded, grinning wider. "Are you hungry, Bob?"

Bob straightened, a hopeful look dawning upon his blue, whiskered face. *Could eat a damn horse.*

"Well then." She turned, hopped off the guardrail and headed across the bridge. "I know the perfect place. You game?"

Bob grinned, teeth glinting as he leaned against the pink door in her mind. *Lead on, sister.*

A small glow of contentment filled Carolyn as she skipped out of town. She hummed a bright tune, wondering if Adam Stillman was busy tonight, and if he was free . . .

For dinner.

5.

OUR WAITRESS (whose tag reads Cassie Tillman) refills Gavin's coffee. She offers me some, I politely decline, and as she walks away a startling realization hits me: our waitress, Cassie *Tillman.*

Jenny

Jenny Tillman

you know . . . the senior who wears the purple eye shadow

and the short skirts all the boys like

The implication sends ice down my spine.

If all these stories are true, or, as Gavin puts it, have Truth in them . . . how many are about folks I know?

For example, Jenny Tillman. Cassie Tillman's younger sister, a high school senior. She disappeared back in March. Got into a big blowout with her mother and stormed out of their trailer in the Commons Trailer Park on the edge of town. She was last seen hitching along Bassler Road, toward the interstate.

Will I read a story about her next? Or maybe a twisted tale about how my next door neighbor—a gentle, seventy year-old retired nurse named Maude—is really a dedicated Satan-worshiper who dines on the flesh of cooked babies and also likes to have orgies with the town librarian and the Ladies Auxiliary. The idea is insane.

Ludicrous. Far-fetched.

So why can't I get it out of my head?

"This story," I say, rubbing my eyes with the heel of my palm, "*this* is when things started getting weird."

"What do you mean?"

I sigh and open my eyes. "The Pital thing was tragic and violent. BUT . . . not so different from what you'd see on CNN. Almost pales in comparison to some of the school shootings we've seen in the news lately. There I was, a few months after the Pital case, a new Sheriff running patrol and I get a call from Dispatch. Someone's called 911, reporting that a truck has hit a teenage girl out by Black Creek Bridge. I speed out there. Freddy Potter's the first on the scene and he's dealing with a dead-drunk Jesse Kretch, who is ALSO swearing to God and Heaven above that he just hit a teenage girl in a pink winter jacket. And there ARE skid marks on the road, blood stains on the ground and markings in a nearby snowdrift that COULD be the impression of a body. But there's no body. And of course, Kretch had been drinking, as usual, so his confession isn't all that credible, except . . . "

"The 911 call and the blood."

"Right. Of course, the call was anonymous and the blood sample we sent to Utica PD's Forensics came back, surprise-surprise, inconclusive. All fine and dandy. That's the way things always work in this town, everything's always inconclusive all the time. But *this* story of yours connects the dots, painting a picture that . . . "

Gavin nods. "Poor Adam Stillman. By all rights, he had a bright athletic future ahead of him, until . . . "

I slap the table, jittering our coffee cups, the salt and pepper shakers, and the book itself. "Did you know? All this time, when hunters were scouring the woods for a 'large wolf-like creature' . . . did you know that this girl killed . . . God, I can't believe I'm saying this . . . that she ATE Adam Stillman?"

Gavin raises his eyebrows, looking so nonplussed that right now, friend or not, I'd like to deck him just to get a reaction. "WAS it Carolyn O'Neil? The story doesn't end that way, does it? We don't really know what she did next . . . do we?"

"GAVIN. Seriously?"

Gavin bows his head and rubs the bridge of his nose between his thumb and forefinger. "You have to understand," he whispers, "back then, I still wasn't sure what was happening. And when they found that poor boy's body, when it was first reported on the news, I didn't know if Carolyn O'Neil even existed."

"C'mon, Gavin. She was sixteen years old. Not the grade you teach but you must've seen her around before, known who she . . . "

"In point of fact, I didn't." He raises his head and when I see how tired he looks, how gaunt and drawn, my ire fades. "You're forgetting I teach at the public school. Adam Stillman attended All Saints High. So did Carolyn O'Neil."

Great.

Now I feel like shit. "Ah, Gavin. I wasn't thinking. Honestly, I . . . wait. *Attended*. She's not there, anymore . . . is she?"

"Two months after the Stillman boy was found, when I finally admitted to myself that maybe—like with Emma and my experience in Portsmouth—I'd written the truth, I did some discrete checking. Apparently, Carolyn's father requested a 'transfer' down south from his engineering firm not long after searchers discovered Adam Stillman's body. They sold their house and left town quietly, without saying goodbye to anyone, a month later."

And there it is.

Like always.

Case closed, end of story, all leads going nowhere, and I'm left holding a bag of clues that keeps sifting like sand out a hole I can't patch, and I can't put all the sand back into the bag again after it's empty. Except . . .

I sit forward. "Jesse Kretch. He swore for weeks afterward that he hit someone that day. And during those weeks, I had to deal with the whole Adam Stillman thing so I forgot about Kretch, just passed it off as his usual drunken rambling . . . but maybe . . . maybe I could talk to him, see if . . . "

"He remembers?" Gavin offers me a sympathetic look one step short of pity. He thinks I'm grasping at straws, and the worst part?

He's right.

"Okay," Gavin admits, "maybe Jesse *does* remember something. Maybe he did see something and he didn't tell anyone about it. But think for a minute, Chris. When's the last time you threw Jesse in jail to sober him up? Broke up one of his weekly scuffles down at The Stumble Inn? When's the last time you even saw his truck driving through town, or saw him out along Route 79 picking cans?"

I open my mouth . . . and realize Gavin's right. It's been weeks. Hell, maybe even months since I've seen Jesse Kretch, certainly months since he'd last slept off a bender in the jail. "Where . . . how do you . . . ?"

Gavin says nothing.

Just points at the book.

"Geez. Really?"

He nods.

Dammit.

THE GATE AND THE WAY

THE WOODS BEHIND Bassler House stank worse than anything Jesse Kretch had ever smelled. He looked up to bitch about it to Scott, but a tree branch smacked him in the face before he could speak.

"Ow! Dammit! Watch it, Scott!"

Small lines burned his cheeks. Scott looked back as he pushed through brush and more branches. "Sorry. You okay?"

"Yeah. Guess so. Stings like a motherfucker, though."

"Pussy."

"Ass."

"Whatever. Just keep movin. We don't have all day. Gotta have Mrs. Wilkins' yard mowed by dinner."

Jesse scowled but said nothing as he followed Scott through the woods behind old Bassler House. They could've taken the easier way along Bassler Road, but that started off the end of South Main Street and looped around town. Way too long. This shortcut—through the woods behind the Commons Trailer Park—was quicker.

But smellier, way smellier. The air reeked of bad milk and old piss. Mounds of bulging white plastic bags dotted the ground, some split open like alien egg sacs, spilling out their moldy contents: greasy food wrappers, rusted and slimy tin cans, diapers and other junk dissolved into unknown gray mush. Enough to make anyone blow chunks if they stuck around long enough.

"Gee-zus. Stinks here. Why we doin this anyway? What's the deal?"

"You'll see."

"Aw, c'mon. Smells like shit up here. Why we gotta . . . "

"Suck it up. Tell you when we get there. Now quit cryin and move."

Jesse fell silent. He loved Scott to death, but sometimes? He was a major pain in the ass.

A few steps later they stopped near the forest's edge, behind the crumbling house. Jesse glanced at its empty windows. They spilled out an inky blackness. He shivered and looked at Scott instead, instantly feeling better.

Jesse always felt good when he looked at Scott. He tried to hide it, though. Didn't want anyone thinking he was queer. But it was hard not to look at him. Tall and lanky and muscled, all the girls loved him. His sharp eyes saw everything. He moved in a fluid way Jesse couldn't. Sometimes it hurt to watch Scott, because he wished he could move and act and talk like him, but somehow knew he never would, no matter how hard he tried.

Scott grinned. "So. Guess what we're after?"

Jesse shrugged, still pissed but trying to hide it. "Dunno. What?"

"Beer and soda cans. Bottles, too."

"Huh? Why?"

Scott popped him one in the shoulder. "Duh. Didn't you see that article in The Tribune the other day about the new recyclin laws?"

Jesse winced and shrugged. "Nope. I just read the comics."

Scott ruffled his hair. Jesse ducked and scowled. He knew Scott didn't mean it, but that always made him feel like such a little kid.

"*Stop*! Butt-hole."

"Dick-breath. Anyway. There's a new law sayin you get a nickel for every can and bottle you turn in. A nickel. For each one. Mr. Greenwood at the Great American's gonna start takin em."

"Yeah? So?"

"Duh. Think of all the kids an drunks sneakin out here to booze up. Gotta be tons of bottles an cans here."

"Still don't get it."

Scott pulled two crumpled plastic bags from his pocket. "Look. These'll hold about a hundred cans an bottles each. If we fill em up, we can get close to ten bucks. We'll split it, five bucks each." Scott winked. "I was over at Brooks Pharmacy yesterday. Guess what they just got?"

Jesse smiled hopefully. "New comics?"

"You bet. Secret Defenders, The Hulk . . . an Dr. Strange."

"Cool." Jesse paused. "Wait. You don't read comics. What're you gonna buy with your split?"

Scott shrugged and looked away. "Dunno. Think of somethin . . . "

He paused and cocked his head.

Jesse broke out in goose pimples, though he didn't know why. "What?"

"Thought I heard somethin. Like a door openin."

Jesse swallowed, his guts squirming for some reason. "Screw this. Let's split."

Scott smirked. "C'mon! Take off your skirt an grow one, willya? Just the wind blowin a door or maybe some shutters closed. That's all." He looked over his shoulder and asked, "You comin?"

"Whatever. Let's hurry, though." Jesse kicked a wadded up newspaper along the way. "I'm readin a buncha issues of Dr. Strange, where he an the Secret Defenders are fightin vampires. I wanna finish em before we cut fatso Wilkins' yard."

They stopped at an open door leading to what Jesse figured was the basement. He tried hard to ignore that sick feeling in his belly, which had gotten worse. He scowled. "We goin or what?"

Scott flashed Jesse a smile he could never refuse. "You bet."

***

He stares at old Bassler House. Noon's high sunlight flickers off shattered glass in moldy window frames, setting off the deep shadows that ooze from those empty windows. Anything could be lurking inside and he'd never know until too late, but he breathes deep, swallows his fear and starts forward. A terrible destiny waits inside this house. He feels this, in his very bones, and also feels that now is the time to do what must be done.

As he walks, an old pistol—a .38, stuck under his belt buckle—rubs against his belly. He clenches and re-clenches sweaty fingers around the handle of Grandpa

Carlton's old Army hatchet, given to him when he was a boy. Little had he known then what it was for.

His footfalls drum out dull rhythms as he nears the house. Three steps. Two. One. He mounts the porch and approaches the front door, pushes it open with the hatchet's blade and enters the front hall. He blinks as his eyes adjust, nostrils twitching at a rotten odor.

He coughs.

It echoes against the silence.

He looks around. Sunlight peeks through crooked shutters, shadows jig on the floors. To his left and right sit empty rooms. Before him, a staircase curves upwards to the second floor landing, and under the staircase, against the back wall . . .

There.

The door to the basement. He starts for it and stops when he hears a muffled thud. A door opening?

He listens for more. Nothing. Except maybe . . . voices. Footsteps. Where?

A scrape. Shuffling feet. Then, a faraway shattering.

His heart pounds as he advances on the door leading to the basement stairs.

***

"Sam Higgins says this place is haunted. Says people see lights in the woods an hear screams at night, shit like that."

Scott paused just inside the basement and touched the rotten door-frame. "Sure. Whatever."

"Sam don't lie. He's okay."

Scott shrugged. "I guess, but I'm tellin ya . . . it ain't haunted. Wise up, chief."

Jesse swung his empty plastic bag at Scott. "You wise up, fart-knocker . . . "

Scott dodged, slipped, and bumped against a table next to the door, knocking over a glass jar. It hit the floor and shattered.

They froze.

Standing still for several hushed minutes, hearing nothing.

Scott relaxed and gave Jesse a weak grin. "Geez. Got me spooked with all those stories. And," he pointed at Jesse, "if you hadn't swung at me I wouldn'ta bumped that table."

Most of his fear had melted, but enough unease remained to make him feel snappy. "Well, maybe if you wasn't so damn clumsy an all."

"Nice. You kiss Mom with that mouth?"

"Whatever. Stick it, ass-breath."

Scott held up his hands. "Okay, enough. I give up. We good?"

Jesse stuck his hands into his pockets. He couldn't stay mad at Scott, not for long. "Yeah. Suppose."

Scott jerked a thumb over his shoulder.

"All right then. Let's move."

***

As he descends the basement steps he notices he's made no progress, like he's been descending an escalator the wrong way. The door at the bottom isn't any nearer. He stops, glances over his shoulder and sees that the rectangle of light on the first floor also isn't any farther away. That, and . . .

Faint whispers hiss around him.

Beneath that, he hears things crawling behind the walls, leathery bodies sloshing and squirming.

He stops.

Glances back at the door above. Its bright rectangle

beckons, and as he looks at the light, the whispers fade, and he feels peace.

But he can't turn back now, so he digs into his pocket and withdraws a folded piece of paper and a small flashlight. He sticks his hatchet pommel-first under his belt, clicks the flashlight on and reads the strange words silently, realizing that after this, there's no return.

Without looking behind him he reads the words printed on the sheet. Harsh consonants rasp against his teeth, twisting his tongue in unnatural ways. His voice, low and guttural, gurgles and croaks and echoes as he comes to the end of the strange invocation. He looks up, shines his flashlight on the door . . .

Nothing.

And then . . .

Rock shifts against rock, and what sounds like a great wind—though not a breath touches him—moans down the stairs. The rock-on-rock sound swells, then fades. The whispers fall silent.

He holds up his flashlight and stares.

The walls and ceiling of the stairwell have been replaced by a cold darkness. He looks down. The steps remain, as does the basement door, but now they float in a nothingness that makes his stomach roll. He doesn't bother looking behind him, figuring the door to the first floor has disappeared also. He imagines the stairs ascending forever into an endless black sky. He shivers and keeps looking ahead. Doesn't need to push his stomach over the edge. This isn't the best time to yack up his breakfast of bourbon and scrambled eggs.

Voices again drift from below, fading in and out like a radio station not in tune.

" . . . this is great . . . we're gonna be friggin rich . . . "

Cold desperation puckers his skin. There's not much time left. He has to move. He stuffs the flashlight and paper back into his pocket and snatches the hatchet from his belt. He then descends, trying very hard to ignore the swirling nothingness all around.

***

There really wasn't that much to see in the basement past some old scattered tools, rusted metal bits and gutted appliances—like old toasters and transistor radios—cluttering a workbench against one wall. Also on the workbench, a few overturned mason jars spilled screws, nuts and bolts into rusting piles. Several pieces of broken and rotting furniture littered the floor, giving the basement its only smell: a light, musty, damp-wood scent that paled in comparison to the woods out back.

But it turned out to be the mother lode. After only twenty minutes their bags bulged with their finds, Scott and Jesse finding most of the cans and bottles in dusty corners or stacked on shelves. At first, Jesse hadn't collected many because they were old and didn't have "refund" stamped anywhere on them, then Scott told him the new law afforded a "grace period" on any aluminum can, so he stuffed his bag full of crusty but not too disgusting cans of Genesee, Coke, Pabst Blue Ribbon and Schlitz. Two cans floating in a bucket of black, mucky water, however, he left for Scott.

Many years ago, someone had split the basement into the main workroom and several smaller rooms connected by a short hall. At the end of the hall, a door led upstairs.

"Man," Jesse said as he followed Scott, "this is great! We're gonna be friggin rich!"

Scott pushed open another door. "Dunno about that. Not if the rest of the house looks like this."

Jesse peeked around Scott into the dark room, saw litter everywhere, but except for a shattered Sunkist bottle in the corner, the room was mostly empty.

Scott cracked his neck. "C'mon. There's one last room. We'll check it out, then head upstairs."

Jesse didn't like the idea of going upstairs, at all. A chill played around his neck. Not fear, really, just . . .

"I dunno, Scott. Maybe we should go home. We got enough, dontchya think?"

Scott's face hardened. Jesse knew what that meant. Everybody did. Scott Kretch wasn't a quitter. He always got what he wanted.

Always.

Scott smiled. "It'll be fine, Jess. I'll take care of ya. Promise."

Scott always promised that.

And mostly, Jesse believed him.

Still, that cold feeling had seeped into his chest, making it a little hard to breathe. His head hurt for some reason and maybe he was just tired, but his ears were ringing, too.

But this was Scott.

Jesse couldn't say no.

"Okay. Let's move it, though. Mrs. Wilkins' yard, remember?"

"Yep."

Scott led the way out of the room and down the hall. Jesse followed him but his stomach churned.

Even with Scott's promise, Jesse couldn't shake a cold, sick feeling inside.

Stupid. Stupid dumbass baby. Lose the skirt and grow one.

Jesse pushed his unease away and followed Scott.

***

He stands at the door and it fills his vision, making it easier to ignore the emptiness behind him. Even so, he's broken out into a cold sweat. He hears them on the other side of the door, walking toward that last room, and fear tightens his throat.

Can he do this?

And do what, exactly? He doesn't know for sure *what* he's supposed to do, doesn't even know if today is the right day. He's read and studied lots over the years, but he's understood very little. When he woke up this morning, his gut just said: today.

He flicks off his flashlight and stuffs it into his pocket. Strange, unreadable symbols all along the doorframe (which hadn't been there before he read the incantations) are glowing now, so he doesn't need the flashlight anymore. He takes the gun out from under his belt, pops out the cartridge cylinder to check the special silver slugs he made by melting down old earrings and necklaces he'd bought or bartered for at Old Man Handy's Pawn & Thrift.

After a few seconds of inspection that doesn't make him feel any better, he slaps the cartridge cylinder back and pulls the hatchet from his belt. He paid two month's wages to make a silver blade for it, because he's read that silver hurts evil things, and though he's not exactly sure *what* waits for him on the other side of that door . . .

He knows it's evil.

So he holds both weapons and waits because he doesn't need to open the door. When the time comes, it'll open for him. That much of his reading he's understood.

Seconds pass.

Feet thump hard against a concrete floor somewhere nearby, then, " . . . what the hell . . . "

The knob twists.

The door sighs and drifts open.

And he steps through.

***

The last room looked different, like it had been dug out. It had no door, just a rectangular opening braced by a wooden frame. Inside, an uneven concrete floor rolled in bumps and ridges, like someone had mixed the cement in a wheelbarrow and poured it by hand. The walls were packed dirt with no windows, and its dirt ceiling hung lower than the other rooms, held up by thick wooden beams supported by intermittent floor joists. Also . . .

"Shit. Lookit that."

Scott swung his flashlight far left, illuminating three rows of strange shapes and symbols carved into the bumpy floor: squares, triangles, hexagons and squiggly lines.

Jesse turned his flashlight clockwise and stopped when he saw the same carvings to his right. "What the *hell*?"

Scott's flat tone spooked him. "Dunno. Maybe . . . "

"Maybe what? Don't dick around. This is some weird shit."

Scott looked at him, wide-eyed. "Maybe all the stories about this place are true."

Jesse felt his gut twitch. "Fuck that noise. Let's ditch."

"Hold on." Scott aimed his flashlight at the back wall. "Is . . . that a door? It don't go nowhere. Filled with dirt. What the hell?"

Jesse saw it; set into the back wall: a wooden, rectangular doorframe. Looked like some crazy bastard had pounded it straight into the dirt.

But who cared? Far as Jesse was concerned, his weird-shit meter was on overload. "Whatever. Let's go."

"Just a sec. Looks like there's a board on the wall next to it. Somethin carved on that, too. Lemme check. Then we can go."

"C'mon . . ."

"Shit." He flashed Jesse that damned smile again as he moved toward the back of the room. "Lose the skirt an–"

He jerked once and stiffened.

His flashlight slipped and fell to the floor.

"S-Scott?" Jesse's suddenly tight throat strangled his words. "C-Cut the s-shit!"

Scott gurgled, and a sour stink wafted from him. He'd pissed himself.

Jesse stumbled on rubbery legs, reaching for his brother. "Scott! What the hell . . . "

Scott twitched. "Nnnngnh!"

No!

Jesse's hand stopped inches from Scott's elbow. "What? What're you . . . "

"Dngnh!"

Down.

Jesse swung his flashlight down and sucked in a

hissing breath between his teeth. Scott had stepped onto a triangle carved into the uneven floor. At the triangle's points, circles contained other strange symbols.

Panic gripped Jesse. He felt like puking and blacking out, all at once. What should he do? No one knew they'd come here. It'd take too long to run for help and he sure as shit wasn't leaving Scott by himself.

Damn! Why Scott? Why not me? He's smarter, he'd know what to do . . . !

Jesse swung his flashlight around the empty room, his mind buzzing, not wanting to touch Scott because he was afraid something would happen to him, thinking maybe he could find a stick or board to push Scott out of the triangle . . . but what if that was bad, too? If magic had trapped Scott, wouldn't magic have to free him? Jesse thought he'd read that in his comics, and that if some weird voodoo-black magic had trapped Scott in that triangle and Jesse tried to push him out with a stick, maybe Scott would go crazy and have seizures and . . .

Wait.

Jesse pointed his flashlight where Scott had seen the board on the wall. Careful to side step the triangle that had trapped Scott, he approached it. Much as he hated himself, he couldn't make himself look at Scott as he passed.

In his comics Dr. Strange was always saying spells and opening the third eye, making weird hand gestures for magic. Maybe the words Scott thought he'd seen on the plaque were magic words that would set him free?

Jesse's flashlight lit up the board. His stomach

swirled and the words carved there blurred. He had to focus very hard to see them, and that made him feel sicker.

He rubbed his eyes. This was stupid. He didn't know what would happen when he read those words!

Jesse forced himself to look back at his brother. Scott's face twisted, his eyelids twitching, lips trembling. Drool leaked from the corner of his mouth.

Tears welled in Jesse's eyes, which made him feel like a damned baby, but he didn't care. This was Scott. The man. His hero.

I'll take care of ya

promise

Jesse turned away from Scott and looked the words over. Some of the last ones jumped out . . .

call upon thee to deliver me forth from this place

"Deliver me forth. That's gotta be it. That means get me outta here, right?"

Like he knew. But what else could he do?

Jesse swallowed and licked his lips. Feeling like this was the worst idea ever, he stuttered . . .

"O . . . uh . . . O K-Keeper of the G-Gate who art the Gate, O Keeper of the Key who art the Key . . . uh, lesse . . . who . . . who w-walks between worlds and across centuries . . . Gee-zus, what *is* this shit? I . . . uh . . . c-call upon thee to deliver me forth from this place!"

He looked back at Scott. A heartbeat passed.

Nothing. Then . . .

A tremor passed through Scott. His head twitched, eyes opening impossibly wide.

And then he screamed, arching his back, arms flailing. Smoke spewed from his shoulders. Jesse's stomach clenched as he smelled burnt flesh. Forgetting about the triangle and what it had done to Scott, he lurched forward, slipped . . .

. . . and then an invisible hand jerked him backward (which didn't make sense; wasn't there a wall behind him, how could he be flying backward?) and as the screaming and jerking and burning Scott shrank to a very small dot and darkness fell over everything, Jesse's mind screamed over and over I wanna go home, wanna go home, wanna go home . . . !

**

He steps into the room (which looks much smaller than he remembers) and sees his younger self sucked backwards into the swirling black vortex that has formed inside the dirt-filled doorframe. Scott abruptly ceases jerking and swaying inside the triangle, head down, hands hanging by his sides, strings of smoke rising off him, and then . . .

He looks over his shoulder and smiles that same damn smile . . . except this isn't Scott anymore.

"*Hey, Jess.*" That voice—like Scott's but not— echoes with countless others, "*Nice to see you again.*"

Too late.

He's come back too late. Sorrow and guilt twists Jesse Kretch's insides into knots. "Damn. Sorry, Scott."

He hefts and throws the silver-bladed hatchet at his brother and it strikes Scott in the back with a dull thud. Scott straightens with a yelp that sounds more pissed than hurt. Smoke pours out around the hatchet and a hot sizzling fills the air as the silver blade sags and melts against Scott's flesh. Sparks and small, greenish flames sprout from the wound, and rivulets of liquid silver run down Scott's back and legs.

Jesse Kretch is pointing his gun even as the

hatchet's silver blade dissolves, but before he can pull the trigger Scott gestures and the gun explodes, taking Jesse's hand off to the wrist and blowing bits of metal and flesh and bone everywhere. Jesse screams once, then an invisible hammer slams him back against the wall, pinning him there.

The hatchet's wooden handle clatters to the floor.

Rocks dig into Jesse's back as he writhes in pain. His stomach clenches, then he pukes down his front, bile stinging his throat and mouth. Wet warmth spreads across his groin, soaking his inner thighs.

Not-Scott turns inside the triangle.

Cocks its head and smiles wider. *"Silver this time. Nice try."*

Pain throbs across Jesse's body. "I-I don't understand. Wha ... what th' hell are ya?"

The smile vanishes. Not-Scott's face relaxes into a plastic expression. *"I am All in One and One in all. Past, present, and future converge in me."*

"So ya knew. Been waitin for me to come back, an it didn't matter *when* I did. You woulda *always* been here ... right?"

"I am Outside Time. I have always been here and will always be here, and you will always be here, at this moment, also."

An icy fist squeezes Jesse's heart.

All this time.

Studying whatever scrap of myth he could find, absorbing what little he understood. All the preparation, the waiting, when he thought he'd been sacrificing so much: love, success, happiness, his life, his reputation, everyone in town thinking he was just a crazy drunk ...

None of that mattered, and it didn't change a thing.

Not-Scott flicks its hand and invisible tethers drag Jesse from the wall toward the triangle, bringing him to a stiff-legged halt inches from it. Though he doesn't want to look into the blazing green orbs Scott's eyes have become, he can't look away and in them he sees terrible, inconceivable things.

"This body is insufficient to house He Who Lies Outside Time. You invoked the Gate. Your flesh should house Him. But this requires your willing submission."

Iron-tight bands squeeze his chest and icy fingers of fear clutch his heart, exhaustion and madness pounding his temples. "If . . . I say . . . no?"

That smile returns, stretching so wide Jesse fears it might split Scott's head in half. *"You will die. And He will fall dormant inside your brother's flesh, just beneath the surface. Your younger self will soon see changes in him. Changes* you've *already seen. Yes?"*

Jesse closes his eyes.

Bloody images spinning in his head.

Of the dead cats and rodents they'd started finding behind their house, of how Scott had shunned family and friends, becoming sullen and withdrawn, disappearing for hours into the woods with no explanations for where he'd been or what he'd been doing, of Scott's troubles with girls, how he nearly got sent away because of what he'd done to that one girl and finally, of police finding him dead in his Utica apartment at age twenty-one, after swallowing an old shotgun's muzzle. And then . . . all the things they'd found there.

Obscene videos, pictures, and magazines; journals filled with insane ramblings.

And the souvenirs.

From all the little girls and boys Scott had apparently killed.

Jesse opens his eyes, forcing himself to meet Not-Scott's burning gaze, swallowing down the nausea inspired by the things he sees there. "If . . . if I go with you . . . will it be different? Will . . . things turn out different?"

Not-Scott's face relaxes. "*Yes. Every decision creates ripples. Every ripple changes things. You've made ripples. Things* will *be different.*"

"F-fuck it, then. W-where we goin'?"

It smiles again, looking more like Scott than ever. "*Far away. To glorious worlds where the Ancients sleep and dream forever.*"

This means nothing to him. Only one thing does, in the end.

I'll take care of ya

promise

"All right." He breathes deep. "I'll go."

And everything becomes a burning, hissing white, then . . .

***

. . . he woke up.

"Scott!"

Jesse sat up.

In his bedroom.

At home. He looked around, confused.

I wanna go home, wanna go home, wanna go home

Everything seemed normal. Dr. Strange and Spider-man posters hanging on the walls, piles of comics sitting on his desk, rumpled clothes lying on the floor. Jesse swung his feet down and sat on the edge of the bed. He closed his eyes, bent over and held his head in his hands. His brain felt jumbled, like he'd been sleeping for hours and now couldn't wake up. Bizarre images mixed in his head with half framed thoughts and ideas that sounded crazy . . . out of his comics, even.

c-call upon thee to deliver me forth from this place
Jesse blinked, trying to concentrate.
Bassler House, and a weird-ass room
But it slipped away.

Jesse rubbed his forehead, feeling muddled. He and Scott had gone to Bassler House. Hadn't they? Some bright idea about snagging bottles and cans for that new five-cent deposit thing.

Jesse looked around his room again.

He frowned. They'd gone out around noon. Mom and Dad had gone shopping in Utica and wouldn't be home until dinner. But his room looked darker than noon . . .

He glanced at his bedside clock.

4:00.

Damn. We're supposed to cut Mrs. Wilkins' yard. She's gonna be pissed. What the hell have we been doin the past four hours?

They must've come home. He must've taken a nap. But why couldn't he remember . . . ?

Scott jerked and seized and burned and screamed
A cold sensation pulsed through him. Jesse bounced off his bed and jogged down the hall toward Scott's room. The door was partly open. He barged in with, "Hey, Scott! Get your lazy ass up! We gotta cut . . . "

Jesse slid to a stop and stared.

His knees buckled and they folded, sinking him to the floor. He opened his mouth and whimpered because there was Scott, lying on his bed, staring at the ceiling. Blood slicked the bed, oozing in thick streams down the sheets, pooling on the floor from a long, jagged gash in Scott's left arm, running from wrist to elbow.

Red meat glistened.

The wound puckered, like a smile . . .

that same damned smile

. . . while underneath just a hint of bone gleamed white. In Scott's other hand, blood-smeared scissors dangled from slack fingers.

A soft fuzziness closed over him. Jesse kneeled there, breathing in the tangy, metallic scent of Scott's blood, listening to flies buzz until his parents came home.

***

A month later Jesse stood in the last room at the end of that basement hallway. His parents had loosened up a little and had been letting him out alone more. He still had to return home by dark, of course, but Jesse was okay with that. The idea of being alone in the dark frightened him more than it used to.

Because something bad happened here.

Something that made Scott kill himself. Maybe even something evil, like in his comics. But so far, he'd found nothing. No carvings. No strange doors leading nowhere. No weird words on boards.

Nothing.

But his nightmares told a different story, nearly every single night.

Self-disgust filled him. Scott had wigged out and

killed himself. Who knows why? Whatever had happened, Jesse knew this: Scott was dead. Looking for things that just weren't there wouldn't bring him back.

He turned to leave, but kicked something that rolled. He knelt and panned his flashlight's beam along the ground, found it, grabbed it and held it up under the flashlight's glare.

An old wooden handle.

Maybe to a hatchet or something.

Funny thing was, though the handle felt worn and smooth, indicating much use, it felt solid. Not rotten or damp, which meant it couldn't have been laying around for long.

Someone had dropped it recently.

Jesse looked at what remained of its blade. It looked melted. The flashlight's beam glinted off the metal. Odd. Didn't look like cast-iron, but more like . . .

Silver.

In his comics, silver sometimes hurt evil things.

He frowned and examined the melted blade closer, noticing scorches and cracks, pieces flaking away, almost as if . . . the silver had been burnt away.

Because maybe it hadn't worked.

silver hadn't worked

For some reason that thought buzzed in his head. He turned the handle over, feeling its smooth grain . . .

His fingertips brushed rough, carved lines near its head. Numbers or maybe letters. He frowned and brought it closer to the flashlight.

His stomach grew very cold.

C. K.

Carlton Kretch.

Grandpa Carlton's hatchet.

Impossible. He'd seen that hatchet *once*, when he and Dad and Grandpa and Scott had gone camping last year. Grandpa had let out that maybe someday he'd give the hatchet to Jesse for his birthday . . .

Holy.

Shit.

Jesse stood and clutched the ruined and impossible handle. Everyone else could pretend Scott went crazy and killed himself, but he knew. Somehow, he knew.

That hadn't happened.

Jesse walked from that room, heading for the town library. The hatchet was proof, of what he didn't know, but *something* had happened to them here. Words *had* been carved into the wall. And though his memories of that day now blurred together, he knew he could remember them, if he tried hard enough.

He just needed time.

To save Scott.

6.

"So THAT'S IT?" I ask as we descend The Skylark's front steps into the nearly empty parking lot so Gavin can take a smoke break. "Jesse Kretch is *gone*?"

With a quick snap Gavin lights the cigarette in his mouth with a battered old Zippo, takes a drag and releases a gray-blue plume of smoke into the black sky. He stuffs the lighter into his front pocket, then sucks on his cigarette some more, its tip glowing a bright orange. He blows out more smoke and says, "When's the last time you saw Jesse? Do you remember?"

I close my eyes, thinking quickly. The answer comes sooner than I'd like. "New Year's Eve. A few weeks after that 911 call. He'd been cutting up rough at The Stumble Inn. Drunk again, ranting and roaring his usual gibberish at the top of his lungs. That time, Deputy Shackleford and I brought him back to the jail so he could sleep it off. Next morning, I got him breakfast—coffee and an egg sandwich from the Quickmart down the road—gave him my usual speech about him sobering up. Also, I remember him being meeker than usual that morning."

And there's nothing after that. I haven't seen him since. According to Gavin, that's because he's not around anymore. "Sonnuvabitch."

Gavin nods. He looks out across the dark parking lot, his gaze thoughtful. "Do you know what the worst thing is?"

I shake my head, if only because I can't imagine anything worse than what I've read so far.

liar

"After things died down no one ever talked about it. Scott, I mean. It was like the town decided it was too horrible to remember, so Scott never existed. Simple as that. We just stopped talking about it, even me, even Jesse's friends. Honestly, I didn't even fully remember Scott until I had finished his and Jesse's story. I'd forgotten, just like everyone else."

"Except Jesse," I whisper. "He never forgot. Just kept it all inside, I guess. He always seemed so sad, y'know? He never really did anything *bad*, from what I could see. Just drank too much and couldn't hold down a steady job. But everyone treated him like he had a disease or something and I could never figure out what it was he'd done to deserve that . . . "

And I can't really think of anything left to say. No snappy or sarcastic quip this time, but still, I'm not swallowing this story whole. At least this one I can verify, to an extent. Tomorrow, when it's light, I'll head out to Kretch's old trailer in the Commons Trailer Park, on the edge of town, right down the road from . . .

Bassler House.

And despite the summer night's warmth, a shiver runs through me. Gavin notices and faces me, eyes bright and penetrating, cigarette tip glowing in the dark. "What?"

"Bassler House," I whisper, trying to stitch together images and thoughts into a crazy quilt tapestry. "John

Finch took Daniel Pital to Bassler House, went crazy and beat him to death. And something in there took . . . or sent? . . . Jesse Kretch away, then drove his brother Scott insane. I've driven past it a few times. Just looks like an old, broken down Victorian farmhouse. But it's more, isn't it? There's something . . . wrong there. Something evil."

Gavin shrugs and looks away again, out across the parking lot. He smokes quietly for several seconds, then says, "I was in Bassler House, once."

"You've been inside?" Despite my best effort, my voice cracks just a little. "What . . . what did you see? Did you see anything like . . . "

"Like what Jesse and Scott saw? No. But to be honest . . . I'm not exactly sure how much I really remember."

"What do you mean?"

He frowns around his cigarette and his eyes dull, as if he's retreating inside. When he speaks, his tone is flat and dull.

"Whatever is happening to me, it's jogging loose all sorts of memories, some from my childhood, some I'd much rather not remember at all. *One* in particular, of the only time we—Fitzy, Father Ward and I—set foot into the damp halls of Bassler House . . . "

THE SLIDING

I'VE BEEN *REMEMBERING* things, lately. Things I don't want to remember, terrible things that happened long ago. I don't know why. Actually, I don't know much about anything, anymore. My writing career is over, I'm on the fourth year of a teaching career I hate, I've been drinking way too much, I'm remembering things I'd rather not and I don't. Know. *Why.*

I've tried to talk with Fitzy and Father Ward about it. They were there, of course. But the conversation always fizzles to a dead end and a change of subject. All they want to remember is the day three high school kids trespassed into the old spook house on the edge of town, and no matter how cleverly I've brought it up over the past few years I can't get their shuttered minds past a certain point.

They think—or NEED to think—nothing happened.

But something did happen. We glimpsed a dark truth: that a shadowed world exists next to ours, one defying explanation. And I'm remembering it.

All of it . . .

***

AUGUST, 1987

I hesitated on the old porch outside the closed window, hand resting on cracked siding. Through the dirty glass the room beyond appeared empty, littered with the usual debris you'd expect in an abandoned house: crumpled wads of paper, old books and magazines, tin cans, beer bottles, broken toys and plates.

"This is stupid," I muttered. "You seriously want to do this?"

"C'mon. You're the biggest guy here. You can't *possibly* be this much of a wimp, can you?"

I glared at Mike Fitzgerald over my shoulder. We'd been friends since my family and I moved here two years ago, but sometimes he pissed me off, royally. "Listen. Your parents may not care *what* you do. I cut my hand messing around with this window and Mom'll have a conniption, then Dad'll ground me for giving Mom a conniption."

"Honestly, Fitzy," Bill Ward said, leaning against the siding, "Gav's right. Maybe this isn't such a good idea. I mean . . . that window wasn't boarded up the last time we came here, and that was almost three years ago. Maybe we should just . . . "

"*Baaaaalls.*" Fitzy folded his arms and hung his head, as if mortified at our apparent cowardice. "What made your wangs shrivel up and fall off? *C'mon*, Bill. We've been in there tons of times. There's nothing even *mildly* creepy about it."

He smirked at me. "Unless, of course, you're from out of town like Nancy-Boy, here."

And that tore it.

Which, of course, Fitzy had been planning on.

I shrugged. "Fine. Someone give me a hand,

though. Looks pretty stuck to me." I grasped one corner of the window, and nodded at the other. "Bill . . . ?" He nodded and joined me without hesitation.

As we carefully tried to pry open the window, I asked, "So what's the deal?"

The story was typical, probably the same in small towns everywhere. Bassler House was an old, three story Victorian farmhouse that had been abandoned for years, and eventually all the kids in town embarked on a pilgrimage here to test their mettle. However, according to Bill, its walls and floors were adorned with nothing more than hastily scrawled Satan-worshiping scripts like pentagrams, 666 and such predictable slogans as *"Satan Rulz."*

"It's kinda lame," Bill said as the window finally screeched open. "It was fun to poke around here when we were little kids, but there's not much to see, really."

"That's only because no one's ever gone into the basement," Fitzy remarked. "Bet there's some seriously cool shit down there. No one's ever had the stones to check it out, though."

I glanced at the crumbling foundation and remarked, "That's probably smart. Doesn't look all that safe, honestly."

Fitzy snorted but I ignored him, figuring that the only way *he'd* ever venture into the basement would be if *I* went first.

And thank God we *didn't* go into the basement that day.

Because I'm not confident we would've made it out.

Several minutes later, after Fitzy had swiped a broken branch off the porch and wedged the window open, I crawled through and stood in a musty room on the first floor. Grit crunched underfoot as I turned in a circle, warily eyeing dark corners, walls shedding wallpaper in curled, shriveled strips . . .

And the open door in the far corner.

"So all the cool stuff's in the other room?"

"Yeah," Fitzy sneered, "check it out . . . if you're not pussy."

Bill sighed as he climbed in after me. "You're an idiot."

As usual, Fizty's reply was brilliant in its eloquence. "Bite me, cock-knocker."

I ignored them and approached the door. A slight chill rippled across my skin, but I told myself it came from a draft blowing through the window, that's all. But when I stepped through that door, I couldn't so easily dismiss the sensation.

Because in the next room *was* a pentagram, but it wasn't hastily scrawled on the wall, nor did it appear the work of drunken kids. Laid with meticulous care, a brick pentagram covered the whole floor in a near-perfect circle.

Bill reached my shoulder, saw what I did and whispered. "Holy . . . "

"What's up?" called Fitzy from outside. Getting no answer, he crawled through the window and when he joined Bill and I, he muttered, "*Damn.*"

Of course we did the most logical thing: we entered the room.

Almost instantly I smelled something rotten. A high-pitched buzzing—which I hadn't noticed before now—filled the air. I squinted and saw flies massing above each of the pentagram's points. As I passed them, that rotten-meat smell wafted upward, making my stomach churn. I couldn't really see very well *what* was rotting there but quite frankly, I didn't want to.

Eventually we found ourselves clustered by a winding stairway leading to the floors above. Bill nodded at the pentagram and whispered, "That's new."

I believed Bill's sincerity but remained skeptical of Fitzy's integrity. "You didn't set this up?"

The bald shock on his face unnerved me. "No *way*," he said, his mouth drawn tight.

We looked around. Unlike the other room, the walls had been painted a stark, blinding white, which maybe you wouldn't expect. A big pentagram laid out in the middle of a room, you'd expect the walls to be painted blood-red or midnight black, scrawled with the requisite 666 or upside-down crosses or weird words written in a strange foreign language. But the blankness of the walls seemed more serious, somehow, more real and very *wrong*, in a way I don't think any of us then could've put a finger on, but after all these years, the best I can come up with?

Alien.

Not human.

But, we were teens and supremely convinced of our immortality, so when no black-robed Satanists burst from hidden crevices to offer us up as virgin sacrifices to strange, unknown gods we relaxed, figuring the pentagram was probably the creation of some lonely and bored Goth kids with no lives and nothing better to do (who were probably virgins themselves). We couldn't explain the whiteness of the room, so, as teens tend to, we dismissed it, and after several minutes, Fitzy grinned and said, "We should trash it."

I glanced at Bill and frowned. "You mean . . . "

"Sure. Toss the bricks out the window. Screw up their little Goth party." He raised his eyebrows. "Think how pissed they'll be."

I shook my head. "That's *exactly* what I'm thinking."

However, this was Clifton Heights. The real world. Nothing much ever happened here. How likely was it that a bunch of Satanist/Goths would hunt us down and drag us from our homes kicking and screaming for messing up their brick pentagram?

This time, however, I wasn't content to lead. "Fine," I nodded at the bricks, "be my guest."

Fitzy's eyes narrowed. For a moment, I thought he'd pass.

But in a flash he grinned, vaulted to the pentagram, grabbed a brick and flung it with rare enthusiasm at the room's only window.

The brick crashed through.

Glass tinkled to the floor.

And when hordes of Satanists didn't stream forth to devour us, we descended upon the pentagram, grabbing and chucking bricks through the window.

I don't remember much about what happened next. We grabbed and threw; grabbed and threw, manic and machine-like. I hate to think that in our fervor we scooped up the rotten matter on the floor but we must've, because minutes later, when we stood in the room's center, panting, the floor lay bare as we absentmindedly wiped our hands off on our jeans.

Our adrenaline burst fading, we eyed each other with dreadful fascination. We'd lost ourselves in our brick-throwing frenzy and it was a bit alarming, to say the least.

And we stood there in the tired weirdness, waiting.

But nothing happened.

Fitzy broke the silence by clapping his hands and saying, "Well, that's that. Let's see if there's anything cool upstairs."

Abruptly, Bassler House became nothing more than an old house in need of exploring. Our momentary fugue dismissed, we tramped up the winding stairs in search of more oddities.

But about fifteen minutes later we descended, mildly disheartened. We hadn't found much. Most of the rooms had been empty save scraps of litter, offering little amusement. Perhaps the most interesting things we'd found was a dented, pitted whisky flask in one room and in a second room, a hole in the middle of its floor, looking as if something had plunged through recently.

I'm not sure how we didn't see it as we descended the steps, but the *smell* hit us the instant our feet touched the floor.

"What the *hell* . . . " Fitzy breathed.

There in the middle of the room was the pentagram, untouched, whole. The flies buzzed as before and when we looked to the window we'd thrown the bricks through . . .

"The window," I said, "it's not broken."

Bill pointed a shaking finger to the window we came in, rasping, "It . . . it's closed. We left it open. Fitzy *propped* it open!"

What happened next is still . . . fuzzy.

We ran out of the room . . . but seconds later found ourselves standing around the pentagram facing each other, hordes of flies buzzing at our feet. We couldn't move or speak, our muscles clenched in fear. Sweat glistened on Fitzy's face; tendons strained in Bill's neck as my fingernails dug into my palms.

And there was something *there*, moving down the hallway. A heavy body sliding toward us, and though it seemed to last forever, it never got any closer.

Between his teeth, Fitzy grated, "Wreck it. Gotta . . . *wreck it.*"

Those words broke the spell holding us there. We again descended upon the pentagram, but all I remember are strange, twisted faces, howling mouths, burning eyes. We grabbed and hurled bricks through the window again.

And when we finished, Fitzy clapped his hands and said, "Well, that's that. Let's go see if there's anything cool upstairs."

Again we ascended, saw very little of anything, except for the dented whiskey flask and the room with no floor, then descended, a little disappointed. When we hit the bottom of the stairs, we smelled the rot again.

"What the *hell*?"

"The window's not broken."

"Where we came in—it's *closed*. Fitzy propped it open! I know he did!"

We tried once more to run but again found ourselves rooted around the pentagram as a heavy *thing* slowly slid down the hallway, much closer, this time.

We struggled and ground our teeth until finally Fitzy managed, "Wreck it. Gotta . . . *wreck it.*"

And again we did.

Only to find ourselves quickly returned to our spots, the sliding even *closer,* now. After the same interminable fight, Fitzy choked, "Wreck it. Gotta . . . "

But I found my voice. "No! Leave it!"

Fitzy and Bill's wide eyes showed their disbelief. "We have to," Fitzy hissed, "it's making this happen!"

And a *force* seized me, an incredible pressure swelling inside my head. My ears rang and eyes watered, and, in my heart, I wanted to destroy that pentagram so bad my hands itched with the desire.

And that's when I suspected. Hell, I *knew*.

The *house* didn't want me to talk. It wanted us to keep wrecking the pentagram, over and over, forever . . . until the sliding reached us. I didn't know how I knew that, how it was possible, but somehow I knew it was true, all the same.

I managed to shake my head. "No . . . it *wants* us to keep wrecking it . . . to stay stuck. It's holding us here . . . for *IT*."

Shocked realization lit in their eyes. "The sound in the hallway," Bill rasped, "it's getting closer."

My mind whirled and I felt sick but I pressed on, following my intuition. "We leave it," I gasped. "We'll leave it alone, go away, and never come back."

The pressure disappeared.

Our bodies leapt free.

But the sounds in the hallway, however, *slid closer*. "Go!"

We pounded away from the pentagram into the adjoining room, arms and legs pistoning. With the loop broken, the window was propped open as Fitzy had originally left it, but as we fled the sliding filled the room, and to this day I'm sure that I felt the hot mist of breath on my neck.

Fitzy, quicker than Bill and I, scrambled through the window first, knocking away the branch and bracing it open with his arm. I've always wondered if he saw It, because I remember his white face and dinner-plate eyes as he screamed, "*Hurry!*"

Bill made it through the window easily. Tall and lanky, I'd always been a little clumsy, so I slid to a stop, put my hands and one foot on the windowsill to pull myself through . . .

. . . and stopped.

Because I wanted to turn around, wanted to see *It* for what it was, *needed* to see It, for real.

But Bill and Fitzy grabbed my shoulders and pulled me through the window. We crashed together onto the old porch in a dusty heap, rotten boards shuddering. The window slammed shut.

And the air fell still.

We glanced at each other for several quiet minutes.

"We oughta get going," Bill finally offered, "Dad'll have the grill hot by now."

"Yeah," Fitzy added, "and I wanted to go into town before dinner."

I nodded silently. We got up, brushed the dust off our clothes and walked away from Bassler House, ignoring the much lower sun, ignoring also the muted sliding, as if something was still chasing us from far away.

***

So here I sit in my office, thinking about what it is I've just written and what I've been writing these past few months. As a professional, my writing career is over. It ended one snowy night on I-95 outside Portsmouth, New Hampshire. I've come to accept this. And to be honest . . . I've changed so much in the past few years, these past few months in particular, that my life as a published author seems a dim fantasy, a memory of a life that happened to someone else.

But I'm a still *writer*. Published or not. There's an old saying, I'm not sure from where: "You're a fighter. And a fighter fights." Well, writers *write*. And I've been doing that a lot lately, writing and writing and writing, but . . .

This is different than the kind of writing I used to do. This writing is uncovering things, unlocking doors, *revealing* things hidden and forgotten, terrible truths that may very well explain all the darkness that's grown inside my soul over the years, leading me to where I am today . . .

Like that moment, at the window.

When I wanted to turn and look, turn and *see* the sliding. I think *that's* the source of everything, maybe even the reason why all this is happening to me right now, with all this uncovering.

Because I want to see.

I've always wanted to see, wanted to see those dark things we dismiss and ignore in the comforting light of day. I've *always* wanted to see that thing hiding in the shadows, just around the corner, that thing in the night, hiding under the bed, in the basement, those dark things that dwell and hide there . . .

I've always wanted to see them.

And I'm only now admitting it to myself.

I saw something that day, and I wonder if that's why I eventually became a writer to begin with. Writing is seeing, isn't it? At the very least, when I write, I *seek* to see.

I don't think the sliding has ever gone away.

I think it's always been with me, since that day. But

maybe I didn't hear it, because in all my writing that got *published*, I wasn't *seeing* . . . except for that first book, about Michael Lockenstein and really, THAT's why I stopped writing the sequel to *Shades of Darkness*, because I had become too scared to *see*.

But now . . . I *need* to see.

Even if I really don't *want* to.

And when I write, things are quiet. Peaceful. But if I don't write, if I dare skip an evening confessional with my iBook, I dream. Of horrible things sliding down the hall, toward my bedroom, shuffling, slithering, sliding . . .

But never getting any closer. And somehow, I think I can hold it at bay . . . as long as I keep writing.

Enough for now. Time to sleep. I can only hope that I've written enough, and that the sliding won't come any closer tonight.

7.

GAVIN HAS SATISFIED his nicotine-fit so we're back inside The Skylark, enjoying the warm cups of coffee that Cassie Tillman refilled in our absence. Gavin sips from his and says, "So you see, you're not the only one who has a hard time getting answers around here. No matter how much I hound Fitzy and Father Ward neither of them will admit anything strange happened that day. But I have a theory as to why."

"And that is?"

Gavin tips his head. "I wonder if they've just come to accept what happened better than me. I ran away and became a moderately successful author who thought he was King Shit, getting as far as possible from my home and who I really was, and the one brush I had with writing about *Truth* scared me into writing for the market and for others only."

I nod slowly. "But Father Ward and Fitzy came home."

"Right. They came home and remained true to their calling, so maybe that's why they don't want to talk about that day. They don't *need* to. They've faced whatever they saw in that house and have dedicated their lives to battling It, while I, on the other hand . . . "

He sips from his coffee and doesn't finish the thought.

"What happened in Bassler House? Do you remember more now, after writing about it?"

Gavin shrugs. "Honestly, I'm still not sure, but I think a *door* of some kind was opened in there. Not all the way, just a crack. And I think something slipped through into our world, and that's what we almost saw. And yes I *am* struck by the similarities between the thing in Bassler House and the thing I dreamed or hallucinated after my accident in Portsmouth. It's led me to another theory, a somewhat dreadful one."

"What's that?"

"That maybe . . . " he pauses, clasps his newly refilled coffee cup, as if seeking warmth from it. He sighs and says, "Maybe that thing I saw after my accident has been with me this whole time, ever since that day in Bassler House when I was a kid. Maybe it latched onto me and has been lurking in the shadows, waiting for just the right moment . . . "

"Your accident," I murmur, a cold sensation playing down my neck.

"Perhaps. And now . . . " He waves at the book, lying open before me. "I've got *this*."

I sip from my own coffee and swallow. The warm bitterness runs down into my stomach, bracing me against a chill I wasn't aware of until now. "So this house. Finch went crazy in there and killed Daniel Pital. Maybe something in there possessed and killed Scott Kretch, kidnapped Jesse Kretch, and *you* saw . . . or almost saw . . . something . . . "

I pause, realizing I'm now assuming that all these stories are true. Though some part of me accepts this, I find I'm not any less afraid.

Actually, I'm terrified.

"So. Bassler House. Is it haunted? Cursed? How does it fit into the big picture? Because Ellen Danvers lost her son on Bassler *Road*. Is there a connection? Is Timmy Danvers in Bassler House?"

Gavin sits quietly for several minutes. I don't speak; worried about rushing him past anything that might help me. Finally, he says, "If Timmy Danvers ever *was* in Bassler House, I don't think he's there now. But the house isn't evil, I don't think. Or cursed, for that matter. As for haunted . . . " He shrugs. "Depends on your definition of the word."

"Not evil? Are you kidding? What about that *thing* you almost saw as kids? What about Jesse and Scott Kretch's story?"

I stop and look around quickly, realizing I'm speaking a little loudly. Thankfully, The Skylark is mostly empty at this hour, and no one seems to have noticed my outburst.

I face Gavin again. "How'dya call that *not* evil?"

"Well, remember, we found a pentagram made of bricks, made by *someone*. *They* called It forth, into that house, or at the very least were in the process of calling It forth. We just blundered across it. Scott and Jesse found something in Bassler House's basement . . . in *that* version of their story, at least . . . that was most likely manufactured by man. So the house itself isn't evil, I don't believe, but there *is* something there. If you'll indulge me in a little armchair metaphysics, maybe there's an opening or a rift on the quantum level, and out of that rift pulses an energy that *affects* people. Like Finch, when he murdered Dan Pital. Or maybe this energy *draws* the kind of people who laid that pentagram, the kind of people who created that doorway in the basement."

Unfortunately, I'm not listening too well because of something Gavin said that caught my attention. I hold up my hand, saying, "Wait. Wait a sec," while searching my memory . . .

There.

in that version

"What did I say?"

I point at him, my mind grappling with a whole new set of implications. "You just said something about Jesse and Scott Kretch. You said 'in *that* version of their story.'"

Gavin fidgets, looking uncomfortable. "Yes. I did."

"What does that mean?"

Gavin sits back in the booth, for the first time looking as unsure as I feel. "I'm not certain. Do you remember those middle grade books we read as kids, the ones with two sides? You read a story through one side, it ended in the middle, then you flipped the book and read a different story from the other side?"

I nod. As a kid I didn't like to read any more than I do now, but I do remember those. "Yeah. They were the only kinds of books I really liked, those and the 'Choose Your Own Adventure' books. Are you saying these stories are like . . . ?"

Gavin shakes his head and leans forward. "Not the CYA books. Those were about choosing your own fate. No, Jesse and Scott's stories are like those flip-book stories: they have the same characters, similar settings, but completely different plots and endings."

"So what are you talking about? Alternate dimensions? Different realities? Is that where Jesse Kretch went? Is that where Timmy Danvers is?"

Gavin holds up a hand, looking a bit flustered. "I don't *know*. Honestly, I don't. I've done a lot of reading this past year in quantum mechanics and metaphysics, even studied something called 'string theory' and as far as I can tell there are no definitive answers for these sorts of things. I think that for whatever reason some sort of energy emanates from Bassler House that keeps most of us away but also attracts darker, more disturbed folks. And, if we are to believe these stories I've written, either Bassler House offers a window of sorts into other realities or these emanations twist or even fragment reality *into* different realities."

He shakes his head. "I've always thought myself a reasonably intelligent guy. In an academic sense, anyway, not so much with life choices, I suppose. Also, as a formerly published genre author, I'd like to credit myself with a fertile imagination and a flexible mind. But I'm no physicist. This stuff is just as baffling to me as it probably sounds to you."

I grunt and rub my temples, which are starting to hurt, when a thought occurs. "Wait. Could all these 'alternate stories' be happening at once? So if I went inside Bassler House, right now . . . "

" . . . another version of you would be there, in a different room, experiencing a different scenario?" He spreads his hands in a surprisingly pleading gesture. "I really couldn't say."

"What about *you*? Do you remember different stories about what happened in Bassler House?"

He shakes his head. "No. I remember just *one* story, maybe because it was about me, and because I write the stories, I can only see and write one story about myself. But I sometimes wonder if that's why

Father Ward and Fitzy remember different things about that day, because maybe . . . in some other reality . . . it DID happen differently for them, and they've latched onto *that* as their memory."

"This is giving me one HELL of a headache."

"Imagine writing the things giving you a headache," he offers dryly . . . but I see it in his eyes, in the shadows lurking there: the strain and the fatigue wearing him down, even as we speak.

"So how alike ARE these stories, then?"

He pushes the open book toward me. "See for yourself."

MONSTER

JESSE KRETCH SQUEEZED the steering wheel of his truck with a white-knuckled grip. Bile stung the back of his throat. He'd thrown up so many times today and he wanted to throw up now, but his stomach was empty and another round of dry heaves would do nothing more than leave him wrung out and aching.

And the voices.

They called to him.

Taunting and jeering. He screwed his eyes shut and bit his tongue to keep from screaming because the voices never stopped anymore. They kept at him day and night, laughing, prodding . . .

They never stopped.

Ever. That's why he had to end this, now.

Jesse grabbed a handful of his hair and pulled. Pain rippled across his scalp and cut through the voices, giving him some clarity. He'd discovered—quite by accident, when he'd punched the bathroom mirror in rage the other day—that pain cleared his head, so as he twisted and pulled handfuls of hair, the voices faded. But they'd be back. They ALWAYS came back.

Which meant Jesse didn't have time to waste. He grabbed his old .38 Wesson off the dash, shouldered open the truck's door and scrambled out onto Bassler Road, reaching behind him and tucking the gun under his belt. It probably wouldn't do much good. However, if he finally faced the thing that killed his brother, he wouldn't let It get him . . .

Like It had gotten Scott.

He rounded the tailgate, reached into the truck's bed and pulled out an old axe. Clenching the handle, he walked away from his truck and plunged into the undergrowth alongside Bassler Road, pushing past the thick brush into the old driveway that he and Scott had walked up so long ago . . .

***

1985

"C'mon, Scott. You still haven't told me what we're doin here. What's the big deal?

Jesse scowled, nostrils twitching at Bassler House's musty scent, and he coughed several times to get the bad-tasting air out. "We ain't tryin to find those nudie books kids' are always yappin about, are we?" He frowned at his older brother. "Cause that's bogus, ain't it?"

It was the whispered Grail Legend of Clifton Heights High that stacks of nudie books lay hidden somewhere in Bassler House. The story had been passed down through generations from sly seniors to gullible freshmen, and the origins of the magazines always varied: left behind by former owners, by vagrants who drifted through town and squatted there, by the football players who partied there every year. Most scoffed at the tale, figuring it was just a scam to filch cash off dumb underclassmen in exchange for a fake "secret nudie map." Others, however, clung to the legend with zealous intensity, swearing on their collective grandmothers' graves that the treasured pornucopia existed and that they'd leafed its glossy pages themselves.

Scott shook his head, frowning slightly. "Nah. Story's bogus."

"Brad Finch swears it's true. Said he's seen em himself."

"Brad Finch is a dumbass," Scott replied calmly.

"Well, why're we here, then? Ain't we gotta mow old Martha Wilkins' lawn by three?"

Scott waved. "Yeah, but she's got one of those new JOHN DEERE riders. That won't take long." Hands on hips, surveying Bassler House's ruined interior, he pronounced, "We're looking for something better anyway. We're looking for beer and soda cans."

"That's stupid. Why?"

"Didn't you read that article in The Tribune the other day about the new recyclin laws?"

Jesse shrugged. "Naw. I read the comics an sports. The other stuff's boring."

"Well, there's some new law sayin people can get a nickel for every soda an beer can they turn in. Mr. Greenwood at the Great American Grocery is gonna start taking them."

"So?"

"So . . . think about all the football parties they've had out here over the years. That's a *lot* of beer cans."

"Still don't get it."

Scott popped Jesse in the shoulder with a playful punch. "*Dumbass*. Think about it. These bags hold about a hundred cans each. If we fill them both up, multiply two hundred cans by five cents, how much we got?"

"Oh! Lesse . . . it'd be seven bucks . . . no, wait." He frowned, biting his lower lip. "Uh. Five times two is . . . uh . . . move the decimal point one, no, two times . . . "

"God, Jess. It'd be ten bucks." Scott paused, smiling at him, "Think how many comics you could buy with that. *New* issues, kiddo."

Blissful comprehension dawned upon Jesse and he grinned. "Wow," he whispered. But then he frowned. "Wait. You don't read comics. What're you gonna buy?"

Scott shrugged, looking around Bassler House's shadowed interior. "Dunno. Think of something later. Cans first." He nodded toward the leaning flight of stairs ascending to the second floor landing above. "Ready?"

"Yeah, but we gotta get goin. I got the new Spider-Man comic from the Pharmacy the other day. The one where he fights Sandman for the first time? I wanna read that before we cut fatso Wilkins' yard . . . "

***

before we cut fatso Wilkins' yard . . .

Jesse stopped and hefted the axe onto his shoulder. It felt good there. Heavy, solid, and commanding. Made him feel strong for the first time in a very long time. Some rational part of him buried deep inside suspected that strength was an illusion, but it was all he had, now.

The sun was falling, its orange glow shimmering off jagged pieces of broken window glass. Bassler House's shadow reached toward him, sliding across gravel and dirt. Jesse breathed, clenching sweaty fingers around the axe's handle, taking it all in for the first time since the monster killed Scott.

Bassler House.

Out here in the middle of an old cornfield left fallow, looking even worse than it had twenty-six years ago, its roof sagging in several places, most of its paint peeled, revealing bleached, bone-white wood. Broken shutters hung limply, fluttering in the breeze against the siding, taping out a light, faraway tick-TACK, tick-TACK, tick-TACK . . .

Like the beating of a heart.

The *monster's* heart.

The front porch sloped downward at one end, its foundation gradually sinking. For decades, no one had ever expressed interest in owning the house so there it had remained, in the bank's ownership, waiting quietly.

Waiting for Jesse to return.

Bitter memories churned his guts; memories he'd never be free of, because every time he closed his eyes he saw it all again: Scott, broken and bleeding, lying on his back, his neck twisted at an odd angle, staring at the ceiling with those wide and terrified eyes.

It was his fault.

He'd let it happen, had let the monster get Scott and he'd never had a moment's peace since, living alone in a small, dirty trailer down the road in the Commons, drinking himself to sleep every night to block out the bad dreams, crawling out of bed every morning to face another mind-numbing day at the lumber mill, when he was sober enough to, at least.

He was a failure. A shambling, drunken failure,

because he'd let the monster get Scott in the summer of 1985. It had been an epic summer, the kind all boys dream about, but it had sunk into darkness after Scott's life was snuffed out with the heavy THUD of deadweight crashing down.

Everyone in town had thought it an accident. When searchers came looking for them, they found Jesse sitting next to Scott's broken and bleeding body, crying in shaking gasps, holding Scott's cold, limp hand.

And no one had believed him about the monster. Mothers buried him in embraces smelling of lilacs, assuring him that "of course death is a monster, dear baby, it's the worst monster of all." Men shook their heads, quietly annoyed at his wailing. Doctors murmured complicated things like "transubstantiated displacement of anger and guilt on an imaginary corporeal construct" while classmates conjured up more vivid and far less charitable words:

nuts
crazy
loony
weirdo
loser

Jesse hefted the axe off his shoulder, its wooden handle slippery in his hands, the old gun a reassuring pressure at the small of his back. His stomach gurgled. He cracked his neck and tightened his sweaty grip on the axe, fanning the flames of his rage before the voices came back. He willed his anger to burn higher and brighter, to protect himself from them.

He'd tried so hard after Scott died to live up to his name. He played all the same sports Scott had liked, trying to *be* Scott, and even though no one ever said it,

Jesse knew he'd failed. He'd never be Scott; he *couldn't* be Scott, ever.

Jesse closed his eyes and felt the voices reaching out from where they waited beneath the house: a light, feathery touch that drove him mad. He breathed in the cooling twilight air, catching the slight whiff of damp rot. "I'm comin," he rasped. "Just like you want. But I'm gonna kill you. ALL of you."

The voices fell silent.

And Bassler House loomed, windowless eye-sockets glaring at him, daring him to come and try.

Jesse breathed once more, quick and shallow. It was time to balance the scales, right the wrongs, atone for his sins. Make up for the way he'd let Scott down, make up for letting the monster kill Scott.

So Jesse stalked up the drive toward Bassler House, his footfalls beating out a dull rhythm that sounded like the gelatinous beating of a lumbering heart, the *monster's* heart, which had been beating in his head over and over since Scott died.

Three more steps, two left, and then with one long stride he mounted the front porch and approached Bassler House's front door, behind which lay all his nightmares and Scott, too, eternally broken and bleeding. Everything good in Jesse's life had died with Scott, and no matter how hard he'd tried, he'd failed at being Scott, for Mom and Dad, for his teachers and his friends, and even for himself, because he was just Jesse and nothing more.

Until today.

Because today he was going to kill the monster that killed Scott.

Jesse raised the axe above his head, screamed and

swung it downward in a scything arc, striking rotten, damp wood with a satisfying, muscle-shaking blow.

The voices in his head laughed, chanting: *not good enough, not good enough, NOT GOOD ENOUGH!*

Jesse yanked the axe from the door and swung again and again, hacking away at the dead wood as the voices laughed and he screamed, remembering when he and Scott first stepped into Bassler House and he'd said . . .

***

1985

"Sam Higgins says this place is haunted. Says people see weird lights and hear strange sounds at night."

"Whatever. Like I believe *that*."

"Sam wouldn't lie. He's okay."

"Yeah, I guess." They stopped at the staircase's first step. Scott laid a hand on the banister and looked up. "Know him from basketball. He's cool. But this house *ain't* haunted, dumbass."

Jesse scowled a little at *dumbass* but couldn't stay mad at Scott because he was the best older brother a kid could have. He always let Jesse tag along wherever he went, hanging out with him like he hung out with his older friends. Scott wasn't ashamed to be seen with him, and he always picked him for kickball at recess even though Jesse couldn't kick worth a damn.

And Jesse couldn't count the times Scott had beaten the shit out of Brad Finch and Jared Simmons for roughing him up during gym, and when girls came over, he never introduced Jesse as his "dumb baby brother" and never told him to get lost. Scott had even dumped one girl for making fun of Jesse.

Scott was the best, and he looked it, too. Tall for his age and strong, he moved in a graceful way Jesse desperately imitated but somehow knew he could never, ever match.

He was *Scott*.

The best brother, ever.

Scott turned, flashing Jesse one of his winning smiles, and proceeded up the steps to redeemable-can glory. "Let's go, chief . . . "

***

let's go chief

Jesse stepped through the splintered door, breathing in the damp odor of wet rot. He blinked, chest heaving as his heart forever pounded in tune with the dark beast hiding in Bassler House's shadowed corners. He knew it lurked somewhere in here, hissing foul breath into the air, poisoning his soul.

By his senior year of high school he'd given up trying to be Scott, the bitter taste of continual disappointment too hard to swallow, anymore. He'd also stopped talking about 'the monster,' sensing that if he persisted, motherly expressions of compassion would sour, doctors would turn unwanted scrutiny on him and the names his classmates called him would only get worse.

So he'd shut up like they'd wanted him to and pretended to get over Scott's death. He'd danced the dance, sang the song, convinced the school guidance counselor he *was* dealing with it and did his best on the outside to live a "normal" life. But all the while, a quiet rage had blazed inside him. Scott was dead. The monster in Bassler House had killed him, and there was nothing he could do to bring Scott back or replace him.

And if he couldn't replace Scott or bring him back, what else could he do?

"I'm gonna kill you," Jesse growled, "kill you ALL, if I hafta rip this whole damn house down to do it."

He looked left, then right. Shadows jigged on the walls and floor as the sun set. He closed his eyes, remembering Scott's sharp cry, that look of FEAR (which Scott never showed, ever) the dull thud of his body, the sharp crack of his neck, the wet gurgle in Scott's blood-choked throat and the pleased mewling receding into the shadows, leaving him alone in the dark with his dead brother.

He opened his eyes, his breath catching. He saw nothing on the second floor landing, but he *knew* that the monster was up there, laughing, hungry . . . waiting for him behind the door at the top of the stairs, the last door Scott had ever gone through, the door that had lead to his death.

He raised the axe above his head, screamed, and pounded up the steps three at a time, each footfall echoing the beating of the beast's dark heart. When Jesse reached the top he plunged forward, heaving the axe behind his head with all his might, screaming through a raw throat.

The monster hid behind *this* door.

Jesse heard its clicking claws digging into wood and its hungry, snapping teeth; heard the beating of its heart.

He swung the axe and it struck the door's center, splitting it down the middle. The door gave away, pieces of wood flying.

A sharp cry came from behind the door.

The monster!

It was here!

And he pushed through the wreckage of the door, axe raised above his head, howling, thoughts bombarding him of the last time he saw Scott, in this room . . .

***

1985

" . . . well, geez," Scott muttered as he pushed the door open and stepped inside, "this sucks."

Jesse peered over Scott's shoulder and looked around. Sunlight streamed through the room's only window, illuminating dust particles, cutting through the room's shadows like a knife, and he frowned as he saw what Scott meant. The room was empty, save for three old Genesee cans and what looked like an old Sunkist bottle shattered in one of the back corners. Certainly not the treasure trove of redeemable cans Scott had described.

"There's nothing much in there, hardly anything at all," Scott said, the disappointment evident in his voice.

"That's okay," Jesse replied, eyeing the room's floor. Near the middle it looked yellow, sagging, maybe even rotten with age. "I dunno if we should go in there. I mean . . . that floor looks like it's about to fall through."

Scott grunted, sounding as if this was little comfort, indeed. "Yeah. Suppose so."

"Hey, what if all the rooms're like this?" Jesse complained. "It'll take forever, an we ain't gonna get enough to buy *one* comic book."

Scott turned and grinned. "Y'know, I bet the football guys hardly ever come up here anyway. Everyone in town says they have their bonfires out back. *That*'s where all the cans'n bottles are I bet, there and in the basement. Probably where they take the cheerleaders to mess around."

Sudden fear stabbed Jesse's heart, a chill creeping up his spine. "T-the b-basement? We're goin d-down there?"

"Yeah, sure. I even brought a flashlight and everything." Scott pulled a silver flashlight out of his back pocket for Jesse's inspection.

Jesse eyed it suspiciously. "S'got new batteries in it?"

Scott tapped it. Metal rang lightly. "Yep."

"Everreadys?"

Scott smiled. "Brand new."

Jesse shook his head. "I dunno, Scott. This house is old, the electric don't work, an what if the foundation ain't no good? I don't wanna go down there."

Scott sighed. "Gimme a break, Jess. We'll just go down there for a couple of minutes, that's it."

"Yeah, but it'll be dark an wet an full of spiders an junk."

"C'mon, Jesse. Take your skirt off and . . . "

"There's monsters down there!"

Jesse snapped his jaw shut, hoping to choke off his fears, but it was too late. He knew what Scott was going to say and was ashamed he'd said something so stupid in front of him.

Scott slapped his forehead and groaned. "*Seriously*? Jesse. Stop acting like such a little . . . "

And then, suddenly, he was mad at Scott. Actually MAD at him. "No! I don't *wanna* go in the basement!"

"Jess, it'll be cool." Scott waggled the flashlight. "We got a flashlight with brand new batteries. What can possibly hurt us?"

A vibrant fear boiled in Jesse's chest, coming from nowhere and everywhere all at once. His heart pounded, his head ached, a ringing in his ears rising and falling. "NO, Scott. I don't wanna go down there."

"Jesse, what's *wrong* with you? It'll be fine, I promise."

Scott stepped toward the hall but Jesse pushed himself into his path. Surprise registered on Scott's face. Jesse had never denied him, not *ever*.

"*What* are you doing? Stop messin around, Jess!"

Icy panic gushed inside Jesse's heart. "Let's just go home," he pleaded. "I'll cut ALL of fatso Wilkins' yard an you can look at any of my comics . . . "

Scott flexed, his larger frame pushing against him. Jesse dug his shoulder into Scott's gut and somehow held his ground. "Jess, you're kinda pissin me off, here . . . "

"No, Scott! I don't wanna go down there!"

"Jesse, get outta my way! There's nothin bad down there, you'll see . . . "

Jesse shook his head, images of dark and slippery and slimy *somethings* spinning through his head. He dropped his plastic bag and placed both hands on Scott's chest. "No!"

"That's it, Jess," Scott said, "we're *totally* going down there now, if I have to drag you, just to show you there ain't nothin to be scared of." He brought his arm up to swipe Jesse aside.

"NO!" Jesse wailed and shoved Scott with all his might.

Scott stumbled backward. Scott, super-athlete, who'd never stumbled, ever.

Until now.

The flashlight fell from Scott's hands, hitting the floor with a dull metallic sound. It rolled away, down the stairs, each successive THWANG echoing over and over all the way to the bottom, and it was like watching an old black and white film with no sound, in slow motion: Scott, falling backwards into the room. Jesse, crying out silently, reaching for Scott's hands, Scott's mouth working as he fell . . .

For several precious seconds Scott Kretch was airborne, and Jesse thought for a moment that maybe Scott could fly.

He was Scott Kretch, after all.

Wonderful, super-perfect Scott.

Why not?

But the thought faded, the moment passing, time returning to normal. Scott slammed onto his back, onto the old, rotten, sagging floor, which crumbled beneath him, disintegrating like paper mache. Scott's lower body slid out of sight, as if he were sucked into the floor, and he cried out as he fell through the ragged hole . . .

And stopped.

One hand clutching what looked like an old floor-beam.

"J-Jess . . . "

Pieces of plaster and drywall crumbled, peppering the floor below, sounding too far down.

"H-hey. C'mon, Jess . . . h-help . . . p-please!"

And Jesse stood there, shivering, his legs frozen, knees locked, heart pounding in his chest and his head, over and over and over and over . . .

"JESS!"

A sudden burst of adrenaline spiked through him

and he shouted and leaped toward Scott, whose fingers were slipping on that damp wooden beam . . .

And a heavy body slammed into Jesse, throwing him aside. As he crumpled to the floor he *saw* it, what he'd known had been hiding here the entire time: a monster, a smear of gray, raising an axe, blurring toward Scott, attacking him, screaming, even as it faded away . . .

Scott cried out.

His fingers slipping.

And with a rustle he fell, his scream cut off by a dull thud and sharp crack . . .

***

Jesse lay on his stomach at the hole's edge . . . an OLD hole, much smaller than he remembered . . . gasping, sweating, mind reeling, trying to piece together what he'd just seen, his heart thudding in time with the monster's . . .

No.

No monster.

There'd been no monster when he'd crashed through the door and there was nothing now save some old cans and a broken bottle, pieces of trash, a doll with a cracked face slumped in the corner and wallpaper peeling in jagged strips. Nothing else here now, but seconds ago . . .

No.

Couldn't be.

Seconds ago, he'd rushed into this room, axe raised high, and he'd seen it happening all over again. Scott, hanging from that floor beam, dangling, about to fall . . .

And even though some part of his mind had insisted it was a hallucination he'd dived at the hole, screaming NO! NOT AGAIN!

Knocking something out of his way.

A small body blocking his path, preventing him from saving Scott, that damn monster, again . . . !

No.

a gray smear, axe held high, blurring toward Scott, attacking him, screaming

a heavy body slammed into him

throwing him aside

fading away

No.

No!

Jesse scrambled back from the hole's edge and stood, panting, confusion mixing with deep, black fear.

He looked around again.

There was nothing except pieces of trash, the sagging floor and its hole, and . . .

. . . him.

Jesse

Jesse whirled, heart skipping double time, head pounding. "Who's there?" he shouted, hating the way his voice cracked. "Who the hell's there?"

He stepped out of the room, looked down the stairs and saw nothing. He glanced to his right and left and saw nothing there, either.

"Nothin," he muttered, desperate to convince himself, "there's nothin there."

Jesse

do you remember?

The voice burned his brain. Cascading emotions washed over him: fear, hate, regret, remorse, disgust and horror, and he suddenly found himself weak, his rage gone and his strength fled.

a gray blur
axe raised
fading away
"P-please," he whispered, "please . . . "
The floorboard creaked behind him.
A soft step, moving closer.
Jesse turned. An indistinct nothingness drifted toward him. As it floated, something whispered in his ears, fading in and out, as if coming from far away over a radio band that wouldn't quite tune in.
DO YOU REMEMBER?
Jesse stiffened.
Tumblers spinning in his head, releasing deeply repressed images and sounds and smells, flooding him with painful remembrance.
no, scott, i don't wanna go down there
jesse, c'mon man, get outta my way
there's nothin bad down there
no!
a gray blur
fading
"Oh, God," Jesse whispered. He felt cold and empty. His head ached, his ears rang, and his heart . . .
pounding, the pounding of the dark and hideous heart
. . . pounded loudly in his chest, threatening to burst in grief and pain and anger.
Jesse opened his mouth but could say nothing. Tears flooded his eyes, ran down his cheeks. He rubbed his temple and tried to push away the pain, stop the aching and pounding and shaking . . .
And then the truth crashed home, destroying all his remaining barriers. Everything Jesse Kretch believed

crumbled to the ground, falling away forever as Scott had fallen to his death.

He was only Jesse.

But he was also *more*.

He was the monster that killed Scott.

He swallowed, his sore throat stinging as he reached with a trembling hand behind him for the gun stuck into his waistband. He pulled it out, tripped the hammer and pressed the muzzle to his temples, cool metal burning his flesh.

It was time to kill the monster.

***

1985

Jesse sat next to Scott, holding his limp, cooling hand, forcing himself not to look at the twisted, broken mess of what was left. He knelt in Scott's warm, spreading blood, crying, his heart pounding like some great, hideous beast's heart. His head ached, his ears ringing with Scott's screams . . .

Scott coughed, his broken body twitching. He tightened his grip on Jesse's fingers for just a moment, and Jesse finally forced himself to look at Scott.

Scott's head was tilted at an unnatural angle. Even Jesse understood that his neck was broken. His face looked mostly normal, though maybe a little swollen and puffy. Blood leaked out of his ears and eyes and nose and thick, red gore clogged up both nostrils. Scott's breaths came out in reedy, sickening whistles. His mouth moved, lips trembling.

Jesse cried as he held Scott's cooling, limp hand but inside he raged and howled and screamed because

Scott was dying, and the monster upstairs, the thing with the axe . . .

the gray blur
axe upraised
fading
   . . . the monster had killed him.

But Scott's mouth continued to move, lips twitching, and even though Jesse read the words there they didn't register, they didn't get through . . .

not your fault

***

It was time to kill the monster.

Cold metal against flesh.

Hammer pulled back, finger tensing against the trigger. Time to kill the monster, make it right after all these years.

His finger twitched.

"It wasn't your fault."

He stiffened. It was the voice from inside his head, but it sounded different, now.

It had spoken aloud.

He opened his eyes and there, standing where the dark cloud had been was Scott, looking exactly as he had the day they'd entered Bassler House.

Scott, before he died.

Before the monster killed him.

Before he . . .

"No," Scott said as he shook his head. "It was an accident. There was nothing you could do. It wasn't your fault."

The gun's muzzle sagged against his temple, confusion filling him. "No," he stammered, his reality twisted to its breaking point. "You're dead. It killed you. It killed you. I *saw* it. It killed you."

Jesse gritted his teeth and jammed the muzzle back against the side of his head. "I'm gonna do it," he rasped. "Gonna finally kill the monster."

yessssss, a smooth, different voice purred, *do it, do it now*

"It lies, Jesse."

Jesse shuddered. The Scott-who-couldn't-be-there stood closer now, right before him. He still looked the same as when Jesse had seen him last. Still the same, always the same.

It was never the same.

It would NEVER be the same.

He pressed the gun even harder into his skin, wincing as it dug into him. His life had been worthless since Scott died, since the monster had killed him, since . . .

He had killed him.

"No."

A gentle grip took his wrist, slowly pulling the gun away from his head. A dizzying wave of vertigo washed over him and he collapsed to his knees. Everything that was Jesse Kretch crumbled away into the darkness. He bent over and buried his face in his hands.

The gun clattered to the floor.

"It lies, Jesse," Scott whispered. Jesse raised his head and saw his brother turning vaporous, indistinct, opaque. "The house lies. It looks inside you, twists what's there, shows you things . . . but it lies. It *always* lies. It wasn't your fault. It was an accident."

In between gulps of air, Jesse forced out, "My . . . life. It's gone. I ruined it. I'm nothin. Never was. Never will be."

The fading Scott knelt, pressing his forehead against Jesse's. "Yes, you are," he whispered. "You're Jesse. That's good enough, man. That's all you'll ever need.

"Go. Be Jesse. Get away from this house. Get the hell out of this town and LIVE. For me."

***

Jesse Kretch stumbled down the gravelly path leading away from Bassler House, numb, tears streaming down his face as dusk fell. He stopped and closed his eyes as the breeze caressed him, washing away everything that had tormented him all these years, leaving only Jesse.

THAT'S IT, JESSE. LIVE. GET THE HELL OUT OF HERE AND LIVE. BE JESSE . . . FOR ME.

Jesse opened his eyes and wiped them with the back of his hand. He shuffled away from Bassler House, the axe and gun forgotten, realizing instinctively deep inside that *this* monster, anyway, had been killed long ago.

He got into his truck, started it up and drove away.

8.

I SIT BACK and force myself to look away from Gavin's handwriting. Dammit if that neat, looping script isn't moving, and I just want to keep reading until . . .

I shake my head slightly, trying to clear my thoughts. "So is Jesse lost in some other world . . . or did he just get the hell out of town? Which story is true? Which one happened?"

Gavin scratches the back of his neck, offering me an apologetic look. "I don't know. Both of those stories about Jesse and Scott came to me within several days, and while I wrote them they *both* felt right. All I know for sure is that no one's seen nor heard from Jesse in months. Even you admitted that. Regardless of which story is true, I believe Jesse Kretch is gone and he's never coming back."

"How *did* Scott die, then? Which version do you remember?"

Gavin opens his mouth.

Closes it, folds his hands and looks out the window, whispering, "I honestly don't remember *how* he died. I just remember him being dead and no one wanting to talk about it. That's all."

I grunt, my head spinning, trying to grasp ideas and images and stick them together into a picture that'll make sense, but it's no good. *Nothing* here tonight has brought me any closer to understanding what happened to Timmy Danvers, what may've happened to Anne Marie Hauer, and it doesn't help me understand why Ellen Danvers won't press charges against her ex, why she doesn't want us looking for Timmy, anymore.

"Bassler Road," I murmur. "It's like Bassler House, isn't it? Maybe Jesse Kretch drove down that road and just disappeared."

Gavin looks at me, his gaze thoughtful. "Yes. Bassler Road *is* a little like the house, I think. Things go missing there."

I nod slowly, the implications dawning on me. "Like Jesse Kretch, Timmy Danvers . . . "

"Or Jenny Tillman," he whispers, offering me a sad, ironic smile.

I pull the book to me and turn the page.

BASSLER ROAD

JARRED SIMMONS JERKED awake, his heart hammering, expecting to see guardrails or trees looming in his headlights, but after several seconds of clutching the steering wheel he realized he was still traveling safely forward on Bassler Road.

"Sonuva*bitch*."

He breathed deep and relaxed. "That was *too* close. Gotta stay awake or I'm dead."

But his eyes felt heavy, exhausted. Everything blurred and mixed together. He felt little distinction between him, his Dodge RAM and the road, which stretched out before him into the night.

He rubbed the back of his neck. His last cup of coffee had worn off and his thoughts felt jumbled. His eyes burned, his face felt heavy and he had to force himself to focus on Bassler Road, which seemed much longer than he remembered.

Granted, he rarely drove this way, so he didn't know how long Bassler Road actually was. He usually left town the other way, southeast, out toward Woodgate and Utica, but his GPS had plotted the quickest route to the interstate along Bassler Road, and his sense of direction wasn't worth shit on a *good* day, so he'd followed the GPS's prompts, no questions asked.

But the damn thing didn't seem to be working, now. Said he should be on Interstate 80, but this was still clearly Bassler Road, framed by dark, looming stands of Adirondack pine, stretching forever into the night's horizon.

Where the hell was the interstate?

A dull pressure throbbed behind his eyes. His temples ached. Not only had he been awake for several days straight, but those shots of Wild Turkey he'd downed a few hours ago weren't helping, either. In retrospect, it had been foolish to hit the road without sleeping it off, but at the time getting away immediately had seemed the best thing to do. This, of course, said little for the logic-enhancing properties of Wild Turkey.

"That's the last time I drink alone," he lectured himself in the rearview mirror, knowing it was a lie. His reflection—that of a balding, chubby-faced middle-aged man—said nothing in return, but the accusation lay there, swimming in watery-gray eyes.

Weak eyes.

Weak.

Jarred frowned at the barren road. The night blanketing the landscape looked like nothing he'd ever seen before, even as an Adirondack native. Thick, swirling, like a living, breathing thing, it swallowed the light cast by his headlights and seemed to press in all around him.

Where was the damn interstate?

He was trying to keep his eyes open and himself awake when he saw it, down the road, on the right.

A white flutter.

Stark against the darkness, waving.

Or thumbing for a ride.

He eased off the gas and as he neared the waving white form, he saw a bag on the ground and long, flowing blond hair. A few more feet and the waving flutter solidified into an extended arm and a raised thumb. Jarred rolled by, slowing along Bassler Road's shoulder.

He parked the Ram.

And when he glanced over his shoulder and looked out the back, a shiver of unease rippled down his back at what he glimpsed through the trees.

Bassler House.

Old Bassler House, out in its unused cornfield, where it'd been rotting for decades. Clifton Heights' own spook house, also a rumored party spot for the varsity football team. Jarred didn't believe in haunted houses so its gothic, shadowed image, seen through night-shrouded trees didn't bother him at all. It was just an old house. A more practical worry nagged him.

He should've passed Bassler House *long* ago. It was just past the Commons Trailer Park. How was he passing it only now?

He shook off the question, focusing instead on the person who'd flagged him down, and *that* didn't make him feel any better, because she was just standing there, staring at his truck instead of snatching up her bag and rushing toward him.

And then another thought, just as unnerving: she was standing right where Bassler House's front drive might open up, as if she'd come from *inside* the old house and had been waiting here by the road, and not just waiting . . .

But waiting for him.

Suddenly, the girl sprang into action. She grabbed her bag, slung it over her shoulder and jogged toward him. Several seconds passed, and as he heard the approaching hitchhiker's feet scrape the gravel shoulder, an odd premonition flitted through his mind: drive off, *right now*, leave her here and find the interstate.

His hand tightened on the shifter.

The urge to drive away swelling.

But the moment passed with a click as the passenger-side door opened to reveal a tanned, young (much younger than he'd imagined) face framed by strawberry blond hair spilling onto soft shoulders. Her white dress turned out to be a faded, tie-dye sundress. Brilliant green eyes danced as the girl smiled. "Hey! Thanks for stopping! *Totally* awesome of you. It's freaking *freezing* out here!"

Jarred blinked, realizing with a hot sense of embarrassment that he was staring like an open-mouthed idiot at a teenage girl young enough to be his daughter. Clearing his throat, finding his voice with some difficulty, he swept empty Styrofoam coffee cups and fast food wrappers off the passenger seat. "Yeah, uh . . . sure. Don't mind the mess. Hop in."

The girl climbed into the Ram with a feline grace that seemed beyond her years. She settled into her seat, deposited her bag between her legs onto the floor, closed the door and put her seatbelt on. With a sigh, she covered her face with her hands and leaned back.

"Thanks so much! Thought I'd be stuck there forever."

Jarred said nothing as he shifted the truck into gear and pulled back onto Bassler Road.

***

Jarred risked several guilty, sidelong glances at his passenger. The instant she'd climbed into the Ram the cab had filled with a sweet, lingering fresh scent, and she exuded a warmth that flushed his cheeks and made his neck burn. Slowly waking desire clashed with intense guilt, making him feel like a dirty old man stealing peeks at such a young, inexperienced girl.

not so young, really

and you don't really know how inexperienced she is

do you

"So," he said, sneaking another guilty peek, "not to pry, but why are you hitching way out here instead of somewhere in town? Gotta be easier picking up a ride there, this late."

Chancing another sidelong glance he caught the girl's shy smile as she gazed into the dark, twirling a strand of hair around her finger. "I live back in the Commons. Just got into a HUGE fight with my mom and said *screw it*, I'm outta here."

She looked at him, green eyes bright and alive. "So I packed my bag and decided to hike out to the interstate along Bassler Road instead of going through town. Didn't want to run into anyone I knew, didn't feel like answering any questions."

She raked her fingers through her hair and smirked, as if amused at herself. "Good thing you came along, though. If not, I'd still be walking." A puzzled frown replaced her smirk as she gazed ahead. "Bassler Road's a lot longer than I thought it was."

He looked back down the road, which seemed endless, framed by high trees reaching for dark skies on both sides, road lights glimmering weakly. "Yeah," he whispered. "That's what I was thinking, too."

"What about you?"

He glanced at her again and this time couldn't help eyeing the girl's trim, curved body beneath that flowing dress, (she couldn't be much older than nineteen) and it took significant willpower to drag his eyes back to the road. He forced himself to, however, not only because this girl was *so* very young but also because he was in no position to ask anything of any woman ever again, not after . . .

No.

Don't start.

"So . . . what about you? I got pissed and stormed out on my trailer-trash mom. How come you're out here, so late . . . *alone?*"

He looked over, startled at the sultry emphasis she put on the word. Her deep, green eyes seemed to be drinking him in, almost *hungrily* as she lounged in her seat, nubile legs tucked underneath her. Guilt and arousal fought for supremacy and he found himself stammering, at a loss for words, feeling like a love-struck, sex-obsessed teenager. "Uh . . . heading to Poughkeepsie. Visiting a friend, spur of the moment, so I packed my bags and . . . "

She nodded, eyes never leaving his.

And he wondered if she sensed his lie. "And you're taking Bassler Road because . . . "

At least *this* he could answer truthfully. He waved at the GPS mounted on the dash, which, of course, still showed him traveling on the interstate he'd yet to find. "GPS said the quickest way to Interstate 80 was leaving town down Bassler Road, but the damn thing doesn't seem to be working very well. Keeps telling me I'm *on* Interstate 80, when . . . " he gestured at the dark road ahead.

"Ah." She glanced ahead, then gave him another one of those quietly smoldering looks (which made her seem so much older), and asked point blank: "So. She leave you, or are you leaving her? And don't bullshit me. I *know* these things."

He opened his mouth to protest but his guilt won out. He looked away, eyeing the wedding band on his finger. He'd no right to wear it, had meant to take it off dozens of times the last few months, but somehow he'd always forgotten to.

"So?"

"I . . . "

He paused, licked his lips, remembering the hot, stabbing pains of betrayal, despair, and failure. He swallowed thickly, his throat raw, but he managed, "She left."

"Divorced? Or just separated?"

"Not divorced. We're just . . . not together, anymore."

"I'm sorry to hear that," she murmured, with what sounded like real empathy. "Did she cheat?"

He looked at her but she'd turned away and he couldn't see her expression as she gazed into the dark night. Before he could answer, she continued. "I bet she did. Before he left, MY Daddy couldn't keep it in his pants. He cheated on Mom all the time, even when she was right there in the next . . . "

She stopped, gasping slightly.

A small sob, her shoulders quivering.

"I'm sorry," he whispered, because he had no idea what to say. So much implied in that small sob, and that last part: "even when she's right there, in the next . . . "

room?

The implications turned his stomach, and like ash cooling in the wind, his guilty lust faded away. He returned his gaze to the road—the empty, endless road—and the silence stretched out between them until he said, "Didn't get your name, by the way."

"Jenny. Jenny Tillman."

"Jarred Simmons," he said, wondering: *why does that name sound so familiar?*

Where had he heard it before?

But before he could ask, the Ram stalled without even a warning rumble. They decelerated abruptly and he cursed under his breath while fighting to bring them to a safe stop alongside the road without power steering.

"What is it?"

Oddly, Jenny seemed calm, apparently untroubled by the prospect of being stranded alone on a dark road with him. Given the implications of her past, this unsettled him considerably.

"I'm not sure," he said, "just had an inspection, oil change and tune-up. Everything checked out fine. Damn!" He hit the brakes, slowed them to a stop, then parked the Ram and turned the ignition off, even though the engine wasn't running. He snagged his cell phone off the dash, thumbed it on . . .

. . . and was greeted with a red X.

Perfect.

No service.

He tossed the cell back onto the dash and glanced over at Jenny. She sat still, hands folded in her lap, eyes fixed forward.

"Well," he said, forcing a light-hearted tone, "guess I'd better get out, check under the hood. You'll be okay in here?"

She said nothing.

And for a moment, Jarred was struck with the bizarre and macabre notion that Jenny Tillman was *dead*. The thought of his fleeting arousal for a corpse made his stomach churn.

But no.

That was insane.

She wasn't dead. That was just the feverish fantasy of a tired, stressed mind. She still sat upright, after all, and he could see very clearly the rise and fall of her shoulders as she breathed.

What the hell was wrong with her, then?

He reached out a tentative hand, perhaps to grasp her shoulder, maybe place a comforting hand on her back, or . . .

slip his hand under her silky hair

massage her neck, caress her soft skin

. . . but he made a fist instead, a vague premonition warding him off. He murmured, "I-I've got to get out, okay? Get the tool box, check the engine. You'll be okay while I . . . ?"

A slight nod. "I'll be fine," she said, but her voice sounded thin, insubstantial. "I'll be fine."

"Okay. Sit tight."

He opened the door and got out quickly, desperate for some reason to be away from his suddenly strange-acting passenger.

An odd, heavy stillness had filled the night and he shivered, shutting the door and walking around back, jingling his keys. At the rear he opened the tailgate and grabbed the handle to a small, red plastic toolbox and as he pulled it out onto the tailgate, he glanced to the front, where Jenny still stared ahead. He couldn't help thinking she was hiding her face from him purposefully and dark fantasies leapt into his mind of her face decayed and teeming with maggots. With a grunt, he pushed those images away, picked up the toolbox and rounded the right-rear bumper toward the front . . .

A flicker caught his eye.

The passenger door hanging open.

And as he approached it, he saw the seat empty, and Jenny gone.

***

There'd been no noise, no creaking of the door, no feet scraping asphalt. But there was the proof before his eyes. Jenny Tillman was gone, vanished without a sound.

He stared for several seconds, unable to accept the visual evidence that, indeed, the passenger seat was now empty, and not only was Jenny gone but so was her bag.

An eerie chill rippled across his shoulders. Had he imagined the whole thing? Conjured up Jenny from the combination of too little sleep, too much stress, a little liquor still coursing through his system? And was that even possible?

"No," he muttered, eyes refusing to believe the vacant seat. "No, NO. She was real. She *was*."

A slight scrape.

A foot, dragging across gravel.

He glanced up, and through the driver side window saw blond hair and green eyes flash by. He walked quickly around the truck's front, driven by a horrible need for validation . . .

he wasn't crazy, Jenny was real, dammit

. . . plagued by the sickening premonition that maybe it'd be better if the whole thing was an illusion, because then at least he'd be alone, and safe.

At the Ram's front he saw nothing for a moment, then he caught the barest flutter of tie-dyed fabric disappearing around the rear. Guts churning, he rushed to the tailgate, wondering what the hell he was scared of. If he'd imagined Jenny it meant one thing: he was too tired and needed rest. If she was real, Jenny was probably high on something and having some twisted fun at his expense. She *was* from the Commons, after all. Trailer trash, just as she'd said.

Coming full circle, standing at the Ram's open tailgate he saw nothing, save darkness and trees . . .

But he heard *something*.

A whisper.

Jarred cocked his head, ears tickling, either with a faint breeze or his fevered imagination, he wasn't sure.

And as he stood in the night, holding the toolbox, he grew certain that somehow he *had* imagined the whole thing. He was strung out, also riddled with guilt. Easy for the mind to play tricks under those conditions. So he brushed off the ghostly sensation of whispering in his ears, turned to close the tailgate . . .

When a cold, slimy hand reached around from behind, clamped onto his throat and squeezed. Jagged fingernails dug into his skin as the hand lifted him into the air effortlessly. His stomach lurched as a rancid smell filled his nostrils: rank, oily, the odor of long dead things rotting in stagnant water. The hand squeezed tighter and shook him. He dropped the toolbox and grasped at the thing's hands, realizing in horror that though his fingers dug deep grooves into the skin, no blood flowed.

Kicking and scratching, he looked down.

A withered, leathery, decaying face with cracked and bleeding lips leered at him, showing slimy, broken teeth.

"Gonna fuck you up, cheater! Fuck you up BAD!"

***

Swaying in the thing's grip, hands clawing and flailing, Jarred tried to scream but only gurgled. He felt the warm flush of his bladder releasing and somehow that was the worst thing; that he was going to die pissing his pants.

The thing threw him into the truck's bed. He fell against a wooden crate for oil and rags and jumper cables and cried out, his back throbbing where the crate's corner had dug him. His throat burned as he gasped for air.

The truck rocked slightly on its shocks. Jarred looked in horror to see the *thing* that had been Jenny crouching on the tailgate, its green eyes burning the night.

"*Jarrrrrrred*," Jenny's husky voice whispered as It swayed with an oddly seductive grace, "don't play coy, baby. You *want* me. I know you do. I could *feel* the lust coming from you the whole time, rolling off you in waves."

Jarred recoiled, disgust and fear churning his guts . . . but that voice. That *voice*. It sent waves of desire washing over him, which mixed with his disgust and fear to create a horrific emotional stew that threatened to drown him. He *believed* she wanted him and could almost believe he wanted her, and even worse, a part of him thought . . . why *not*?

Why not let her have him, and let her take him?

Because then it would finally be over.

OH NO, NO JARRED, the thing whispered in his head, *IT'S NEVER OVER, LOVER. NOT OUT HERE IN THE DARK. IT'S JUST YOU AND ME AND THE DARK AND WE'RE GOING TO BE HERE FOREVER AND EVER, JARRED.*

FOREVER AND EVER.

"N-no," Jarred whimpered as he cowered against the truck, "g-get a-way!"

"What's wrong, Jarred?" the thing cooed. "Is it because I'm not Angela? Not a fat little secretary to screw just because you can?"

"S-stop it!" he screamed, hands groping for something, *anything*, "STOP IT!"

Darkness covered parts of Its face and the desire pulsing through his guts almost convinced him she was whole, desirable and fresh. But weak light from the cab illuminated a slip of decaying, leathery skin; enough to hint at the phantasmal reality hiding in the shadows.

"Because that's all it was, wasn't it? You weren't even attracted to Angela. You just knew she'd let you screw her and that's what *got you off*. The power. The power of a stupid little lawyer in a stupid little town, a big fish in a small pond screwing his secretary and ruining his dedicated wife's life."

Jarred whimpered as he blindly groped in the crate for something to defend himself with—a tire iron, a crowbar, anything—and desperate hope surged as his fingers curled around something wooden wrapped in worn, cracked tape.

The thing settled onto its haunches, gathering itself. *"Let's get it on!"*

It sprang forward, a dark blur of decayed flesh, gnashing white teeth, blazing green eyes. Without thinking, he yanked the wooden object free of the crate and swung it with every ounce of strength he had, and only as it passed did he see . . .

It was a bat.

An old, worn Louisville Slugger.

His son's old baseball bat. The one he'd given Bryan for his twelfth birthday, back when things had been good between him and Linda, back when they'd been *happy.*

And as the bat swept past, images flashed by, of the last time he'd seen it, at Bryan's last Little League game, after he'd spent the whole morning giving his son some pointers from his own high school baseball days. Bryan hit four homeruns that day; a Webb County Little League record.

But Bryan was gone now. Both he and his sister Jane refused to speak to him.

The bat swung by.

And Jarred felt a force vibrate in his shoulder, A strange resonance flowing down his arm, into the bat, a sensation that had been absent from his life for years, perhaps ever since that last baseball game.

Love.

Intense love. Parental love, the love a father feels for his son, his love for Bryan and Jane and his love for Linda, coupled with a desperate desire to see her face glowing with that love once more.

The bat connected with a squelching *thud.*

His arm shook and a fantastic splash of the whitest light he'd ever seen brightened the night as the baseball bat glowed and pulsed upon impact.

The thing shrieked, landing on its back, scrabbling and clawing. The sickening smell of burning meat filled the air and the thing rolled and kicked and scrambled its way off the tailgate.

Jarred lay there, frozen. He wanted to cower and hide, but a trembling kind of courage drove him forward, out of the truck's bed, baseball bat held before him.

As he shakily stepped down onto pavement, the thing stopped flailing and crouched on all fours, glaring at him, growling. The bat had dug a wet, seeping trench in the thing's right temple, above the eye, exposing rotten, blackened viscera and a strip of gleaming white skull.

But the thing's tortured flesh changed.

Swirling like silly putty. The trench filled in and the thing's face melted and churned until it slowly hardened into a new visage, one that sent cold shock flowing through him.

It stood slowly, smiling at him cruelly with Linda's dead face.

"No," he rasped, his fingers tightening on the bat's handle, circling away from it. "You're not Linda."

The thing laughed and snapped its teeth. "Why not? This is the dark, after all. Dead things abide here. You and I both know Linda is dead, don't we?"

Jarred lifted the baseball bat and pointed it, noting with a detached sense of awe that it still glowed faintly. "No," he said again, more firmly this time, "you're *not* her."

The thing feinted and Jarred felt ashamed as he skittered back several feet, almost slipping and falling. It laughed as they continued to circle each other. "You'd like to think that, wouldn't you? Fact is, I *am* Linda, and she's me. We're all here in the dark, waiting for you. Only fitting, after all, seeing as how *you* killed Linda . . . "

The bat shook.

Its light dimmed and his legs weakened at the knees. "No, no, *no*. I didn't kill her. I never, ever wanted . . . "

The thing spread its hands. "Well, *you* didn't draw the warm bath, pour a bottle of sleeping pills down her throat and cut her wrist for her. *She* did that all on her own. Gotta admire her efficiency, by the way. Most people botch their suicides, cause they don't really want to bite it, but she *wanted* to, all right. Even had a back-up plan, swallowing those sleeping pills before slashing her wrist."

His vision blurred as tears stung his eyes, and the bat trembled, wavering. "N-no, no, no, *no!* I never wanted that to happen! I didn't want her to die! I would've done anything to make it up to her . . . *anything!*"

The thing smiled at his grief. "Well that's too bad, buddy boy, cause she died, choking on her own vomit. Guess she really meant it when she said she couldn't live with the thought of you sleeping with someone else." It waggled a scolding finger. "And it's too late for apologies, Jarred, because Linda's here with us in the dark, and she wants her pound of flesh." An oily tongue licked ruined lips, dribbling saliva all over. "And we're only too happy to oblige."

And then, sudden understanding strengthened Jarred's knees, stiffening his arm as he once again held the bat rigidly before him.

This *wasn't* Linda.

It couldn't be.

He didn't know much about religion or God or Heaven or Hell but he thought only two choices existed. He'd gone crazy and was hallucinating, or the never-ending road and its thick, unnatural darkness was *real*. If he was hallucinating, so be it. Nothing mattered anymore, so what could he fear?

If this was real, however—the road, the dark, this *thing*—then Linda didn't belong here. She deserved better for her years of selfless sacrifice raising their children, loving him unconditionally at first, tolerating and suffering him later . . .

She deserved better. She didn't deserve this.

But *he* did.

"No," he whispered, the bat glowing and throbbing anew, "you're not Linda."

The thing stopped.

Arms hanging slack, face expressionless.

It stood that way for several seconds, and then its face twisted, skin melting and sliding and folding. Even in the midst of his newfound resolve, Jarred's stomach clenched at the sight.

Finally, the features hardened again into the ruined face of the thing called Jenny, chunk of upper-right temple missing, strip of bare skull gleaming in the moonlight.

"Well, well," its teeth clicked, "the spoiled little boy finally grows up a little. Doesn't matter, because the dark is forever, Jarred." It paused, face splitting into a horrible grin. "Time to get it on, lover."

Two notions struck Jarred in a heartbeat. One, the thing knew nothing about the source of the bat's power, and two, it was *lying*.

It screeched and leapt forward, its face melting and sliding as its entire body shifted and changed. Jarred stood his ground, squaring his feet and shoulders just like he'd taught Bryan so long ago, and as he cocked the bat behind his head it flashed, lighting the night with a pure white light . . . and he saw his arms around Bryan, helping him hold the bat high at just the right angle; shoulder dipped, head up so his eye would stay on the ball and as the distance closed and Jarred looked down the thing's gullet at the writhing, damned souls nestled there he remembered his pride as Bryan belted his fourth and last homer of the day, remembered Bryan jumping into his arms afterwards, unembarrassed by his father's embrace . . .

Its hot sulfur stink filled his nostrils. Cold green eyes penetrated his soul.

And he swung hard as he could, the bat flashing with the brilliance of a thousand suns, filling the darkness and canceling the night. The thing screeched and everything exploded into whiteness.

Homerun.

***

He slowly came to, sitting on the edge of the tailgate, crying quietly, cradling his son's baseball bat. Eventually (how long didn't matter, because he now understood time had no meaning here) his sobs subsided, tears drying up. He heaved one last sigh, wiped his eyes with his forearm and looked up.

The horizon had lightened. The sky still looked dull and gray but the night was over for now, though he suspected it would return soon enough.

He looked down; saw streaks of grime and dried patches of gore on his clothes, physical remnants of his battle and a horrifying reminder of his fate, of where he was.

the dark is forever

He hefted the bat onto his shoulder. Stood, closed the Ram's tailgate and walked to the driver's side, leaving the toolbox behind. He had a feeling he wouldn't need it where he was headed.

Climbing into his truck he tossed the bat into the passenger seat, buckled his seatbelt and turned the key. The Ram started right up, its rumble a welcome sound in this gray dawn's stillness.

He shifted and pulled onto Bassler Road, which stretched out into the gray horizon forever, lined far as he could see by crowded Adirondack pines. He still wasn't sure exactly what or where this was but somehow, though he knew the journey would be long, there *was* an end somewhere, a place of forgiveness and maybe even peace.

And maybe, if he were very lucky . . .

He drove on.

Not surprised at all to see his son's baseball bat glowing faintly from the corner of his eye.

9.

"JARRED SIMMONS RAN his truck off Bassler Road in April," I say, eyes closed, rubbing my temples, trying to massage away the persistent ache that's taken root there. "He drove right into a huge Adirondack pine. Airbag malfunctioned and he suffered massive head trauma. According to the tox screens, he'd also been plastered."

"His wife had committed suicide four months before," Gavin says, "his children had disowned him and due to the revelation of the whole affair his law practice was failing. I'd say the man was suffering."

"Well, at least this story I can verify."

"How?"

I open my eyes, drop my hands and drum my fingertips on the tabletop. "*Because*, Gavin. Jarred Simmons is still in a coma, at Clifton Heights General. Has been since he got out of surgery after the accident."

Gavin raises an eyebrow, looking pleasantly surprised. "You've kept tabs on him?"

I wave away his quiet admiration. I'm really not that altruistic. "The case just seemed so . . . odd. Forensics guys determined by tire marks that

Simmons drove right off the road. No signs of braking, no skid marks, nothing. Like he *wanted* to die."

I nod at Gavin, knowing the answer to my question before I even ask it. "You've visited him too, haven't you?"

Gavin folds his hands on the tabletop and stares into them. "Yes. I would've liked to visit Mr. Simmons on a regular basis. I have this feeling that there's more to his story, yet."

"Right. Because somehow he's still driving on Bassler Road and maybe someday, if he finally reaches the end . . . "

"He'll miraculously wake up. Or pass on. Or his brother, who holds power of attorney, will finally feel an impulse to disconnect his life support and let him go. I don't know. There's so much we don't understand about comas and the human brain. ANYTHING could be happening in his head, things completely beyond our comprehension." Gavin shrugged. "In any case, I wanted to sit with him once a week, get a feel for where his story is going, but that doctor of his . . . "

Though it's late and I haven't slept very well since the disappearance of Timmy Danvers, I perk up, because Bassler House isn't the only place around here I'm curious about. "Dr. Jeffers, right? Had a run-in with him when Brian O'Hara—the high school's star quarterback—got hurt at a kegger he threw back in September. He suffered a concussion, got checked into that hospital and quick as spit Dr. Jeffers 'transferred' him to some 'special alcohol addiction treatment center' downstate. The kid vanished and his parents moved out of town almost immediately after. And because the parents gave Dr. Jeffers consent . . . "

" . . . you couldn't investigate," Gavin concludes with a sour expression. "That's the way it always seems to work with Dr. Jeffers. He *always* gets consent. *Always.*"

Gavin leans across the table, his expression grave. "Do me a favor, Chris. You ever get sick or injured; if Meg is ever sick or hurt, if you can . . . go to a walk-in clinic in Booneville or Old Forge. Go see Fitzy at Utica Memorial. Do *not* go to Clifton Heights General, if you can help it."

And he sits back and runs a hand through his hair. "Because I'd hate to see you OR Meg 'transferred' somewhere . . . "

A BROTHER'S KEEPER

CRAIG HARTLEY STOOD at the tiny hospital room window, sweating. It was summer and eighty degrees and here he was, stuck in a room with an ancient air conditioner that grinded and wheezed and grumbled but had very little effect. Nothing he could do about it, of course, but stand and sweat and hate hospitals in general, especially small town, backwoods hospitals like this one.

He watched townspeople scuttle along the sidewalks outside and smirked. *Look at them, running around in the shadow of the place that'll kill them someday. Idiots.* That's why he'd left, of course. So he wouldn't become one of them.

His smirk faded. He'd carved out a good life for himself, dammit—but now it felt like he'd never left. He still felt nineteen: still defiant, reckless, insecure, still scared of his father's bullshit, still haunted by . . .

No. Didn't believe then, won't believe now.

A dry spot on his scalp itched.

He turned to inspect the room, avoiding the burnt thing lying in its middle. He ignored the gurgling tubes and wheezing respirator that jiggled that burnt thing . . .

The thing that used to be his brother.

Buddy.

Tubes breathed for him, IVs flushed and drained him and the itchy patch on Craig's scalp burned. He couldn't ignore it or push it away. According to Pop, it bore testament to Buddy's sacrifice. So Pop had always claimed, anyway, before disappearing into the swamps on a trapping run three years ago. Drowned, most likely. *God rest, Pop.* Awful that he couldn't muster more emotion than that, but it was all he had.

Enough.

Craig swallowed.

He turned and looked at Buddy, his stomach twisting. Every inch not wrapped in gauze was burnt gut-red. Cracked skin had congealed into molten, oblong globs. Buddy looked half his size; the fire having burnt considerable tissue away. Against his will, Craig imagined a thin layer of gristle coating Buddy's charred frame.

Layers of gauze also hid Buddy's face. If Craig didn't know better, he'd think Buddy was a badly done movie prop. Small bumps stuck out where ears should be. The mouth—intubated with a plastic air tube—was only a burnt hole. The crisped remains of Buddy's nose peeked from underneath the gauze.

An insistent cardiac monitor sounded Buddy's heartbeat with a rhythmic *ping*. Somehow, Buddy's heart was still beating.

"He's dying, Craig."

Craig glanced over his shoulder at Dr. Stanley Jeffers, chief resident. Tall, gaunt, with bloodless lips and a black widow's peak, he looked like a classic Universal Movie Mad Scientist instead of country hospital doctor.

Craig shivered. Dr. Jeffers had freaked them all out as kids, and Craig imagined that no matter how many peppermints he distributed when treating pediatrics, Dr. Jeffers *still* freaked all the kids out.

Craig's scalp burned.

And he thought he smelled Old Spice, Pop's favorite cologne.

Dammit. Man's dead and drowned, out in the swamps. Can't hurt me now.

"How long?"

The doctor frowned. "A few days. We've done all we can. The trauma is too severe. His body is breaking down."

"What happened?"

"After your father disappeared and the farm was repossessed by the bank, Buddy boarded at Miss Walpole's and worked the landfill. It was burning night. A load of burning garbage shifted and fell on Buddy, pinning him to the ground." Coal-black eyes stared at him. "It's fortunate you came. He needs your help."

Something twitched in Craig's belly. Shame? Or despair? He ignored it. "I can't do anything about *this*. Nothing *anyone* can do."

"Not necessarily."

Craig turned and studied the doctor's pinched face. "What do you mean?"

"Measures *can* be taken. Your father left explicit instructions in his will regarding either of your deaths, as well as a healthy trust fund. He left *specific* instructions regarding efforts to save Buddy's life, particularly."

Craig snorted. "I'll never understand why you let

Pop peddle his hoodoo here. Surprised no one ever sued your asses off."

Dr. Jeffers shrugged. "We've an open mind." A heavy pause. "Your father healed many people over the years."

Craig glanced away, cheeks burning. "Placebo-effect. Healing power of the human mind. Trick people into feeling better, they heal."

Another silence, filled with pumping, wheezing, gurgling, ping, ping, *ping* . . .

Craig looked everywhere but at the doctor's intense gaze. "Don't understand how Pop could've saved that much money. He did fine on the farm, conned lots of hill folk with his hoodoo." He glanced at Dr. Jeffers, suspicious. "Not enough to set up a trust fund, though."

"As I said, your father healed many people. Many *grateful* people."

So that's how the old man had paid for his college tuition. And to think, he'd let Craig believe it had been Buddy slaving away on the farm.

But he shook his head. "No way. He's burnt to hell and I'm too old to believe in Pop's hoodoo."

"Nevertheless, Buddy is fading quickly. He needs blood. As his brother, you're a compatible match."

Craig looked away. *What the hell am I supposed to do?*

As if reading his thoughts, Dr. Jeffers whispered, "Save his life." A pause. "It's what your father would've wanted."

So many words he had for that man, if he were still alive. So many words, bundled up tight with bitter feelings. *Bastard. Even when you're dead, you can't stop, can you? If only you were still alive. I'd take those words and shove 'em down your damn throat.*

"We need blood, son. Desperately."

Craig faced the doctor and smiled stiffly. "What the hell? You get some blood and I go back to my life. Why not?"

Dr. Jeffers' grin spread taut over his face. "Indeed."

But as he followed Dr. Jeffers out of the room, Craig's scalp itched and burned.

***

Craig sat in a small, featureless examination room. Several racks of empty blood bags stood next to him. He knew nothing about medicine, but there seemed too many bags for just a simple blood transfusion.

Seated, shirt rolled to the elbow, Craig felt a prick on the inside of his forearm, as painless as the wide-hipped, dour-faced nurse had promised.

As Dr. Jeffers entered and the nurse exited, Craig felt many emotions and surprisingly, one was pride. Finally, he was doing something for Buddy. He may not believe Pop's hoodoo, but it felt good to give back to his brother.

Dr. Jeffers checked the IV lines and smiled. "This is a good thing you're doing. Not many people would sacrifice so much."

Craig offered Dr. Jeffers a smile in return. "It's only a few pints. Haven't given to the Red Cross lately. Got some karma to redeem."

Dr. Jeffers' smile grew. He withdrew a syringe from his jacket pocket. "Yes. A few pints. So modest." He paused. "'Karma to redeem.' Apt words. Tell me, Craig—did you truly disbelieve your father's faith?"

Craig did his best not to scowl. "You mean his crazy

hoodoo magic? Don't get me wrong. Pop raised us best he could, hard but fair. Never laid a wrong hand on us. He provided for us."

Dr. Jeffers tapped the syringe, then secured it in the IV's port. "But you didn't approve of his practices." A statement, not a question.

Craig blinked as a warm fuzziness touched him, but he pushed the encroaching fog away. "C'mon, Doc. Casting spells, binding spirits, mixing herbs, composing arcane incantations? That's no way to raise kids, especially one like . . . Buddy."

"You turned out fine. Good college degree, high-paying job, fancy car, even?"

"*I* got the hell out. If it'd been up to Pop, I would've stayed here forever, working the farm with Buddy."

An intense wave of vertigo hit him, tugging down his eyelids. Looking up at the syringe jutting from the IV port, he mumbled, "Lissen . . . Doc . . . what's in that syringe? I'm losin it, here."

The doctor smiled again, looking very eager, for some reason. "We need to get you prepped, Craig. You've quite a procedure ahead."

Whatever was in the syringe, it was acting fast. Craig's tongue felt heavy. "Boy—you guys take blood transfusions seriously, huh?"

Dr. Jeffers knelt next to him, his smile turning somber. "I'm afraid I've misled you. This is more than a blood transfusion. We're going to save your brother's life, and pay back your *Weirguild* to him."

Cold suspicion stabbed Craig's heart.

Because he *knew* that word from somewhere. "Wait-a-minute. Whatdidja say?"

"Weirguild. Your life debt to Buddy."

The sedative slammed into Craig, finally. His head swayed and his tongue flopped. Dizzily, he searched Jeffers' face . . . and saw a glittering pendent hanging around the doctor's neck, under his open-collared shirt.

It was a simple yet ornate pendent, in its own way. Pewter, braided by gold, a circle with an inverted 'Y' inside. Similar to one his father used to wear.

A sudden panic spiked through the medication's warm, fuzzy glow, and Craig jerked back . . . only to find his arms and torso restrained.

When had *that* happened?

A line of cold drool leaked from the corner of his mouth, down his cheek. Dr. Jeffers fingered the pendent while he talked. "Your father was a great man. His knowledge of the netherworld was vast. He taught me many things before he left us. You can't imagine how many lives I've saved because of him."

Craig's shoulders twitched.

"Believe it or not, he *was* proud of you. But he was prouder of Buddy. I was the attending physician when you and Buddy were born, the night of your mother's death. You were conjoined at the head. Impossible to sever cleanly."

Craig's scalp burned.

"I had to cut nearer to one scalp than the other, and the blood loss was going to cause irreparable brain damage to the twin I cut nearest to. It was inevitable."

Every nerve screamed as Craig slumped further down. He felt a small tug on his arm. Unable to turn his head, from the corner of his eyes he glimpsed tiny red streams flowing upwards, away from him.

All the while, his scalp burned.

"I watched, amazed, as your father touched your souls, even in the womb." His eyes flickered. "In Buddy, he found such a willing spirit. In you—not so much."

Craig's head rolled back and the white, blurry ceiling filled his vision.

Dr. Jeffers must have leaned close, because as Craig faded away, warm breath tickled his ear. "Everything you've achieved is because of Buddy. It's time to repay the Weirguild, Craig. It was your father's last wish."

There were no more words, only darkness . . . and a breath of Old Spice, sharp on the air.

***

Light.

Sound.

With a gasp, Craig awoke into pain.

He lay on his back. Above him, a rectangular mirror reflected his naked torso. A white blanket covered the rest of him. He tried to move his head and found it secured. He squinted in the excruciating glare. Bone-white forms drifted by.

He tried to scream but he hissed, nothing more.

A masked face leaned close.

Piercing eyes, the bridge of an aquiline nose.

Dr. Jeffers.

Craig tried to push against the restraints but his brain fired blanks. Tenderly, Dr. Jeffers gave his brow a rubbery caress. "Good news. The transfusion was successful. Buddy has several more days. We've got room to work, now."

No! Getmethehellouttahere!

As if sensing his anger, Dr. Jeffers chuckled. "You

may wonder why we've woken you. We've adjusted the anesthesia so you *will* feel pain, but not unbearably so. We're simply following your father's last request. He felt your Weirguild would be more meaningful if you were awake for the procedure, to create a sense of balance. All these years Buddy suffered quietly, watching you live a life forbidden him. *Never* did he blame you. Ever. It hurt him, though. Badly. I saw it in his eyes every day."

A white wraith floated near. Craig recognized the gray eyes of the big-hipped nurse. Dr. Jeffers turned, accepted from her a silver scalpel without a word, then faced him.

God, no! Please!

Stop!

He felt it, then.

A sting first.

Followed by a sharp stab, a line of fire, then worse ... *pressure.* As the cut lengthened, his insides pushed against flesh and muscle.

"For thirty-three years, your brother suffered. Never once did he complain."

OH GOD! I'M SORRY!

"Your father hoped someday you'd understand what Buddy gave up for you. As a physician, it's my charge to fulfill that hope."

Hu-hu-help m-me. Someone help me . . . PU-PLEASE!

"There." Dr. Jeffers probed the incision. Fire streaked along Craig's abdomen. Jeffers reached up and adjusted the mirror's angle. "You may watch, of course. In fact, your father insisted upon it."

Craig tried to shut his eyes and hide in the darkness . . . and found he couldn't. They'd taped his eyelid open. No matter how he strained, they remained so. He sobbed silently. The mirror above reflected his mouth sagging in a lopsided *O*.

"He wanted you to see everything taken away. Just as Buddy watched you grow, you must watch yourself diminish."

Unable to stop himself, Craig looked into the mirror. The incision in his abdomen was perfect. Straight. The organs inside pulsed and quivered. It was almost . . .

God help him.

Beautiful.

Blood pooled to the incision's edge but didn't run over. Dr. Jeffers' hand descended again. Craig stared. Though there was still pain, it had started to feel very far way.

"Unfortunately, though the blood transfusion helped, Buddy's kidneys and liver are failing." Dr. Jeffers turned and gazed into his eyes. "This will be your first repayment to him."

He resumed cutting, skillfully parting flesh. As Jeffers made three more identical incisions across his stomach, Craig marveled at their symmetry, balance and order.

The blood flowed.

And he lost himself in its red, shining brilliance. It swirled into little whorls and spirals. As Jeffers cut, tendrils of crimson ivy crept across Craig's skin. Craig was reminded of those plastic spirographs he and Buddy drew pretty little designs with as kids.

Bloody spirographs, all over him.

All for Buddy.

But the grotesque fantasy broke. His rapture vanished and Craig screamed silently.

DADDDYYYYY!

Dr. Jeffers peeled the skin back. Craig glimpsed squirming organs—purple, pink, smooth and rubbery and turgid, sliding around his guts—before his mind shut down. He saw no more, open eyes regardless.

***

Black spotted to a gray mist that slowly dissolved into a reflection of Craig's open chest. Ribs had been sawed and pulled back, revealing two white, shivering lungs.

"Good news." Dr. Jeffers' face eased into view. "Buddy's immune system accepted the transplants. No signs of infection or rejection."

He felt down Craig's open chest to his abdomen, which had been stitched up. Bright, throbbing red muscle gleamed in the mirror. "Nearly 70 percent of Buddy's skin was burnt beyond repair. We took some grafts from your stomach to close over his abdominal incisions. He'll need more, of course." He passed a strangely comforting hand over Craig's brow. "That will be later. Our final step. For now . . . "

He turned, accepted again the scalpel from the dour-eyed nurse, and descended into Craig's chest cavity. "As you can imagine, Buddy's lungs were badly damaged by smoke inhalation. One was recoverable, the other, however . . . "

In the mirror, Craig watched Dr. Jeffers cut into the bronchi. A great slash of pain exploded in his chest, powerful enough to make him jerk in spite of the anesthesia. He moaned, panicking as blood filled his nose, choking off his breath.

"Don't be alarmed. Blood and mucus flooding the

trachea and nasal cavities is expected. The naso-gastric tubes will suck it out. We'll intubate if we have to, of course."

He paused, shifting his hands so the nurse could assist holding Craig's lung as it fell slack from its bronchi.

The pain dulled. True to Jeffers' word, two lines suctioned away blood and mucus from his nose. The blood on his lips, however, glimmered like fantastic lipstick on a mime or clown. He stared at his reflection as the doctor and the nurse pulled away the quivering, gore-spotted lung. He *was* a clown, with shining red lips, red rivers running from his nose, and a glistening, red wet belly.

He was still imagining himself as Bobo the Gibbering Clown in Dr. Jeffers' Traveling Weirguild Roadshow when the room went away.

***

They took parts of his intestines next.

"We don't need everything, of course," Dr. Jeffers said pleasantly as he began. "Just enough to patch Buddy up. His stomach was burned badly, buried beneath all that smoldering garbage."

Dr. Jeffers and his nurse gently coiled slick, gray lengths of his intestines into a gray bin. "Perhaps you're wondering how all this is possible?"

Dr. Jeffers extracted another length of intestine from Craig's gut, which pulled free with a sucking sound. He threaded it to the nurse, then returned to Craig's side.

"Procedures like these are not possible using *conventional* medicine." Craig's eyes were still taped open. He'd no choice but meet the doctor's gaze. "This is all due to your father's occult knowledge. Without it, both you and Buddy would bleed out instantly; die of shock, or the transplants wouldn't knit together properly."

He looked about to continue, but stopped. Instead, he laid a hand on Craig's shoulder. "Rest. The last—and *hardest*—follows."

A warm, fuzzy cloud of anesthesia descended and covered the world.

***

"We'll increase the sedation for this, just a bit. It'll be the most painful step, your final repayment to Buddy."

They started at his feet, cutting through skin and muscle, slashing tendons and ligaments with looping, circular cuts. Then . . . they *peeled*.

Pain.

Oh, God . . . the pain.

Craig wailed silently as nerves blazed like fireworks until they died, ripped away in the skin and muscle torn from him. As they pulled away thick, corded tissue from around his thighs a writhing stick figure emerged. This awful thing jigged and jittered as gentle hands cut, lifted, and folded. Spiny red limbs dripped with gossamer threads.

And then . . . the last.

They cut under the chin first.

And even full of drugs, he felt pressure swell from that point around his neck, a phantom noose pulling tight in the scalpel's wake. Then, gloved fingers dug under the edge and slowly peeled the skin up and away from his face.

Finally, it pulled free.

His skull popped out of its skin and hair cap with a

plop and thumped wetly onto the table. He stared with horrified fascination into the mirror above at the reflection of his new face; the bald, gristle-spotted pate, cavernous eyes and cheekbones, looming nose-hole and grinning-death teeth.

It was the last thing he saw before . . .

***

He awoke.

And something felt different.

He was sitting upright. The light was dimmed. Though a warm blanket still enveloped him and deadened the pain, things seemed clearer. He didn't feel any restraints . . . but he couldn't move. He couldn't close his eyes either, and he realized with a cold rush that was because he didn't have eyelids to close, anymore.

A mirror hung on the opposite wall. In it, his reflection: a pitifully thin figure, reclined, wrapped in gauze with eye, nose, and mouth holes. Wet redness seeped through in spots. Cardiac and respiration equipment loomed at his bedside. He swallowed and felt a plastic tube in his throat.

The door opened.

And in walked Dr. Jeffers wearing his office clothes, followed by a handsome smiling young man dressed in khakis, a white polo shirt, with a leather jacket slung over his shoulder. Though his face looked slightly inflamed—like he was recovering from an allergic reaction—he bore a strong resemblance to . . .

Craig couldn't scream, of course.

But the escalating *ping, ping, ping, PING!* of his heart monitor did it for him.

Looking concerned, Dr. Jeffers moved to adjust

one of the IV drips, presumably his sedation. Craig's warm, heavy blanket pressed down harder and the *pinging* slowed.

"That's better." Dr. Jeffers pulled up a chair, the man—the impossible man—following suit. "We nearly lost you after that last procedure. Would hate to lose you now."

He paused, waving a hand at the young man sitting next to him. "Here he is. Alive, healed . . . in the flesh. Your flesh, more accurately."

Son of a . . . son of a . . .

BITCH!

"The swelling has receded nicely." Dr. Jeffers ran a finger down Buddy's face. Buddy grinned and knocked it away playfully. "Fortunately, most of that was done with rather pedestrian analgesics and anti-inflammatory creams. In a week's time, he'll be completely healed."

M-m . . . my face. That's my face . . .

MY FACE!

Dr. Jeffers turned back, looking regretful. "Sadly, there are limits even to your father's knowledge. We weren't able to repair Buddy's vocal chords and removing yours seemed too risky. Your father *explicitly* stated in his will you were to survive the procedure, so I didn't want to risk losing you."

Buddy smiled and nodded. He looked at Craig, gratitude shining in his eyes. Confusion swirled into Craig's broiling hate.

"Also, his ears are completely cosmetic. He's both deaf and mute, but he's picked up sign language very well." Dr. Jeffers paused, signed something and Buddy chuckled, his laughter strange, scratchy and mewling . . . but *sound* that could be heard, all the same.

Damn you, Pop . . . DAMN YOU!

"Of course, there's not much we can do about Buddy's mental limitations. However, your father DID set aside two sizable trust funds. One to fund your care and another, larger one to see that Buddy never has to work again. That, and . . . "

Dr. Jeffers glanced at Buddy and grinned. Signing as he talked, he said, "In a week, Buddy will be quite an attractive fellow. I don't think he'll lack for female companionship."

Unbelievably, Dr. Jeffers mimed a generous hip thrust, at which Buddy broke out into scratchy peals of laughter.

Kill you . . . goddamn . . . kill you . . .

Dr. Jeffers sobered and waved a hand. Buddy calmed down. "Most importantly, Buddy is immensely grateful. You have repaid your Weirguild and more than that, you've acted like a true brother."

He stopped signing and raised his eyebrows. "We didn't transplant your vocal chords, but we did cut them so that you won't be able to tell anyone the truth, and it's doubtful—with the amount of tissue we've taken from you—that you'll ever be able to write anything or make any meaningful movements ever again. Buddy will never know the truth, but it's better that way, don't you think? That he'll always believe you *offered* this, freely."

Dr. Jeffers looked at Buddy, who rose and knelt next to the bed. Gently, he cupped the back of Craig's head and stared with baby blue eyes Craig wasn't sure he'd ever really *seen* before today. Buddy touched foreheads with him and grunted something that needed no translation.

Thank you.

Craig broke into little pieces inside. *Aw, Buddy . . . I'm sorry . . . so sorry . . .*

Buddy nodded once, grunted again and stood. Dr. Jeffers stood also. They walked for the door.

Wait! Buddy, don't leave me! Not after this! Buddy! Don't LEAVE!

Buddy gave a big, friendly wave and a thankful smile that burned into Craig's memory. Dr. Jeffers clapped him on the shoulder, and Buddy—now Craig—walked out the door.

NOOOOOOOOOOOO!

BUDDDDDDDDDDDDDDYYYYYYYYYYYYYY!

Dr. Jeffers followed but stopped in the doorway, hands in his pockets. "Don't worry, Mr. Hartley. Our staff is caring and professional. We have fine equipment. You should live for a very long time. Thirty-three years, at the very least."

He offered Craig a thin smile. "Also . . . you'll finally get to have those words with your father."

He turned and closed the door.

IO.

"OKAY … THAT'S … that's just … "

I straighten and cover my mouth, which tastes a little like bile. Honestly, it's touch and go. But I swallow and manage to say without stuttering, "I hope Cassie Tillman doesn't come back, ask if I want anything more to eat or drink. She does … I'm puking. Definitely."

Gavin sips from his coffee (even THAT'S enough to twist my guts a little) and says, "I imagine. *I* didn't have much of an appetite for several days after that one."

I force myself to breathe evenly and say, "I'm guessing that 'Buddy Hartley' is no longer at Clifton Heights General? That he's … "

" … been 'transferred downstate to a special burn-care facility'? You'd be guessing right. At least, that's what they told me when I called. They didn't say WHERE, of course. 'Doctor/Patient Confidentiality' and all that. I found 'Craig' Hartley's number using Directory Assistance, but no one ever answers. Of course, 'Craig' is also now mute, so maybe he just doesn't answer *any* phone calls. Draw your own conclusions."

A slow flush of resentment is building inside me, pushing the nausea away. "And I can't *do* anything, can I? Can't confront this Dr. Jeffers and it's not like I have any evidence to warrant staking the place out, sneaking in there and looking around . . . "

Gavin's eyes widen a little, as if alarmed I'd even suggest such a thing. "I wouldn't go into that place for *any* reason, Chris. I mean . . . it's not like the hospital itself is evil, but from what I can tell, Dr. Jeffers' will is absolute. If he were to catch you breaking in . . . "

I can't help smiling. "Oh, come on. Even with all the strange things we've talked about tonight, isn't that a bit much?"

He leans forward, gaze burning and intense. "I'm serious. Everyone in that building, right down to the lowliest intern, does what he says and follows his smallest whims to the letter. He's like a demigod. He decides who lives and dies in there. You need to be wary of him."

I nod, not sure how much I believe his warning but also unable to shake the nausea inspired by this tale. Besides, I have another question. "Clive Hartley. This story said he disappeared into the swamps a few years ago, and Craig seemed to think he was dead. Dr. Jeffers didn't seem to think so, though, and I've heard . . . things."

Gavin raises his eyebrows. "What kind of things?"

"Just stories. About a man who wanders the woods, peddling folk cures, even craziness like vengeance curses. Is it possible that he's . . . "

Gavin purses his lips. "I think by now, Chris, it should be clear . . . just about *anything* is possible, in this town . . . "

LONELY PLACES

MUSKY AIR FROM the fireplace clouded the small hunting cabin. From across a wooden table, green eyes burned into Derek Barton's soul. He didn't want to be here, but he'd nowhere else left to go.

"What's happening to me?"

A leathery voice creaked. "Somethin powerful, boy. *Old Magic* powerful."

Fear slithered in his guts as he stared at this . . . man. Rumors called Clive Hartley many things—brujo, shaman, zombie, the walking dead, even—but Derek had never believed them, always figuring they were bullshit stories and nothing else.

Now, however? He desperately hoped the stories were *true*, because if not . . . he was *fucked*. "People say you *know* about this kinda shit. Ya gotta help me."

Clive Hartley leaned into hissing lantern light, bright green eyes narrowed, deep lines creasing his thick skin. "Somethin's growin inside ya. Ken see it in yer eyes."

"*Please.*"

A pause. Hartley folded his hands on the wooden table. "Tell me how."

Derek shuddered as pieces of himself fell away inside.

***

THE NIGHT BEFORE

"Quiet! We're gonna get busted!"

Derek Barton grunted, working his crowbar into the crack between the door and its frame at Handy's Pawn & Thrift, which sat on Hurd Street, a cracked gray strip of asphalt with nothing but the pawn shop, the Salvation Army and a few empty lots on the east end of Clifton Heights. No one came here at night, not even the cops. They patrolled Main Street and the bars on the other side of town, where all the action was this late.

He jiggled the crowbar and wood groaned.

"Shit!"

"Shut the *hell* up." Despite the cool night, beads of sweat dotted his brow. Liquor sloshed in his belly, making him slightly queasy. He closed his eyes and breathed deep.

Eddie Bannister said, "*Fuck*, man. Let's ditch."

Derek opened his eyes and scowled over his shoulder at Eddie. "Don't be a pussy. This'll only take a minute."

A worried frown pinched Eddie's thin face. "What if there's an alarm?"

Derek pushed against the crowbar and the door bowed out of its frame. "Dumbass. An alarm? For this shit hole? If there was, it woulda gone off by now." He was making that up, of course, but it sounded good enough.

"C'mon, Derek. We get caught by cops an I'll lose my job, for sure."

"We ain't gonna get caught unless you don't shut yer . . . "

He levered the crowbar once more, hard. Another sharp whine, then something cracked and metal tinkled to the ground. The door swung open and banged against the siding.

"*Shit*! Let's go, before—"

Derek whirled, jabbing the crowbar in Eddie's face. "No. Fuckin. Way. You said you were up for this. In or out, dickhead? Time's a'wastin."

Silence fell.

Eddie swallowed. "We split it, right? Down the middle?"

"Absolutely."

Wide-eyed, Eddie nodded. "O-okay."

Derek grabbed Eddie's arm and pulled him towards the doorway. "Let's go."

***

After twenty minutes they stood nearly empty-handed. The old register had been easy to jimmy but had only offered a hundred dollars, which wasn't nearly enough to help Derek pay off his debt to Jimmy Jones after splitting it with Eddie. They'd found nothing valuable on the shelves, either. Mostly junk and odds and ends.

And with each shelf ransacked, Derek's stomach tightened with unexpected guilt. Old Man Handy had always treated everyone in Clifton Heights square, minding his business. When Derek's father had made him quit ice hockey in the tenth grade and he'd hawked his gear here, Handy hadn't said a word, just paid up.

Pa. That sonuvabith. I loved hockey. Probably the only thing I ever did love an he didn't give a rat's ass, just needed me to work so his fat ass didn't have to.

217

He swallowed, the memories coming hard and fast and against his will; memories of Pa coming home drunk to sit on Derek's chest while he cowered in bed, memories of Pa sticking an old .38 under his chin, clicking the trigger and saying, "Yer nothin."

Click. "Nothin, hear me?"

He hated Pa and he hated Clifton Heights, too. He just wanted to get out so he could *be* something, *anything* other than what he was . . .

Loser.

Thief.

Pa's son. And he was doing a fine job of *that,* wasn't he, losing big in poker the other night and owing Jimmy Jones a thousand bucks he didn't have and everyone in Clifton Heights *knew* you didn't fuck with Jimmy Jones. He'd been able to beg two days out of Jimmy to raise the cash, but tomorrow morning when Jones showed up and he didn't have it . . .

Something glimmered in his flashlight's beam as be panned the back of the store. Looked like an old trunk or something. "Eddie!"

Footsteps trotted over. "What?"

In minutes, they broke the trunk's rusty latches with the crowbar, but they opened it to nothing but mounds of musty clothes and dirty rags.

He sighed. "Fuck me sideways."

"Man, we should split."

He hated to admit it, but Eddie was right. "Fuck this." He pushed off the trunk's clutter. Something like a static shock passed through the fabric and jolted his hand. "Damn!"

"What's wrong?"

He examined his palm, expecting to find it cut. It

wasn't, but it glowed an angry red and tingled as if he'd touched something hot. "Dunno. Somethin under here." He grabbed a bundle and unwrapped the rags under his flashlight.

Roughly the size of his palm, it was an ugly wooden head, strung on a rawhide necklace. Its lips grinned blood red, pointed teeth painted in jagged black lines. Pale yellow eyes bugged lizard-like on opposite sides of the head, staring from under painted eyebrows. Worst of all was its full head of *hair*, because that's exactly what it felt like: dry, rustling old human hair.

It felt warm, even seemed to get warmer as he held it. He shivered and abruptly realized that for some reason he wanted to wear it, wanted to feel its warmth against his chest . . . and *there* . . . he heard something beating softly, far away.

Drums.

With voices.

A song? Someone singing with drums beating in the background, over and over. Something hissing and buzzing, too, in time and rhythm like maracas . . .

Eddie reached for it.

Derek jerked back. "Get the fuck off!"

"The hell's wrong with you?"

"Hands off, dumbass. This whole thing was my idea, remember?"

"I just wanna look at it." Eddie's voice grated harsher than normal, something bright flashing in his eyes. "What's that on its forehead?"

Derek brushed back the fake hair with his thumb. Sure enough, something was etched into the wood, two dots under a gently curved line. He rubbed it and a pulsating heat gripped him.

Drums.

Buzzing and hissing.

Singing, or maybe voices screaming together . . .

Ia! Ia! Ia!

"Hey. Derek."

"What?"

"I'll let you keep *all* the cash for that thing."

His fingers closed over the charm, not caring about anything now except this warmth spreading through him. He met Eddie's hungry gaze. "No deal. Keep the cash. This is *mine*."

Eddie's eyes flashed again as he bared his teeth. "*Give it.*"

Derek tensed, grinding his teeth, biting off clipped words. "Fuck. Off. *Bannister*."

Silence.

Hot, throbbing silence, as Eddie's burning eyes drilled into his own.

Eddie reached again but Derek dodged, grabbing the crowbar with his free hand and slamming it against Eddie's temple. Eddie screamed, the air misting red as Derek swung again . . .

And again.

***

"That's not all, aye? There's more."

Derek bit his tongue. He wanted to scream. Giggle hysterically, or maybe even puke. He wanted to push away from this table and this crazy redneck witch doctor and run away.

But he didn't, he just sat there, trembling.

"Lookit me, boy."

He swallowed and gazed into those burning green eyes, surprised to find something almost like sympathy there.

"I can't help ya if you don' tell me *everythin . . .* "
***

THE NEXT DAY

Derek's stomach clenched as a hot knife carved a path along his intestines. Gasping awake, he scrambled off the couch in his apartment over Chin's Pizza, stumbled to the bathroom, fell before the toilet and vomited.

With a lurch he spewed clumps into the bowl. Next came bile, then dry heaves, his head pounding, tears stinging his eyes. Finally, nothing remained but gossamer strands of glistening drool hanging from his lips.

He wiped his mouth on his sleeve and flushed the toilet. He didn't look at the swirling mess. He closed the lid, stumbled back to the couch, collapsed and closed his eyes.

He couldn't really remember much about last night. Strange, hazy thoughts swirled in his muddled head. *What happened? I don't remember anythin after drinkin an bitchin with Eddie about losin that money an havin to pay Jimmie Jones, an us makin' crazy plans to . . .*

. . . do what, exactly?

He rubbed his unshaven face, glancing at the wall clock. It was almost two in the afternoon. He'd slept most the day away.

He closed his eyes and thought hard, rubbing his forehead. He needed cash bad because he'd gotten fired from the lumber mill two months ago after John Finch got killed and someone else had taken over, someone who actually *minded* Derek occasionally showing up to work late and drunk. He'd used up most his meager savings paying rent and utilities, his last ditch attempt at cards the other night to raise some quick cash clearing him out.

He'd been drinking his last dollars away with Eddie last night, jawing about the places in Clifton Heights they could break into, only half serious, really. They'd debated over the Salvation Army or Old Man Handy's place . . .

The phone rang.

He groaned and fumbled on the table next to the couch, finally getting it after several tries. "Eddie, this better not be you bitchin bout last night cause I can't remember what the fuck we . . . "

Soft, feminine sniffing.

A sob.

His irritation quickly faded. He sat up, stomach sloshing, but somehow he held it down. "Shelly? What's wrong?"

"*He knows, Derek . . . he f-found out. About us.*"

"SHIT! How?"

The voice on the other end broke. "*The necklace you b-bought me. At the f-fair last spring? He found it. I must've gotten distracted, left it out somewhere.*" Her voice crumbled. "*He hit me, Derek. In the stomach.*"

"Shelly . . . does he know it's me?"

"*No. Don't think so.*"

"Where's Cody?"

"*He's at school.*" Her voice steadied. "*Derek, let's go. Now. You, me, Cody . . . today.*"

His stomach churned, frustration mixing with helplessness. How far could they get, if they tried to run? They had no cash of any kind, especially after last night's wild plan failed, and . . .

Last night.

Fog still swirled there.

What happened? Ice tickled his spine. Slowly, he looked down and saw it on the coffee table. The charm.

Beating drums. Buzzing, hissing. Hooting cries.

Ia! Ia!

And hunger.

Eddie. What happened to Eddie? His stomach fluttered as he tasted a faint, copper-saltiness on his tongue, and he thought of puking, again.

No.

No, no, no, no.

Trembling, he looked down at the clothes he'd worn and slept in last night: jeans, Timberland boots, red flannel over a gray T-shirt, all stained dark red. Shriveled bits of *something* peppered his boots and shirt.

His mind twitched. Drawn by an irresistible fascination, his gaze slid back to the charm. "Fuck *me* . . . "

"*What?*" Shelly's voice pierced his fog. "*Derek, listen. He got called to work. Probably the only reason he didn't . . . but he said he'd be back. To t-teach me a . . . *" She broke down.

He couldn't speak.

Because he knew too well what kind of lessons she meant; lessons this scumbag *excelled* at giving out. She'd met him at her strip club, the Aces Wild, three years ago. She'd been a desperate mother and thought she could tough out the lessons in exchange for the cash waved in her face.

Until she'd met Derek, someone who'd grown up

with the same kind of lessons, someone who *understood* what she'd endured better than anyone ever could.

They'd waited and planned an escape, a bid for a new life together but it had all fallen apart because he was a worthless loser who'd not only gotten his ass fired, but was now in debt to Jimmy Jones, of all people.

He was nothing.

Click.

"Nothin."

Shelly's voice brought him back. *"I'm packing the car, getting Cody, then leaving. I c-can't take this anymore."*

Wild desperation tightened his throat, making it hard to breathe. "Shelly, we'll never make it with no cash . . . I can't . . . somethin's *wrong* . . . "

"I love you. Hurry." She hung up.

The phone slid from his hand and hit the floor with a plastic rattle.

He stared at the charm.

Its yellow eyes swelled and stared at him. He picked it up. Its heat pulsed against his hand. He stood shakily to a knock on his door and a harsh voice.

"Barton? Open the fuckin door. It's Jimmy. Time to pay up, asshole."

***

Derek stood and stared at the door shaking in its frame, his feet rooted to the ground, seemingly incapable of thought or action. Too much was happening too fast with last night and Shelly and Cody and he couldn't think or move but he had to do something, *be* something before . . .

"C'mon, Barton! Don't make this any harder'n it's gotta be. You don't open this door right now, I'm gonna fuckin kick it off the hinges!"

And there was drumming.

Buzzing and hissing.

And voices crying out, chanting to the beat of the drums . . .

Ia! Ia! Ia!

Derek squeezed the wooden charm in his hand tightly, feeling it glow and pulse warmth into his palm, up his arm, out into the rest of his body. He looked down, startled to see himself gripping it so tightly.

"That's it. I'm fuckin done playing with you!"

A crash of a boot against wood, Derek's front door slammed open and a looming Jimmy Jones filled the doorway, jabbing a meaty finger at him, wide meat-slab face red and scowling. "Gave you two days, limp dick. Where's my goddamn money?"

Jimmy and Derek had gone to school together. His old man had worked with Derek's for years, went out drinking with him, too. Jones had been something of a football star at Clifton Heights High; though a knee injury his senior year had frightened scouts away and ended a potential college career before it had even started. Still, he was a construction foreman for Webb County, ran a backroom, illegal poker club at The Stumble Inn that drew people from as far away as Syracuse and he was a *somebody* while Derek was *nothing*, as Pa had reminded him whenever he could, with his fists or belt, or that cold .38 jammed under his chin, late at night when he was a kid.

Click.

"Nothin."

"Where's my money, Barton? No one stiffs me an you know it. I gave you two days cause your old man an mine was tight, but I'm gettin paid right now, an I'm either takin it in cash, or takin it outta yer skin."

Derek swallowed down a tight, dry throat, the charm burning in his hand. "I . . . I just need a day or two more, Jimmy. That's all. I promise I'll . . . "

"Bullshit!"

In two quick strides, Jones covered the distance between them and swung a haymaker too fast to duck. His sledgehammer fist slammed into Derek's chin, launching him back over the coffee table onto his couch. Pain shot through his jaw into his temples, thousands of little lights sparked across his vision . . .

And the charm burned hotter in his hand.

As the drumming and buzzing and hissing and chanting filled his head.

Ia! Ia! Ia!

Jones grabbed his shirt and jerked him face-to-face, so close their noses almost touched. "Last time, Barton. Or yer gonna be eatin dinner from a straw for a month."

Derek gagged on Jones' tangy, sweaty scent, which made his stomach churn not with nausea but something . . . *else.* He clutched the charm tighter, his nostrils flaring as he inhaled deeply of Jones' smell. Desperate fear, spiced with anger, gripped him, hunger swelling inside. The charm burned in his hand, and he heard . . .

Ia! Ia! Ia!

Everything seemed to stop.

And he rasped, "*No.*"

He lunged upwards, jaws snapping, and latched onto Jones' neck. Teeth sawed through flesh as Jones' screams gurgled into wheezing rasps. Derek's teeth ripped muscle into bloody strips and still the drums beat and the voices cried.

Ia!

His face swelled.

Enormous pressure stretched his cheekbones.

Blood spurted in gouts from Jones' neck, covering Derek's face, streaming down his throat. He tore out a chunk of flesh, chewed once, then swallowed. Jones' twitching corpse flopped to the floor.

Muddied thoughts swirled in his head. He needed to run. Think. Plan. Find help. Get to . . . *Shelly* . . . before *he* killed her. First, the body. Jones, the . . . *meat*. He needed to . . . needed to . . .

He fell upon Jones, the scent of blood and meat consuming him. Pressure throbbed behind his face. His stomach surged briefly, as if he was about to vomit everything back up, then it settled and throbbed with hunger pains he'd never known.

Time passed.

Slowly, he stopped, fighting to clear his mind.

He took one last bite, swallowed it with a snap, sat back on his haunches for a deep breath, and looked into the hallway mirror.

And screamed.

As the voices screamed with him.

Ia!

***

"Lemmme see it."

Derek fumbled in his pocket and withdrew the charm. It still pulsed warmly. He hated relinquishing it and even as Hartley took it, jealousy twisted his heart. *He can't have it! It's mine! Ia! It's mine!*

He rubbed his face. It no longer felt stretched but when he moved his jaw it still clicked, like he'd grown extra hinges or something. He looked mostly normal again, but he remembered well what he'd seen in his apartment's mirror.

Something tall, with spidery-limbs that had stretched and ripped his clothes. Gray, rubbery skin. A long, flat face with a gaping jaw that hung impossibly low, ringed by jagged teeth dripping with blood and tissue . . . and wide-set, yellow eyes.

Something lean and hungry.

Something evil.

"Not evil." Hartley caressed the symbol on the charm with a withered thumb. "Old, aye. Not evil."

He swallowed, wincing because his throat still burned raw. "What is it, then?"

A ghostly smile flickered on Hartley's creased, leathery face. "A piece of the Old World. There's lots of 'em, scattered all over."

"But what the *hell* is it doing to me?" Hartley held up the charm. "This here charm's filled with an Old One. Algonquin pro'bly, by its sign. Maybe Mississauga. It's workin its will on ya."

He massaged his jaw, which still hurt from how it had *stretched* when he'd attacked Jones. "How the hell did something like *that* end up here?"

"Algonquians mostly squatted up north in Canada, Mississauga round Poughkeepsie. Close nuff to here. Maybe got traded, pawned off after bein handed down a few hundred years. Who knows? Yer not the first to run into an Old One, specially round these parts in partic'ler."

"So what happens now? What the *fuck* is happenin to me?"

"My Algonquin's rusty, but I think this here symbol means, 'he in lonely places always hungers.'" Hartley offered a flat grin. "Ye know all bout the hunger part, I'm guessin."

His guts twisted as he thought of Eddie . . . and Jones.

He squirmed. It was probably his imagination, but his clothes seemed tighter than usual, his legs and arms sticking out several inches from the cuffs and sleeves. "And?"

Hartley dangled the charm from its strap. "I'm guessin' this here is an old conjure for what they used to call a 'Wihtikow', roughly translated as Wendigo. Some dialects even call it Ithaqua . . . "

Ia!

Ithaqua!

" . . . god of the wastes. Either way, it's a thing of great power an hunger."

"These . . . things . . . whitaka . . . "

"Wendigo. Ithaqua. Whichever's easier."

"Whatever. They . . . uh . . . eat . . . "

"Aye." Hartley nodded. "*Anythin* livin or dead. An they never stop, are always hungry."

"An I'm . . . "

"Yep. 'Pears so."

"How? Why?"

Hartley shrugged. "A Wendigo spirit . . . or Ithaqua . . . is nat'rally attracted to those who hunger." His eyes narrowed. "*You* hungerin for somethin, boy?"

Derek opened his mouth . . . but stopped.

What did he hunger for? What did he . . . want?

Respect.
To *be* something.
Anything.
He closed his eyes and breathed. "Aw, *shit.*"
"Aye. Have ye worn it, yet?"
Thin hope flared. "No! Not yet. I want to, though. Real bad."
Hartley smiled. "There's a chance, then. Ye haven't pledged yer soul to it, yet."
"What happens if I do?"
Harley smiled, eyes burning.

***

LATER

Derek stood on Bassler Road before a small, dingy trailer too trashy even for the Commons Trailer Park. It had been a short trip through the trees and their snapping branches, and he'd run with uncanny speed, darting through brush with barely a rustle, his feet anticipating every rut and dip in the ground. He'd smelled his way here on the breeze, smelling *her:* the fresh scent of her hair and skin. He'd smelled her fear also, which meant *he* was there.

Derek had come too late.

Click.

"Nothin, hear me? Yer nothin."

Swirling odors overwhelmed him: Shelly's fear and pain; *his* aggression and hate . . . all burning, spicy odors and there he stood, pulsing with them. Even from here, he heard the cries.

A scream and a meaty *smack.* Broken glass tinkled and a shrill, young voice cried, *"Mom!"*

He leaped forward, sprinting up the driveway, hurtling onto the trailer's leaning porch and slamming through the trailer's screen door. There was abrupt silence, except panting and breath whistling through a swollen nose. Shelly cowered on the floor, hugging Cody.

"*You*? Un-fuckin-believable."

There he stood, looming over Shelly and Cody, left fist glistening wetly with Shelly's blood and snot. His twisted, fat little face sneered at Derek, just as it had every day of his life until he'd gotten big enough to fight back.

Dad.

Dear old fucking Dad.

His old man turned his shoulders and swung his jiggling beer belly around, which was stretching a stained yellow undershirt to its limits. Clutched in his other hand Derek saw it, dreadful and gleaming: the .38. The same one Pa had stuck under his chin night after night.

The hammer *clicked* and snapped his focus back. His old man pointed the gun at his head and lumbered towards him. "So *you're* the one? More balls'n you *ever* showed growin up, for sure."

Derek glanced at Shelly, brown hair spilling over her face, limp strands plastered to her cheeks with sweat and blood. Her eyes darted back and forth between him and Pa.

Pa stepped so close Derek could smell his sweaty aggression, as he had for so many dark and lonely nights. "So now. Young rooster thinks he can diddle the old man's prize hen? That it?"

He said nothing, just swallowed and reached up . . .

But pain and stars burst in his eyes when the .38 slammed into his temple.

The floor rushed up to meet him and his forehead cracked against wood. Pressure built inside his skull as his old man bent over him. "Teach ya a lesson about touchin what's mine, boy . . . "

No.

Snarling, he lunged upwards and felt himself *changing* even without touching the charm, as his jaws latched onto a mouthful of cloth and flesh at the old man's belly. Pa screeched a high, shrill note as Derek bit down and twisted.

With a jerk, he ripped a mouthful of fat and cloth away. Blood pumped from a ragged hole in Pa's undershirt as he gurgled and crumpled to the floor.

Derek spat out wadded, bloodied cloth and chunks of flesh, slumped forward and breathed into his hands. Pa's blood tasted sour. Impure. Bad. On the floor, Pa curled into a shivering fetal ball.

Derek grunted and wearily stood.

Shelly and Cody had crawled into the den. She stared at him, trembling . . . scared of *him*. Maybe more than she'd ever been of Pa.

Derek bent, grabbed the .38 and tossed it to Shelly. It landed at her feet. Next, he pulled out his wallet—filled with the cash he'd taken off Jones' corpse before *eating* the rest of it—tossed it next to the gun, bent down and grabbed Pa's wallet and tossed that, adding it to the pile.

"You packed?"

She nodded, her eyes wide. He could only imagine how his blood-streaked face looked. He waved at the door. "Go. Quick."

She collected the wallets, jammed them into her back pockets, palmed the .38 and slid it under her belt. She stood and pulled Cody up. The boy stayed a half-step behind, eyes unblinking. She opened her mouth. For a second nothing came out, until, "Are you . . . "

"No. Gotta finish this."

He toed Pa's moaning form, then met Shelly's gaze. She nodded and shuffled for the door. Passing him she stopped, reached out . . . but pulled back at the last moment. He didn't blame her.

She searched his eyes and swallowed. "I'm sorry."

"Me too."

Cody looked at him for several seconds but said nothing. Something lingered in the boy's gaze. Sadness, but not fear, and something else. He wasn't sure, but he thought . . . maybe . . .

Shelly pulled Cody out the door.

Derek closed his eyes.

Something stirring deep within.

He opened his eyes and looked down at his wheezing father. He'd almost screwed up. Like always, he'd almost screwed it up . . . but not this time.

Not ever again.

Reaching under his shirt, he pulled out the charm, its newspaper wrapping scratching his skin. Dim heat pulsed through newsprint. He stood that way for several minutes, thinking hard. Had he done this for Shelly? Or himself?

Didn't matter.

It was time to *be* something.

Finally.

He tore the newspaper away. The charm blazed and filled him with something wonderful and powerful and awful. Reverently, he pressed it against his skin and something inside rushed towards a crescendo.

Bones and joints popped.

Ligaments snapped and stretched. Glorious pain filled his limbs as they grew. Facial plates cracked, the skin on his cheeks ripping. The world blossomed into a rich aromal tapestry of blood, meat and sweat. He turned and grinned, jagged teeth clicking.

He took his time.

Pa screamed.

For a long while.

II.

GAVIN IS TALKING about researching Wendigoes and old Native American myths, something along those lines but I'm not listening too closely, not really. I can *hear* the words coming from his mouth, can recognize them as English but I can't distinguish one word from the other as they flow along into a steady stream of babble . . .

Because I'm too busy staring at this damn book open before me, at its script—Gavin's flowing script—which *still* seems to quiver and tremble and even *undulate* across the page. I'm starting to wonder what will happen if I keep staring at these words, what will happen if I keep reading them, what will happen to them, to *me*? Will they slide off the page, down onto the dull and scuffed Formica tabletop, slither over to my hand, melt into my skin, ride my blood to my brain and burn themselves forever there?

Okay.

Hell.

That's enough of *that*.

So I close my eyes, hold a hand up to pause Gavin's talk as I *try* to sort things out in my head, too many things, strange and confusing and frightening things I *don't* want to think about, at all.

But I've got no choice, really.

Because I asked for this.

I *wanted* to know.

"So," I manage, "Derek Barton *ate* Jimmy Jones, then his old man? *That's* why we haven't had to worry about that illegal poker club over at The Stumble Inn these past few months? Jones hasn't been around to run it because . . . "

I open my eyes, peer at Gavin, part of me wishing to Heaven I'd never started this but also knowing deep in my gut, now, that it was inevitable. "I bet if I called Henry Chin, Barton's landlord, he'd just say Barton skipped town and his rent, and he probably wouldn't even think to mention a small little thing like cleaning up huge bloodstains on the floor after Barton cleared out."

Gavin nods slowly. "You knew Barton, then?"

"Not really. Questioned him a few times after Emma Pital killed John Finch, because back then Barton was still working at the lumber mill. Never saw him after that, honestly. And I'm sure his old man's landlord would say the same thing—that he just skipped rent—and also his job probably has no idea where he went, and if I checked with Aces Wild where Shelly Livingston danced they'd probably have no idea where she went, either. Same thing with the school regarding her son, Cody. Eddie Bannister I've never met and quite frankly at this point I don't give a rat's ass WHAT his story is, because it'd just lead to a dead end, too."

Gavin offers me a weary smile. "You're starting to get the hang of this."

"Here's the kicker. Barton and Bannister broke into Handy's Pawn and Thrift, Barton killed and ATE Bannister in there . . . and Old Man Handy DOESN'T report the break-in, much less the blood all over his place? What the hell?"

Gavin offers me a shrug and cryptic expression. "I have a feeling I'll be writing lots of stories about *that* place."

"Great. Just great. Meg loves shopping for odds and ends there, and maybe it's evil. WONDERFUL."

"Well, perhaps not evil, just . . . "

I wave him off, massaging my aching temples with my other hand. "Yeah, yeah. I got it. Holy God, Gavin. Demons, evil houses and doctors, ghosts, redneck voodoo zombie witch doctors and monsters . . . what the hell else have we got in this town?"

He tips his head at the book. "How about gods . . . "

ON A MIDNIGHT BLACK
CHESSIE

NOW

BRADLEY AGAIN TURNS onto the strange road bathed in the moon's phosphorescent glow. He understands this place now. Understands what it is, where it came from, and how it came to be.

Ned sits on the passenger side, still drunk, forehead pressing the window as he gazes at the glowing scenery. "Wow. Am I awake or dreamin?"

"Neither," Bradley whispers. "Or maybe both."

Toward Ned he feels a resolved sadness. Bradley no longer hates him so much but rather pities him, for he's caught up in something much larger than himself, much larger than Bradley or anything else, and is completely helpless in the face of it.

As Bradley is.

And as they drive down this softly glowing road, Ned continues to stare. "Geez. Don' recognize this at all. You lost?"

"No," Bradley says as he slowly pulls up to the glowing church at the road's end. "Not at all.

"I'm home."

THREE DAYS AGO
FRIDAY AFTERNOON

Bradley Sanders had just pulled shut his office door at Webb County Community College and was in the process of locking it when he heard: "Hey, Brad. What's up?"

He breathed deep, feeling his insides warm.

And he turned, smiling at Emma Hatcher, a colleague in the Mythology Department here at Web Community. Young and vivacious but also highly intelligent, she'd proven very stimulating company this past year.

Very stimulating indeed.

He regarded Emma's approach with surreptitious appraisal as she glided toward him. Not swinging her hips, exactly, but swaying in a graceful way that couldn't be so plainly described as "walking." She seemed more suited to Broadway than a backwater community college in the Adirondacks.

She smiled. "Heading home to good old Clifton Heights?"

He shuffled books and office keys and his satchel. "Well. Urm. Yes. And you . . . ?" He nodded toward the exit, feeling both foolish and wonderful.

"Yeah. SO done with this place for now. Especially with summer session starting Monday." She smiled. "Walk with me?"

He happily grinned like an idiot. "My pleasure."

She fell in step with him. "Y'know, some folks from the other departments are meeting at the White Lake

Inn tonight. An 'end of the semester' mixer around nine. The Inn's only about thirty minutes away from Clifton Heights, I think. Just after Old Forge and Otter Lake."

She paused.

Offering him a gentle grin. "Of course, you'll probably be too busy playing with your trains, I suppose."

He snorted good-naturedly and looked down, heat rising past his collar. "I'll have you know I enjoy *many* other stimulating pursuits besides model railroading."

Her eyebrows raised.

Glistening, playful lips curving upwards. "Such as?"

"Well. Er. There's perusing yard sales, especially the Commons Yard Sales at the Commons Trailer Park, just outside of town. Browsing thrift shops over in Eagle Bay and Inlet. Of course, my studies. And . . . well . . . "

"Hah!" She bumped shoulders with him. He shivered, even at this platonic gesture. "Admit it. At heart, you're a big kid obsessed with his train set."

"*Layout*, Emma. It's a model scale layout of Clifton Heights. A *set* you put under a Christmas tree for children to play with."

She chuckled. "Methinks you've been working too hard on your *layout*. Bit overprotective, aren't you?"

He shrugged. "Perhaps. It's addictive, really. Like building my own world."

"Well, Maestro . . . if you're not too busy building your own world . . . tonight. Nine. See you, maybe?"

And with that they pushed through the exit into the sunny afternoon. Emma glided off toward her white Mazda Miata, looking over her shoulder, smiling, her eyes dancing.

He waved.

Grinning like a fool.

She grinned, waved back, gliding toward her car. She opened the door, tossed her purse and books and satchel inside and flicked him one more jaunty half-wave.

She got into her car and drove off.

While he stood there staring, satchel in one hand, books pinned under his arm, cursing himself delightfully for being a thousand times an idiot.

But a happy idiot.

Until he considered her parting rejoinder, and felt his joy recede.

if you're not too busy
building your own world

Subdued, Bradley shuffled to his car.

FRIDAY EVENING

Bradley's train layout filled over half his basement, its wooden tablework skirted with blue cloth that just touched the floor. Underneath he stored his supplies and extra parts. Unused rolling stock: boxcars, flat cars, oil tankers, engines and cabooses. Boxes of automobiles. Unassembled houses, gas stations, stores and warehouses. Miles of track, assorted spare parts (organized into rectangular sorters), shakers filled with powdered terrain of all kinds: grass, dirt and gravel. Bags of shrubs and pre-assembled trees of every size and shape and color. Rolls of plaster, tubes of clay for landscaping. Miniature lights for homes and stores and churches.

Everything he needed.

Packed into green totes, stored neatly under the layout, behind the royal blue curtain.

Over the last few years, he'd spent hours casting plaster streets and roads and sidewalks, stringing electrical lines, aligning buildings to scale and landscaping hills and knolls, applying grass and dirt and gravel, bushes and trees where needed.

He'd spent hours down here.

Cocooned in the peace of his basement every night, or on afternoons like this one, and on holidays and weekends, also. Next to teaching and studying, modeling trains had become his love. An obsession, he freely admitted. He loved every inch of his layout, this version of Clifton Heights that only existed *here*. Loved it, as a Creator must love His world.

He smiled.

Claiming godship of a model train layout might be petty, but he'd take it.

What else did he have?

He forced himself not to think about that as he poured plaster into the roadbed he'd outlined with molding tape, branching a new road off Front Street, one that didn't exist in real life, advancing into the layout's last bare section, the final thing he needed to finish his world.

A section of Clifton Heights all his own, of *his* making.

Though he'd intended his layout to generally resemble Clifton Heights he'd tweaked his version in places. Most of his alterations were cosmetic, accounting for railroad tracks that didn't exist in real life. And some buildings he'd moved around simply because he thought they looked better this way.

But that was fine. *Realism* wasn't necessarily *reality*, after all. Realism offered its *own* reality.

This was *his* world, wasn't it?

So he poured one last drop of plaster, picked up a flat length of balsam wood, placed it edge down over the newly-poured street and scraped the excess plaster off the road's surface. He put the wood aside, grabbed the moist towel hanging from his belt and dabbed the plaster that had leaked under the tape. Tomorrow, he'd paint the road black, lay down some gravel for its shoulders and begin landscaping.

He dabbed away one last spot of plaster, stood and examined the new road. He tucked the damp towel under his belt and grunted, then turned to his workbench, where he'd laid out the buildings he intended on using. Six different styles of residential homes and a church.

But not just *any* church.

For he'd modified it. Removed the steeple's cross, painted over marks of mainstream faith with a slate gray, because this was *his* church. This was his world, after all. This church should worship *him*.

He smiled. "The First Congregational Church of Brad," he chuckled.

But of course he couldn't name it after himself, so instead he'd decided to call it "The Church of Luna." Dedicated to the various moon gods and goddesses he'd encountered in his studies. Which made wonderful sense, seeing as how tonight was May 5th, the month's first full moon, which would last until Wednesday night.

His sigil? Carefully painted onto the front and back doors with a toothpick dipped into black paint, a pagan moon symbol:

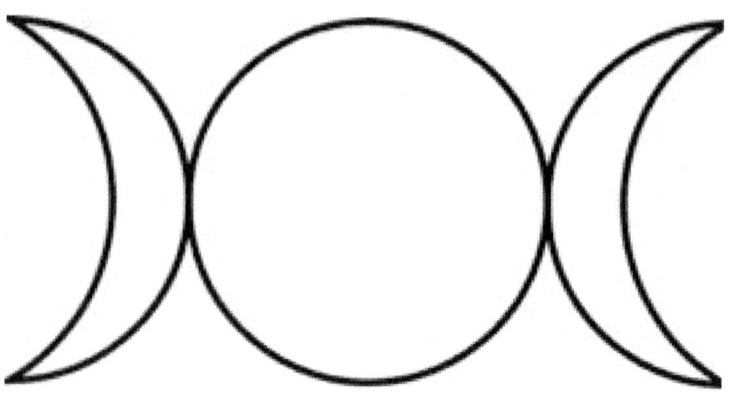

And he knew exactly how he'd arrange things after he'd finished the road and surrounding forestry. Houses on either side, with varying-sized lawns, and the church at its end.

Yes.

A road leading to *his* church, The Church of Luna, because all roads in this world lead back to him. And, as a final touch, he'd already decided on a graveyard behind the church, framed by hills and a forest. Of course, many pagan beliefs favored cremation over burial but that didn't matter. This was *his* world, one he'd built with his own hands, the product of his toil and care and sweat; his blood, too.

He could do what he pleased.

He glanced at the wall clock.

It read three.

He thought about breaking for an early dinner; reading from Edith Hamilton's Mythology to prep for Monday. After, he'd cut wire mesh for the surrounding hills, mark out building plots and begin laying ground cover: lawns, shrubbery, and the forest. Perhaps he'd even tinker with The Church of Luna's graveyard . . .

Or . . .

meeting at the White Lake Inn tonight
an 'end of the semester' mixer
around nine, you should come
if you're not too busy building your own world

He rubbed his nose, staring at the completed sections of his layout, at its curving tracks, rolling hills, precise town blocks, brilliantly verdant lawns and forests, and that newly poured road, thinking about building and molding his world, also thinking about how loud and crowded it'd likely be at The White Lake Inn, how he'd much rather spend the evening here, making a world from nothing . . . but for *Emma*.

Emma, on one hand.

The train layout on the other.

Everyone needed variety. He was an adult, capable of balancing more than one interest, and he respected and liked Emma, wanted to be around her, learn more about her, maybe even . . .

take her to bed

. . . and he'd begun caring for her, personally. *That* he couldn't deny.

But did she reciprocate?

Could she reciprocate and feel attracted to him? He was ten years older, stodgy, and spent all his free time building model trains, for goodness sakes. Their only common ground was mythology. The idea of a liaison between them seemed far-fetched. What if he revealed his feelings and she *didn't* reciprocate?

He'd feel foolish. Also, if that ruined their pleasant friendship, he'd be devastated.

But what if she *did* reciprocate?

What then?

He bit his lip, staring at his layout for several more minutes, and then finally decided even a Creator could relax. God took a day off, didn't He?

But as he left the basement, thrilling at the prospect of seeing Emma socially for the first time (even if in mixed company) he couldn't repress a small guilty twinge as he shut off the basement lights, casting his unfinished world into darkness.

FRIDAY EVENING

Bradley sat at the end of a table at The White Lake Inn, staring at nothing, sipping his Heineken occasionally, cursing himself, for the night had turned out *exactly* as he'd feared.

It had begun fine. Emma, excited to see him, had squealed, slip-stumbled off her stool and hugged him briefly around the neck with one arm. She'd followed that up with a quick peck on the cheek.

Completely platonic, of course.

As she'd kiss a brother or cousin.

But his heart had swelled with pleasure. And, those present from other departments, folks he didn't recognize, had acted pleased to meet him.

However, after some small talk Bradley faded into the background, gradually disappearing like he always did. Occasionally Emma glanced his way and smiled, but she seemed far more interested in a young man sitting next to her, a young man with longish, curly black hair and big blue eyes.

So things had transpired as they always did: he became part of the scenery. His attention drifted as they chatted about sports and reality television and the next episode of that zombie apocalypse show; politicians and whether or not the budget will get passed, who was up for tenure, who was a son-of-a-bitch and which son-of-a-bitch was up for tenure.

An idiot.

He was an absolute idiot to think it would've gone any differently.

But then things changed. Everyone at the table scattered. The women headed to the lavatory and the men either to the bar for more food and drink or to the jukebox.

Leaving Emma and him alone.

He fumbled over a dozen witty conversation starters but failed to initiate even one. Luckily, after finishing her current glass of wine, Emma asked, "And how are you managing, Quiet Mouse? Hanging in?"

He shrugged and in a rare moment of inspiration, decided on the truth. "Actually, I'm bored to death. Having a dreadful time." He offered her a jaunty smile that surprised even him. "You?"

To his delighted surprise Emma snorted and had to cover her mouth with both hands. She coughed and managed, "Oh, God. Some of them *are* kind of shallow, aren't they?"

He opened his mouth but paused for a moment, realizing he didn't mean that at all. "No, not really. I'm just a crusty old academic, I suppose, more comfortable in solitary pursuits than social ones. I can lecture eloquently about how our hopes and dreams and fears are reflected in our myths and legends and what that says about being human, but I'm not so good at acting like one, I'm afraid. Or at enjoying their company."

She gave him a knowing smile. "So not true. Really. We get along, don't we?"

And there it was.

An invitation for him to broach his true feelings. Did he dare? "Well, yes . . . but . . . "

The moment slipped away as she reached over and patted his hand. "I'm sure any single woman your age would be mad about you."

woman your age

The ladies returned, followed by the men with refilled pitchers and promises of hot wings and chili cheese fries and all too quickly, as if he'd never spoken, Bradley faded into the background once more, occasionally sipping his now lukewarm beer, feeling numb, realizing he was flirting very near to pouting and not sure if he cared.

And then Emma yawned, running a hand through her gorgeous, silky black hair. "I'm done, folks. Bushed. Summer session starts Monday and I've done nothing to prepare."

Knowing chuckles circled the table. Bradley flickered a smile, though he doubted Emma noticed.

But Emma turned and met his gaze, smiled and asked, "Walk me out, Brad?"

He blinked. Stupidly, he felt sure, but he did his best not to stammer. "Yes. Certainly. Really, I probably should get going myself."

"I bet." Emma winked as she shrugged into a light spring coat. "Probably eager to get home to your precious trains."

A slight flush of . . . *anger*? pulsed through him. Was she joking, or . . .

The group's laughter sounded amiable, the young man who'd sat next to Emma—a Math instructor, he thought—saying he'd love to see Bradley's layout some time, to which he nodded numbly.

But Emma's remark bothered him.

Was she mocking him? In public, no less?

But he shook it off. Hell, she'd asked him to walk her out, offering a chance for them to be alone, so he prepared his best face and smiled. "We gods are busy, Emma. Can't keep my Creation waiting, now can I?"

This reply apparently served well because everyone laughed again and Emma's smile was rewarding: bright and mirthful. Joking, she'd been. Obviously.

Surely.

As they left The White Lake Inn, Emma flashed him a hopeful look. "So I've a favor to ask, one I wanted to pose in private."

His heart stirred inside, beating faster, making it hard to breathe. As they faced each other, Emma's red lipstick glistened in the neon glow of the Inn's beer signs, eyes shimmering in the night. He struggled not to sound too desperate. "Anything. Name it."

"Could you cover my class next Friday?"

His mouth hung open for a second, stomach twisting in disappointment. He closed his mouth, scrambling to recover. "I . . . well. Yes, I'm certain I could." Hating himself for acquiescing so easily, he asked, "What for? No troubles, I hope."

"Nooo . . . " she bit her lip. "I have . . . ah, hell. I can tell *you*, right?" She cocked an eyebrow. "If you can't trust a friend, who can you trust?"

At the word "friend" his stomach twisted more. "Of course," he murmured.

And amazingly enough, Emma looked embarrassed. "I'm sort of . . . going away next weekend. With a friend. A . . . *work* friend."

"Someone from the college, then." He understood her reticence, now. Inter-faculty dating wasn't expressly forbidden but missing class to vacation with a fellow faculty member wasn't likely to be received well.

"Yes. Ned Simmons, the one who said he'd love to see your layout sometime."

Bradley nodded. Yes. The one with the curly black hair and blue eyes, whom Emma had shown so much attention.

"We're going to Maryland for the weekend. Ocean City. We're leaving early next Friday morning." She twisted her hands, looking sheepish. "I *did* sort of tell the Department Chair I had a family affair, so . . . "

He nodded, hoping the night hid the frustration he felt burning behind his eyes. "I see. Of course. I assume your leave was approved, long as you found your own substitute."

Emma's apprehension dissolved, her face breaking into a beautiful smile that crushed him, because he understood that it wasn't for him. "Yes! You can cover? You're the best. You were the first person I thought of, because I knew my kids would be in good hands and also figured you wouldn't blab."

He forced a small smile. "Of course. As you said, what are friends for?"

She grabbed his elbow, squeezing it. "Great! You're teaching Intro to Mythology this summer, right?"

He nodded, wanting to say something, anything, but caught flatfooted and speechless.

"That's in the afternoon, I'm always home by then, so we can't hook up at school. I'll come by your place, say . . . Wednesday night? Drop off my lesson plans?"

His place.

Wednesday night.

Faint hope bloomed inside. Emma at his home, at night. Them, alone together . . .

yes, you idiot, so you can help her go off on a dirty weekend

Still.

Desperate measures.

"Sounds excellent. Maybe we could eat . . . "

"Sure!" Emma smiled and slapped his shoulder. "I'll bring over some pizza and beers. The least I can do. And hey—I'll bring Ned over, if that's all right. He's crazy about trains. He'll love your layout."

A crippling sense of futility burned in him. "Well, actually, I was thinking more that . . . "

But she struck him dumb with a heartfelt look of gratitude. "Thanks, Brad! You're fantastic."

With that, she headed to the parking lot and her car, leaving him on the Inn's front walk, fumbling his keys.

"Friends," he murmured, rolling the word around in his mouth.

And it tasted like ashes.

***

Bradley had taken a wrong turn somewhere. Hard to believe, having spent hours driving around Clifton Heights' roads during his layout's conceptual stages, but there it was: he was lost. Didn't recognize this road at all. No buildings, no streetlights, and the transition had been instantaneous. One minute, he was passing the Great American Grocery on the corner of Asher and Front Street, the next he was *here*.

On this dark, murky, hazy road.

He braked gently, parking the car, and sat for several seconds, listening to the night, which sounded curiously empty and devoid of life.

Silly thought.

Then why did his hand tremble at the door handle?

Snorting, Bradley unhooked his seatbelt, opened the door and slid out. The air felt cold on his skin; unseasonably cold for this time of year, even in the Adirondacks.

He stood on the center stripe and glanced over his shoulder. Sure enough, the bright streetlights on Front Street glimmered in the distance. But the other direction, where this road led . . . ?

The back of his neck tingled.

His breath echoed in his ears.

His belly swirled. "This is ridiculous. Just an old road, is all."

But to the best of his knowledge, no road branched off Front Street here.

Except . . .

No.

Ridiculous.

He squeezed his hands into fists and turned, looking down the road to where it seemed to disappear into the gray, indistinct haze his car's headlights couldn't penetrate . . . as if there *were* no more road, or anything, at all.

yet

because it isn't finished

No.

Ridiculous.

Fog, that's all. The Adirondacks was notorious for its heavy fogs.

He looked up.

No stars.

Nothing except a bloated full moon, casting the fog and the road itself into an eerie phosphorescence that somehow didn't make the night any brighter.

Of course, the full moon. May 5th.

But where were the stars?

"Cloud cover," he murmured, "What was the forecast today? Clouds. That's all."

Clouds.

But how could clouds be so selective, shutting off everything *but* the moon?

He turned and looked back into town, saw the lights of Front Street, which looked farther away than before, saw also the nearly insubstantial red glimmer of Great American, and just barely saw the turn he was supposed to have taken onto Adams Street.

But he'd missed it and kept driving because he was tired, frustrated and depressed, and had driven onto a road he didn't know, driven into . . . this.

He faced forward again, trying very hard to shake the impression that the road ahead disappeared into a drifting gray nothingness.

Fog.

That's all.

And then an immense fatigue weighed him down. What he really needed was to get into his car, turn around, and go home to bed.

So he did exactly that, not thinking about how quickly he got back into his car or how his keys jingled in his trembling hand as he stuck them into the ignition, ignoring the relief that flooded him as the car started and he turned around and drove away.

SATURDAY MORNING

Bradley awoke slowly, pain throbbing in his neck where it bent; his face sore, resting on his forearm . . .

Wait.

Neck sore where it bent.

Face resting on his forearm.

He blinked and raised his head experimentally, wincing as the pain's dull throb stabbed down his neck, into his shoulders. He gazed around, confused. Couldn't be hung-over. Only drank one beer last night . . . but strangely he couldn't remember much after leaving the Inn. He'd taken a wrong turn, hadn't he? Gotten spooked by some weird fog before finally finding his way home.

And as foam crunched under his fingertips, he realized: he'd fallen asleep on his train layout.

He inched his head higher up, feeling his stiff neck pop. Slowly he uncoiled, sitting up and leaning back in his rolling chair.

He closed his eyes.

Cupped his face, kneading his forehead with his fingertips, fumbling his thoughts, groping last night's fragmented memories. They drifted there in gray mists; he just had to pull them together.

He'd stayed up later than he'd intended after

coming home last night. That much he remembered. In a fit of depression over his failure with Emma, he'd started landscaping the area around the new road. He'd laid some ground cover: grass, brush, trees, and gravel shoulders along the new road, then began landscaping. He'd cut some wire mesh, started molding it over mounds of crumpled department meeting agendas, formed some hills, secured the mesh down tight, started laying strips of wet plaster . . .

He blinked.

Realizing he remembered *nothing* after that. And when he looked down, he sucked in a hissing breath and stared at the completed mountain range and forestland surrounding the new road he'd poured yesterday afternoon, taking in the ground cover, knolls, rock ledges, brush and trees, lawns, a stand of trees on one side of the road . . .

And the houses, arranged in varying widths from each other, along a road leading to the Church of Luna, complete with a sign out front and a graveyard behind, through which ran a track he'd extended from the main town line. The track ran to the layout's end, made a sharp left and joined into another previously unfinished spur, running against the basement wall.

Finished.

It was all finished.

as it should be

He spread and inspected his fingers, spackled with grayish-white bits of crushed plaster, peppered also with glued-on bits of powdered ground cover, stained with faint streaks of black paint.

He rubbed his hands.

Staring at the newly completed hills, forest, track,

homes, church . . . and graveyard, feeling the gritty proof of last night's manic endeavors on his fingers.

And it looked *perfect*.

The hills blended into plains seamlessly. The brush and rock face and tree placement looked natural. Houses sat all perfectly aligned with the road and each other, lawns and shrubbery immaculate, driveways pristine . . .

And that graveyard.

A chill skittered down his spine as he gazed upon the miniature graveyard behind the Church of Luna. A graveyard bordered by brown plastic fencing, replete with rectangular gravestones.

He reached out.

Touched a gravestone with his fingertip, wiggling it. Firm and secure, inserted into the foam base, glued down *into* the foam. Sound practice, what he did with all his trees and telephone poles and street signs. Based on their width and size and texture, he guessed he'd snipped off Popsicle sticks and painted them. They could be purchased in bulk at hobby stores anywhere. He had a box. There it was, open on his workbench.

The gravestones.

He peered closer.

Of course, he'd painted them gray. But . . . had he somehow written epitaphs on them, also? How was that even possible? Such detailed work—if he'd managed it—far exceeded dedicated realism.

It bordered on the fanatical.

As he peered closer, however, he saw that he hadn't *written* epitaphs but instead inscribed a symbol very similar to the pagan moon symbol he'd painted on the Church of Luna's doors and sign:

But what did the symbol mean?

He couldn't remember.

And the reality hit him, then. "Impossible," he whispered. "Should've taken me days. The plaster alone would've taken all night to . . . "

There.

Lying next to the box of craft sticks on his workbench, a hair dryer. At some point in his fugue he must've brought it down here and quick-dried the plastered terrain so he could finish everything in one night, which wasn't necessarily so unusual. He'd heard stories of modelers using a hair dryer to speed up the cementing process; had even done it once himself, in his layout's trial stages.

But that method was for small tasks: ballast along the tracks, gravel shoulders along country roads, never for an entire plaster mountain range. The work should look sloppy, rushed . . .

But it looked beautiful, nearly perfect. Maybe the best work he'd ever done.

He stood slowly, pushing up from his chair,

rubbing his gritty, plaster-crusted hands, staring at his work, trembling slightly.

Why the alarm? He'd just gone a little overboard last night is all. Consumed by his loneliness.

That's all.

Which of course didn't explain why he slowly backed away from the layout, resolving to go upstairs, wash and dress, eat breakfast and study at his campus office, telling himself he needed to work without distraction on Monday's opening lecture. It didn't explain why it took such great effort to turn from the layout and walk away.

***

On the way to campus, Bradley made several trips up and down Front Street, scanning all the side streets he knew, following Front Street as it curved into Old Barstow road, even following Old Barstow all the way to the New York State Electric and Gas Payment Center on the edge of town.

He turned and came back, repeating the circuit several times, but no matter how hard he looked, he found no sign of a side road with a dead end.

None at all.

SATURDAY AFTERNOON

Bradley was sitting in his office at his desk and laptop, staring at the results of his Google Image Search when someone rapped on his open office door.

In truth he felt grateful for the interruption. So far, his attempts at study had failed. He'd barely gotten anything done. Granted, he was teaching "Introduction to Mythology" this summer, which he'd taught several times before and could probably teach cold, if needed. But he liked having intimate, fresh recall of the material, no matter how many times he'd taught it.

So it had frustrated him, finding himself doodling that odd symbol he'd apparently painted on those tombstones, and no matter how often he'd crumpled his doodles and refocused on his studies, his attention had drifted again.

To unbidden images of an empty road disappearing into gray mists.

not so empty anymore

No.

Ridiculous.

But the more he tried to repress the memory of the road shrouded in gray mists, a road that he couldn't seem to find by the light of day, the more he'd doodled that strange symbol, over and over, until he'd finally given up, put his studies aside, opened Google Image Search on his laptop and typed in "moon symbols", a safe bet because it looked so similar to the image he'd painted on his Church of Luna.

He'd found his answer quickly.

And was still sitting and staring, amazed and maybe a little afraid when the knock repeated, accompanied by a cough and a "Brad? Got a minute?"

He started, slightly relieved for some reason at being interrupted. His relief dimmed, however, when he swiveled in his rolling chair and saw Ned Simmons—that Math fellow Emma was going on holiday with—leaning in his doorway, grinning.

"Hey . . . Brad. Ned Simmons. We met last night at the Inn."

Bradley stared, groping for something to say and finding nothing. Ned's smile faltered. "Ah . . . uh. Sorry. Were you busy? If so, I'll just . . . "

And then as usual—damn them—his manners kicked in. He smiled, waving dismissively. "Not really. Just trying to prep for Monday and failing horribly."

Ned chuckled, folding his arms. "Yeah, summer session. Used to teach it myself but since I got tenure two years ago I don't bother with it. Guess I figured I didn't need to impress folks, anymore."

"Yes," Bradley murmured. He'd yet to be offered tenure. "I see your point."

And as he took in Ned Simmons' wiry form, rakish curly black hair and big, sensitive blue eyes (eyes that would be gazing upon Emma next weekend), he found that, deep inside, he *hated* Ned Simmons.

But with great effort he smiled. "What can I do for you, Ned? Also. How'd you figure I'd be here?"

Ned managed to look sheepish. "Well. Ah. I looked you up in the faculty directory, called your home and when you didn't answer I called Emma, asked her where you'd most likely be, in pretense of wanting to see your train layout."

"Ah. Interesting. So, in other words, you didn't want Emma to know why you *really* wanted to see me."

Ned held out a hand. "Don't get me wrong, I was totally serious last night. Would love to see your layout sometime. My Uncle Mark had one, filled his whole basement. My cousins and I spent hours playing with it."

He bristled inside at the idea of *playing* with a train layout. One didn't *play* with someone else's creation, and he loathed the idea that Ned might want to *play* with his. But he kept his tone light. "What did you want to talk about, then?"

Ned shrugged and looked away, shuffling like a nervous teen on his first date. He swallowed and looked at him again, that silly grin plastered all over his face. "Well . . . this is going to sound cowardly, I know. But Emma. She's rather . . . "

Bradley raised his eyebrows and remained noncommittal, determined not to make this easy. "Yes?"

"Well, she's pretty special. Unique. Full of energy and always moving, talking, thinking . . . so expressive, so alive she makes *you* feel alive just being around her. Y'know?"

"I suppose," he remarked dryly, wondering how Ned could miss his sarcasm. "I see her every day. Maybe I've built up a tolerance for her."

"Yeah, maybe." Ned rushed on, clueless, and Bradley despised him even more. "Anyway she's fun to be around and we've had a blast on a bunch of dates . . . "

Try as he might, Brad couldn't repress the jealousy stabbing his guts. "Dates?"

Ned waved. "Yeah. Movies. Bowling. Hiking . . . that sort of thing."

movies
bowling
hiking
that sort of thing

Sorts of things Bradley had known nothing about; that Emma had never once mentioned at all.

But why would she?

They were *friends*, of course.

And friends didn't discuss some things, apparently.

"Go on," Bradley prompted, unable to keep a chill from entering his voice. Energized by his topic, Ned didn't seem to notice.

"See, that's the thing: those dates were all one-shot deals, right? I never really planned on us getting back together, it just kept happening."

Though he didn't feel any sympathy for Ned (rather burned inside with a cold envy) he saw the young man's dilemma. "But spending a whole weekend with her . . . that's a bigger commitment. More than fun and games."

"Well . . . yeah. Those other dates we were busy doing stuff, having fun. We go away for the weekend . . . we can't be busy the whole time . . . "

"Why yes," Bradley remarked, raising his eyebrows, not even bothering to hide his sarcasm now, but Ned still missing it, "you'll have to make intelligent conversation for once."

Ned snapped his fingers and pointed. "Right! The car ride *alone* to Ocean City will be over four hours. For the first two I figure I'll manage all right, have enough to say . . . but after that . . . "

Bradley sighed, fighting to keep his exasperation in check. God. What did Emma see in this stumbling lout? Past his youngish, rugged good looks, of course. His athletic build, excellent fashion sense . . .

He forced himself to speak politely. "So. You came to me because . . . "

Ned shook his head. "I dunno. I know all the right things to say on a date, right? Make them laugh, get them all dewy-eyed, weak in the knees, show them a good time, maybe even . . . "

Bradley coughed.

Ned blushed and offered a weak grin. "Ah. Don't suppose you want to hear about that, do you?"

Somehow Bradley kept his face blank, even managed a small, wooden smile. "Well. It wouldn't be polite to kiss and tell, would it?"

Shock and even embarrassment reddened Ned's cheeks. At least the man had some sense of propriety, not that it made him any less loathsome.

Ned waved. "No, of course not. I just mean that Emma's more than someone to share a few good times with. She's bigger than all that. She's like . . . "

"A force of nature?" he offered, still sarcastic and ironic but telling the truth, now. It was how *he* felt, after all, which of course made this doubly unpleasant, that someone as young and attractive and suave and modern but so damn shallow could feel the same way about Emma.

His Emma.

Ned snapped his fingers and pointed at him again. "Exactly, and you feel so small next to her, right? See, I'm a numbers guy. Good with equations and formulas and processes. Can calculate shit in my head instantly, but get past my smooth lines and that's all I am, Numbers Boy, while she's so much more, she's . . . "

" . . . one with the universe," he finished quietly, no trace of sarcasm or irony in his voice now, just a touch of sadness, and, if he admitted it . . .

Defeat.

Resignation.

"Yes!" Ned finger-snapped-pointed again. "Exactly. It's like she *knows* things, like she's got access to the secrets of life or mystical knowledge or something."

Bradley smiled, almost genuinely. "She teaches mythology, Ned. 'Mystical knowledge' is her thing."

No finger-snap-point this time. Ned sighed and slumped against the doorframe. "Yeah. So what chance do I have? I mean . . . how can a guy like me connect with someone like her, on a deeper level? Or at least not sound like an idiot on the way to Ocean City?"

"And you want to pick my brain for ways to connect with Emma, don't you?"

Ned straightened, smiling nervously. "Well you guys are always together. Eating in the café, talking between classes. You're so similar, like she's your little sister or something. I thought . . . "

He rubbed the back of his neck. "Hell, I know it's forward but I was thinking maybe we could grab dinner at the Inn and talk."

A variety of responses occurred to Bradley, most of them involving violence and aggression and profanity and none of them, of course, suiting his nature at all.

So he sighed and stood, grabbing his jacket from off his chair. "Dinner, then. Was getting hungry, anyway."

"Great! That's awesome." Ned fairly beamed. "And I wasn't kidding about seeing that layout, sometime. I'd love to. Seriously."

Bradley smiled tightly, nodding at the door. He followed Ned out and locked his office door behind him, quietly, calmly . . .

like she's your little sister, or something

. . . burning inside.

SATURDAY NIGHT

Driving Ned Simmons home late at night after too many rounds of beers and Tequila wasn't exactly what Bradley had been expecting, especially after dinner had started so tolerably well. Much to his surprise, after seating themselves and ordering, Ned hadn't started prying for advice about impressing Emma. Instead, they'd chatted about strictly mundane things: social matters of the Heights, whether or not the reconstruction from last fall's flood would be finished by summer's end, about this town resolution or that, little bits and pieces of gossip from the hallowed halls of Web County Community College.

And, not surprisingly, they talked about model railroading. Ned had yet to build his own layout (not enough space in his studio apartment over in Oakland Arms) but he had boxes of supplies just waiting to be opened. He even attended an annual train show in Steamtown, Pennsylvania and was something of a novice train spotter.

So throughout dinner Bradley had felt stirrings of grudging respect, maybe even (God help him) a reluctant approval of Ned.

But things changed after several beers, beers that quickly turned into tequila shots, and the Ned Simmons that was revealed *after* the liquor stripped several layers away . . .

Well.

Bradley's hands tightened on the steering wheel thinking about it, how Ned, after his third or fourth shot, looking slightly disheveled, eyes glassy and distant, had burped discretely and said, "Women. Remarkable, wonderful creatures. No wonder we want to hold onto as many of them as possible, even with all the headaches they cause."

Bradley remembered frowning, not sure if he'd heard correctly. "Sorry. Did you say . . . *many*?"

Ned paused, sucking on his lip in that wary, embarrassed way drunks had. Then he snorted and grinned. "Ah. Probably shouldn't talk about it, eh? Like discussing my exes with my girlfriend's *Dad*."

And with that all his affinity for Ned dissipated like fog in the morning sun. A stony coldness crept over him, and he'd had to *force* his hands to grip each other on the tabletop rather than reaching for Ned's throat.

"I don't follow."

"Well, see," Ned began with a flourish, warming to the subject, "there's this girl in Utica, been shacking up with her occasionally over the past year. Dental hygienist. Nice girl. No Emma, mind you. Not even close. But she'd make a solid wife, right? Kinda woman who'd be fine quitting work to raise my kids, attending PTA meetings, running bake sales for the local charities, that sort of thing. See, Emma's wild, philosophical, alive . . .

"But she'd hardly give up her studies and teaching to go home and be barefoot pregnant for you, would she?" Bradley muttered.

Too drunk on tequila, Ned had missed Bradley's verbal jab. "Yeah. Don't know if she's the marryin, have-kids-kinda girl. Problem is, she's like a drug. She gets in your system and is addictive as hell."

He knocked back his bottle of Guinness, drained it and thumped it onto the table. "Helluva choice.

Helluva choice." He burped again. "Then there's *Haley*."

Ned had gripped his hands tighter, nails biting into the backs of his hands. "Haley?"

Ned had blushed and waved. "Yeah. A junior at Syracuse. Met her at a party, she didn't tell me her age . . . but that was months ago. It didn't mean anything but she keeps calling me, and she was *hell* in the sack. Hell in the sack."

In that moment cold and bitter feelings coalesced into a sharp point inside Bradley, but he'd just smiled, raised his hand and beckoned to the waiter, saying to Ned in the most affable tone he could manage, "I know what you need, Ned."

"More to drink."

NOW

And so here they are on this strange glowing road that only exists at night, except now Bradley's not lost, and instead of turning down an empty, mist-covered road leading into gray nothingness he's arrived at a place he's known all along he was coming to, a place made for him, *by* him.

Bradley parks his car.

Kills the engine.

Wondering if, even before Ned started drinking, he'd planned this. Ned *had* wanted to see his layout, after all.

So here's his chance.

But as Bradley gets out of the car and stands before the Church of Luna—glowing with the same phosphorescence covering everything else—he knows, deep down, that he was meant to come here, Ned Simmons regardless.

For all this is his.

Wrought by his hands and heart, and at this moment he calls it "good."

The passenger door slams shut. Ned mumbles, "Holy . . . shit. Too much booze. Everythin's all glowin an shit."

And then Ned squeals like a kid at Christmas, pointing, his face childlike in the moon's glow. "Look! Tracks run behind that weird church! And . . . man! A Chessie! It's a goddamn Chessie!"

Without another word Ned runs and stumbles across the church's front lawn, slipping on night-slicked grass into the graveyard and up to the black, sleek engine and its lone passenger car sitting on the tracks behind the church.

Bradley follows slowly, at ease, in no hurry. Of course, he'd half expected the train to be here, once he discovered what that symbol painted on the gravestones meant.

He's not too long in joining Ned, who's staring at the thrumming midnight black Chessie. "A Chessie," Ned whispers. "A Chesapeake and Ohio River Valley engine. But I've never seen one all black like this. And this . . . "

He reaches toward a white symbol like the ones painted on the tombstones. "This is supposed to be the shadow of a cat, the Chessie symbol. What's *this* mean?"

He touches it.

And stiffens as if gripped by an immense cold. He trembles, jaw hanging open.

"It's the mark of Charon," Bradley whispers. "A moon of Pluto. Also, in Greek mythology, the ferryman of the dead, who transports people across the River Styx to Hades."

Ned's hand drops limply to his side. He turns, his eyes blank, gaping slack-jawed at Bradley, the black mark of Charon glimmering on his forehead. "And it looks like you just paid Charon's toll. Or maybe I did, for you," Bradley amends. "This is new to me."

A door to the engine's only passenger car hisses open. A tall form leans out, dressed in a black rendition of a steam engine-era conductor, and the face beneath its cap is smooth and white and blank. Slightly bumpy protrusions suggest eyes and a nose and cheekbones and craters . . .

like on the moon

. . . but no actual face regards them. The voice, however, rings clear. "All aboard."

Ned Simmons sways like a man sleepwalking. He looks at Bradley and whispers, "Not coming back, am I?"

Bradley shakes head. "I don't think so. But maybe that's for the best."

For Emma.

And *me*.

Ned blinks and nods sluggishly, lips moving, as if to say more but nothing comes out. So he turns, shambles away and boards the train, disappearing into the passenger car past the faceless conductor, who leans out further. "Will you be coming also, sir?"

Bradley shakes his head. "Not tonight."

The faceless conductor nods and withdraws into the train and immediately a mournful, low horn blows.

Metal shifts deep within the Chessie marked with the sign of Charon.

It chugs away; off on a railroad running through the woods that he's fairly certain doesn't exist in the daytime.

And he turns away, leaving the graveyard, knowing that for sure, Emma will be upset—perhaps even distraught—when Ned's disappearance becomes news. But based on what he's learned tonight, Bradley feels sure he can share Ned's sordid past with Emma and convince her that more than likely, the young raker simply moved on to other pastures.

There will be questions, of course.

Especially because he'll be recalled as the last person to have seen Ned. But he's sure he can weather the inquiries. There's no evidence left behind, after all. Bradley can say that because Ned was drunk he drove him back to his apartment and that was the last he saw of him.

And Emma?

She'll get over Ned's apparent abandonment, because *he'll* be there. That's what friends are for, of course, and perhaps this will finally open Emma's eyes to their potential.

And if not?

That'll be unfortunate, especially when the next full moon comes around, because despite his peaceful nature, Bradley has a feeling he won't turn out to be a very forgiving god at all.

12.

AMBIGUITIES. SHADOWY, SURREAL ghosts seen out of the corner of the eye, like hallucinations dreamed during a fever, things that can neither be confirmed nor denied. These are the things I've been reading about.

Though Webb Community College is ten miles out of town, between Clifton Heights and Old Forge, Bradley Sanders lives here in town. I've seen him around a few times, been introduced to him twice. And he *does* have an impressive train layout in his basement. Every Christmas he opens his home to the neighborhood for tours. I had night patrol this Christmas and missed it but luckily Meg convinced Grace—our sitter—to take her. She gushed for days about its meticulous detail in copying nearly every facet of Clifton Heights. I'd hated missing that and had vowed to make sure I was free next year to go see Bradley's layout with Meg.

Not so sure I'll be doing that, now.

A resigned weariness settles over my shoulders. "I suppose if I called Web Community College, asking after Ned Simmons . . . "

"They'd tell you the same thing they told me,"

Gavin says tiredly, looking as weary as I feel. "That Ned Simmons ended the May semester as always on the high recommendations of his Department Chair, then was never heard from again. Didn't return any phone calls during the summer break, and when someone finally got a key for his apartment, it looked unlived in for months. Essentially, he left everything behind and vanished."

"And I imagine the college simply washed their hands of the matter and hired someone to replace him?"

A slow nod, eyes focusing on some distant point over my shoulder.

"What about Emma Hatcher?"

A sigh and a slight shrug. "A month ago, she tendered her resignation and apparently left the area. Of course, the resignation was mailed, not delivered in person, and according to *her* landlord a UHAUL picked up her things and her last rent payment was slipped under the door. She snuck out of here like the proverbial thief in the night."

"Maybe I *should* look up this Bradley Sanders, then. Ask him a few questions." Even as I speak I realize I'm grasping at straws again. This Gavin knows, too.

And after gazing out the window into the dark for several minutes he finally looks me in the eyes. "What would you say, Chris? That you're questioning him on suspicion of building a magic railroad that whisked two people off to the Underworld because they pissed him off? Either he'll laugh in your face or you'll find yourself on a midnight train ride also."

"C'mon. Whatever the guy is, whatever he can do . . . he's not a god."

Gavin scowls slightly, as if frustrated that I'm missing the point, somehow. "Of *course* he's not a god." He gestured at the street outside The Skylark. "It's this town. Things hide in the shadows and the woods, houses *do* things to people, certain roads go on forever . . ."

"And some people *think* things and they become real?"

"'But thoughts are things, my friend,'" Gavin whispers, "'when you imagine a thing, you MAKE a thing.'" He smiles at me. "Sir Arthur Conan Doyle, from his story 'Playing With Fire.' And again, it's this town. Maybe like Bassler House, not only does it draw a certain sort of folk, but when other sorts of folks imagine things, believe in things so passionately . . ."

"They become real."

He shrugs. "Maybe. Who the hell knows, right? We don't have much in the way of proof, do we? Past a handful of people who have either died mysterious deaths or folks who have left town, quietly vanishing without a trace, what can we prove? Nothing. What do we know? Precious little. Something else you might be interested in, by the way."

"Do I really want to know?"

Gavin taps the side of his nose with his index finger. "I'm not sure how much bearing it has on anything but I did a little digging into Sanders' academic background. Apparently, before coming to Web Community he taught Mythology and Old Religions at Miskatonic University up in Massachusetts. Now *there's* a place that's more closed-mouthed than this town. I couldn't get one word out of them about Sanders besides confirming his previous employment."

"Great. Just what we need. More mystery."

I stretch, rub the back of my neck and glance at the diner's clock over the front register.

11:00.

God.

I've been here nearly six hours, reading and listening to . . . what?

Truth?

Fiction, fantasy?

Nightmares?

Regardless, it's gotta stop. I came here needing to hear something and while I've certainly heard *something*, I'm not sure what or how it can help me find Timmy Danvers or if any of these things mean anything, at all.

It's time to get down to business.

"So. Have you written about what happened with Ellen and Timmy Danvers yet? That's the next story to read, right? Fits the chronology."

He shakes his head slowly. "Not yet."

A glance at the book confirms this. The next page is empty, and I don't have to flip through the remaining pages to know the rest are empty, too. Don't ask me how I know; I just *do*.

"Why not? I need to know what's going on, Gavin. No more metaphysical bullshit. I need to know what happened to Ellen Danvers' boy and why she doesn't want us looking for him anymore. Why haven't you written it, yet?"

He sits up straighter, his eyes flashing. "Because," he says firmly, "that story's not finished. You're part of this one, Chris. And to finish it, you need to go see Ellen Danvers and have *her* tell you why she doesn't want anyone looking for her son. Then the story will be finished, then I can write it."

And with that, he reaches out, snaps the book shut, gathers it up and stands.

"Where are you going?"

"Home. While you go to Ellen and finish the story so *I* can write it."

He turns and exits the diner.

Leaving me alone and suddenly very afraid.

13.

THE COMMONS TRAILER PARK

ELLEN DANVERS OPENS her trailer's screen door and smiles sadly, as if she's expected me this whole time and has been wondering what's taken me so long.

"Evening, Sheriff," she whispers. "What can I do for you?"

For a moment, the absurdity of my intentions strikes me speechless. We've gotten everything we can from Ellen. She's got no more information to give, past her wild tale.

So why am I here?

In Gavin's mind, I'm here so Ellen Danvers can tell me what *really* happened to her son. In mine . . . well, at this point I really can't say. But I can't stand here on the porch forever so I smile and lie. "Just stopping by to see how you're doing, Ellen, let you know the State Police and my men are still searching for Timmy."

The last part is true, at least. Even though Ellen now claims there's no need to search for Timmy, the initial report of a missing child set off a chain reaction that can't be called back so easily. With the wheels turning on a missing child report the search will continue for a few days, despite Ellen's protests, because according to the State Police Department's psychologist, even though Ellen has returned to work and resumed life as normal, she's merely experiencing classic symptoms of denial and soon enough reality will crash in around her and she'll once again beg us to find her son.

But standing here, looking at Ellen's peaceful, strong green eyes, I wonder who's more in denial: Ellen, or the State Police psychologist, because far as I can see, Ellen Danvers really and truly believes her son Timmy will never be found.

And she's made her peace with it.

She flicks an understanding, sad smile. "I'm very grateful for that, Sheriff. I really am, and I understand that my initial reaction is the cause for all this. But I really wish you and the state police would stop searching. It's a waste of time. You won't ever find Timmy, believe me."

"Unfortunately, Miss Danvers . . . "

"Mrs.," she corrects with that same sad smile. "My husband died in a tractor trailer accident out on this road when Timmy was just a baby."

Of course he did.

Because this is *Bassler* Road.

"Right. Sorry, Mrs. Danvers. Anyway, the initial report of a missing child has set some pretty big wheels into motion and they need to at least conclude their search of the surrounding area before they can call it off."

"I understand. It's just unnecessary, is all. Timmy's in a safe place now."

So here it is.

And suddenly, this whole night makes a little more

sense. Though Gavin hasn't written it yet he must know *some* of this story and because I'm part of it, before he could write it down, before he could finish it, *I* needed to understand, needed to believe . . . or at least needed to hear the story firsthand.

I remove my patrol hat, run a hand through my hair and say, "Ma'am. Mrs. Danvers. I think we need to talk."

Her face is composed and still, eyes wide and bright. "About what, Sheriff?"

I breathe in and let the breath trickle out, feeling all my resistance escape with it. "About things I can't report. About a case I can't solve, a story that'll never see print or the light of day, ever."

And she looks at me—hell, *through* me—her gaze penetrating. "Why?"

Another deep breath. "Because. I'm the Sheriff of this town. I'm responsible for it . . . "

so the Guardian may protect the threshold

" . . . responsible for its welfare and the welfare of everyone in it. Even if I can't write it down in a report, can't solve it or arrest anyone for it . . . I *need* to know. I'm the Sheriff," I repeat. "This is my town. I need to know, need to understand."

She nods slightly and I can tell by the shine in her eyes and the acceptance I see there that I've crossed a line. And, as I felt earlier tonight when I first opened Gavin's damned book . . .

Life will never be the same again.

She tips her head inside and holds open the door. "Come on in."

* * *

Quickly enough I'm seated in an old recliner in the

living room, a pleasantly steaming cup of coffee warming my hand. Ellen Danvers sits on the edge of the couch, elbows on her knees, hands clasped tightly, staring down. When she speaks, her voice falls soft and gentle onto the floor.

"I'm going to tell you a story. And you're probably going to think I'm crazy." She looks up and smiles. "They do think I'm crazy, don't they? The doctors."

I shrug . . . sip my coffee and say, "Not crazy. Grief-stricken. In denial. That's what they think, mostly."

Her smile widens a bit. "Mostly. Huh." She looks back down and shrugs. "Hell. Maybe I AM in denial. Maybe this whole thing is a desperate fantasy made up by my grief-stricken head because I'm so messed up."

She looks up just then, eyes narrowed, face slightly pinched in thought. "Thing is . . . the world can't always be figured, can it? Things can't always be explained, like how my son disappeared in only ten minutes out there on Bassler Road. How'dya explain that, Sheriff?"

I assume a poker face and say, "We can't, yet. State police's forensics is still working on it."

She waves my response off. "Doesn't matter. They won't find him, no matter how hard they look."

I clasp the warm coffee cup in my hands, trying to ward off a chill settling onto my shoulders. "Where is he?"

"Somewhere . . . away. Somewhere safe."

"That doesn't tell me anything."

She sighs and looks to the floor again. "I'm going to tell you a story, Sheriff."

"Seems that's all I've heard, tonight."

A slight smile and she continues. "Maybe you'll

believe it. Maybe you won't. But like you said . . . you're the Sheriff and you need to know these things. So here's my story, about Timmy and what happened to him. It's also a story about someone named Mr. Nobody . . . "

MR. NOBODY

"MOMMY! NOOOO!"

Laughter echoed through Ellen Danvers' small kitchen as she knelt and bent her son Timmy backward over her knee. He giggled while she pretended to lose her grip.

"Jeez, you're heavy! What've you been eating? Hippos?"

His face split into a toothy grin. "N-no! Just p-puppies!"

"PUPPIES!" She shook him in mock fury. "That's it! You're gonna get it!"

His blue eyes widened in anticipation. "No!"

"Too late!"

She raised clenched fingers, her fake scowl threatening to break into a grin. "Now. You. Die!"

"Noooo!"

With an exaggerated downward thrust, she planted her hand into his belly and tickled him. He laughed and jerked, and alarm shivered through her as her grasp slipped. Timmy was only six, but he was so big for his age. If she wasn't careful, he could squirm free, hit the floor . . .

Worry crept in, spoiling the moment and she

stopped, gently grasping his shirt, tipping him up. She hugged him tight, closed her eyes, breathing deep. His speeding heart trip-hammered against hers and a mournful ache pierced her breast.

"Mommy? You okay?"

She squeezed him tighter.

"Mom?"

Finally, she released him. He stepped back, eyes wide and bright. She brushed strands of black hair off his forehead. "Yeah. I'm okay."

"Can I watch Nick Jr. before bed?"

"Sure. Only one hour, though."

Timmy grinned, dashed from the kitchen into their living room and THUMPED onto the couch. The television blasted a noisy fanfare.

Ellen wobbled upright and limped to the kitchen sink. She leaned against cool, stainless steel and stood there for several minutes before slowly finishing the dishes.

***

Ellen shuffled around the trailer's small den, weary after another long day at Great American Grocery, her feet throbbing as she gathered up Timmy's things. A bittersweet moment every night, with Timmy finally in bed and his stuff picked up, she could relax on the couch, watch some television . . .

And also try not to think about Danny, or worry about what he'd get up to next.

Down the hall, near the end on her right she toed open the toy closet, which was really an oversized linen closet without its lowest shelves. She dumped stuffed animals into a blue tote, Matchbox cars into an old Quaker Oats container, then closed the door.

Brushing something with her elbow.

A piece of paper fluttered to her feet.

She knelt and picked it up, shivering, though she wasn't sure why. It was a picture showing two childlike stick figures. The shorter one wore a red T-shirt and blue pants. With scribbled black hair over a round smiley-face, it was obviously Timmy.

The other figure was taller and wider. All black but scuffed around the edges. Its most striking feature: black wings instead of arms, and blazing red eyes. Scrawled over it, Timmy's childish script read: MR. NOBODY.

Her stomach flipped over. There was something WRONG with this picture, with *Mr. Nobody.* Something . . .

Wait.

To the left. A creaking sound, coming from Timmy's room.

Ellen stood, grabbed the doorknob to Timmy's bedroom door and gasped. Cold, so cold. But strange, liquid warmth was flowing against her feet . . .

She looked down.

Blood.

Oozing under Timmy's door and lapping against her bare toes.

"Timmy!"

She twisted the knob but it wouldn't turn. She slammed her shoulder against the door; jerked and slammed again.

It flung open.

She stumbled in and smelled it instantly: a rich, sharp, metallic odor.

Blood.

On the floor. Splashed on the headboard, soaking the pillow and Timmy's head. She couldn't tell for sure in the dark, but his head looked wrong. Lopsided, caved in. Numb, Ellen stumbled mindlessly forward . . .

And into Timmy's closed bedroom door.

***

Ellen blinked and winced. She touched her forehead where she'd head-butted the door. Was she really *that* tired?

An image flashed of Timmy's misshapen head. She gasped and looked down but saw only aged carpet. She grabbed the knob to Timmy's bedroom door. It felt cool, but not *cold*. She eased the door open and peeked inside. Everything looked fine. Timmy slept facing away but from here, his head looked normal.

And why shouldn't it?

A cool breeze touched her skin.

The window.

Open, its curtains fluttering.

Ellen crossed the room. Still holding Timmy's picture, she eased his window shut, but despite her best efforts it squeaked and Timmy shifted under his blankets, clutching his stuffed Thomas The Train to his chest. "Whatcha doin?"

"Just checking, chief." She came to his side and straightened his covers. "Why'd you open your window, kiddo? It's raining and cold out there."

A slow blink. "I know. But if my window's closed, Mr. Nobody can't come in. He asked me to open it, so he could come in and see me." He frowned. "Sorry, Mommy. Didn't mean to make you mad."

"I'm not mad, kiddo. It's just that . . . "

"Is Mr. Nobody here?"

"No one's here, sweetie. Just you and me." She held up the picture, though she doubted he could see it in his nightlight's soft glow. "Did you draw this?"

Another slow blink. "Uh-huh."

"Who is he, honey? No one's been talking to you at the playground or around here, have they? You know what I've told you about talking to strangers."

She shuddered involuntarily, because she saw it all the time: on television, in the newspapers, kids snatched from their homes, parks or playgrounds, even walking to the bus after school. Snatched away, gone, without a trace, never seen again.

In fact, hadn't that been in the news lately? A little girl from Utica taken from her single mother's apartment, a little girl not even ten years old. Something odd about that, something she'd heard in the newspapers, saw on television . . .

But it wouldn't come to her.

Timmy yawned, snuggled deeper into his blankets, nuzzling Thomas the Train under his chin. He mumbled, "Mr. Nobody's not from around here, Mom. He's from far away, from a special place. He talks to me when I'm sleepin."

Ellen shivered.

Only a dream?

Maybe, but even so. "And he told you to open the window, so he could come in?"

"Mm-hm."

Dream or not she didn't like that at all. "Don't think Mr. Nobody's coming tonight, kiddo. And *some* little boy needs his sleep, or he'll be stumbling around like a zombie tomorrow."

"Kay. Night, Mommy."

She kissed his forehead. "Night, chief."

***

" . . . and the search continues for missing Utica girl Anne Marie Hauer, who was allegedly abducted from her Utica home on the West Side only three weeks ago, though authorities have yet to uncover any signs of forced entry into the Hauer home or Anne Marie's bedroom. A person of interest in the case is Matthew Harmon, age twenty-four of Utica, a boyfriend of Anne Marie's mother, Emily. According to Emily Hauer, Mr. Harmon was allegedly watching Anne Marie the night of her disappearance but when Emily returned home from working as a nurse at Utica General neither Anne Marie nor Mr. Harmon were to be found. He's not been seen nor heard of since and authorities wonder if . . . "

The phone rang.

Ellen blinked, shifting on the couch where she'd drifted off.

The phone rang again.

She straightened, rubbing her sleep-blurred eyes, reluctant to get up and answer. Probably work, needing coverage for tomorrow night's shift . . . *again* . . . because they were still shorthanded after Shelly Livingston bailed from town about a month ago. And on Ellen's only night off this week, no less.

The phone, ringing.

She sighed, pushed herself up off the couch and made her way to the kitchen. She grabbed the phone off the hook, mumbling, "Hello? Mark, I covered Shelly's shift last week, and I don't really . . . "

"Hey, babe. What's cookin?"

Oh, God.

Not work. She wished to God it was, she'd rather cover every one of Shelly Livingston's night shifts for the rest of the year than talk to *him*.

Danny, and he sounded drunk.

Again.

"Gotta see you, babe."

She twisted the phone cord, leaned against the wall and closed her eyes. Where was he? On the way here? Or was he already parked outside?

"NO, Danny." She pressed the heel of her palm into her forehead. "Not like this."

A sharp edge crept into his voice. *"I gotta see you, babe. Can' stop thinkin bout you, bout US."*

Ellen swallowed and forced an even voice. "Danny. Judge said you can't be within a hundred feet of us until you've finished your probation, stayed sober for two months. It's only been three weeks! Go home, sleep it off, and I . . . "

She breathed deep. Dare she say it? Wasn't this a sign that Danny wasn't worth it?

"Just go home. I won't tell Judge Miller, I promise. Just go home."

"This is cause a him, ain't it? That snot-nosed brat. He don' like me, so you don' want me around no more."

Her eyes snapped open, adrenaline flushing her veins. She pushed off the wall, gripping the phone so hard her knuckles hurt. "This is because you can't stop drinking, because of what you did last time when . . . "

"His fault. He tole Judge Miller somethin bout me, didn' he? That's why I got this damn restrainin order, ain't it?"

She glanced down the hall, her heart throbbing with fear. "No. He doesn't know anything, I swear."

His voice cut like ice-cold steel. *"Don' matter. I'm gonna take care a things for good. Then nothin'll keep me away. Specially not your dead husband's brat."*

Anger swelled inside her. "Don't you talk about Jeff. *Ever.*

The line hissed and she imagined his drunken sneer. *"Jeff's been dead an gone for years. Get used to it. Ah'm the man a the house now. Or will be real soon."*

She clenched her teeth and tried to ignore the fire in her belly. "You're drunk. Go home. You come over here and I'll . . . "

A low chuckle, rippling with static. *"I'm already here, babe. An I got my bat. You know the one, right?"*

The bat.

Which he kept in his truck for 'self-defense.' He bragged about, always showing it off, especially around her and Timmy.

And then an image flashed.

Of blood oozing under Timmy's bedroom floor, of his caved-in head.

got my bat

"You just sit tight," Danny hissed, *"cause Daddy's* home.

The phone clicked.

Its dial tone shrilling in her ear.

***

Panic thrummed through her as she dialed 911, that *image . . .*

Timmy's lopsided, bloody, crushed head

. . . flashing before her eyes, over and over. She heard a click, put the phone to her ear . . .

"You've reached 911. All our operators are busy.

Please be prepared to explain the nature of your emergency . . . "

She threw the phone down and raced out of the den toward the bedroom. She slammed the door open, dove across her bed, reached under and pulled out a safety deposit box, which she pulled into her lap as she sat up. Opening the nightstand's drawer, she rummaged for keys, crying out when her fingers touched metal. She yanked them out, fumbling at the box's lock until she popped the lid open.

A .38.

Jeff's old gun. She'd only fired it once and then only at cans out back but that would have to do. She grabbed some cartridges and clumsily loaded it . . .

A rattling sound.

A window in its frame.

Timmy.

Oh, GOD!

got my bat

She stuffed the last cartridge in, slapped the cylinder shut, and lurched off the bed and out the door, desperately hoping she'd loaded it right . . .

She flung open Timmy's door.

And saw him sitting up, pointing to his window, Thomas the Train under his other arm. "Mommy! It's Mr. Nobody! He came, just like he promised . . . "

Outside the window on the ledge she saw a dark form hunched against the glass.

And the window was opening.

She screamed and fired. The window shattered and the shadow vanished.

"Mommy!"

She sprinted across the room, pressed her back

against the wall under the window, hesitated, then reached up and blindly fired twice out the window. The revolver's barks shattered the night, then faded.

Silence.

He's out there, though. Gotta be. And he wants to hurt Timmy.

got my bat

"Mommy! Why'd you shoot at . . . "

She stuffed the .38 into her front pocket, turned to the bed and scooped Timmy up, knocking his stuffed Thomas the Train out of his arms in the process. He cried out, "Thomas!"

But she didn't stop, lurching around the bed, out of the room with Timmy crushed to her chest. She shuffle-ran to the den, mind racing. She'd used up three shots. She should reload but the fear thrumming inside demanded she leave *now*.

"Shush, it's okay, we'll be okay . . . " She stumbled to a halt at the front door. Quickly and as gently as possible, she set Timmy down and snagged the car keys off the lamp stand next to the door. Her breath roaring in her ears, her heart hammering, she unlocked the door, cracked it open and peered outside. Danny was out there somewhere. She knew it, but her car and freedom were only several steps away . . .

"Fuck it," she whispered as she grabbed Timmy's hand firmly, careful not to hurt him. "Okay, sweetie . . . down the steps quick as we can, get in the car and we'll head to cousin Grace's house and things will be fine, okay?"

Timmy said nothing, sucking his thumb, nodding while tears glimmered in his eyes. Ellen forced a stiff smile and counted. "One . . . two . . . three!"

She flung the door open and burst through, taking the front steps as fast as she dared, afraid Timmy would topple and fall. He didn't though, and they were almost there . . .

Headlights snapped on from the far end of the parking lot, blinding her. Danny, in his truck! Waiting for her! But the window, who'd been at the window . . . ?

The truck's engine growled.

No time for thinking. She opened the passenger door, plopped Timmy down, crawled over him and pulled the door shut behind her. Squirming behind the wheel, she jammed the key into the ignition and nearly screamed as the Escort sputtered to life.

Terror speared her heart as Danny's truck roared and its tires squealed. She threw the car into reverse and hit the gas. Tires spun and gravel pinged off her trailer. Danny's headlights swelled, filling the car with blinding light.

Pointed toward the exit, Ellen slammed the Escort into drive and floored it. The trusty little car shot forward, opening a small gap, but she still felt Danny's truck back there, gaining.

She sped down the trailer park's fairway, plunged out the exit and swerved left onto Bassler Road, tires squealing and sliding on rain-slicked asphalt, the steering column whining in protest. She wrenched back too hard, nearly throwing them into a tailspin that she barely recovered from.

Blazing headlights arced behind, filling the car.

She pushed down the gas and her car lurched forward, widening the gap a little more. The highway wavered through her streaked windshield as wipers smeared water everywhere.

"Mommy! You forgot to buckle me!"

Cursing, she reached across Timmy, grabbed the seatbelt one-handed and yanked it over his lap, fumbling for several precious seconds but the car swerved again, bald tires sliding on wet asphalt. She let go of the seatbelt, grabbed and twisted the wheel, tapping the brake, bringing the car back under control.

Danny's headlights loomed in the rearview mirror. She stomped the gas down and they sped back up but a desperate voice in her head yowled *tooslowtooslow!* as Danny kept pace.

"Mommy, why'd you shoot Mr. Nobody? He's my friend!"

"Honey, I know this is hard to understand, but that wasn't Mr. Nobody, that was . . . "

Static and whistles burst from the car radio, sounds of voices and music melding together, the radio scanning multiple channels. She glanced at it, openmouthed and amazed as lights flickered and strobed behind the channel finder. The thing hardly ever worked, so why'd it turn on now?

" . . . *and if anyone has any leads regarding the case of missing Anna Marie Hauer, from Utica, please call* . . . "

She gaped at the radio.

"Mommy! Look out!"

She looked up, forgetting the radio and slamming the brakes, twisting the wheel. The Escort slid forward on wet asphalt toward a tall and wide figure standing in the middle of the road, black as night, with no face, just glowing red embers for eyes, dark feathery wings cradling Timmy close to its chest . . .

No!

Timmy's here, he's . . .

The Escort plunged off the road and into the ditch, slamming Ellen against the seatbelt. Her chest burned and she couldn't breathe.

An engine roared.

Old brakes squealed and the Escort rocked in the wake of a larger vehicle speeding past. Ellen looked up and saw Danny's battered truck skidding to a stop several feet away.

Fear pumped her heart. She strained against the seatbelt, clawing at its catch. "Timmy! Gotta go, now!" She turned, reaching for his seatbelt . . .

Which dangled, unhooked.

mommy, you forgot to buckle me
she reached, fumbling one-handed
but the car swerved

And the empty seat stopped her cold, snatching the words from her mouth. The passenger door hung open, the ditch stretching away into the raining night.

She stared. "Timmy?"

The wind, whispering.

The rain, tapping.

The Escort's engine ticking, Danny's truck thrumming, its door slamming shut. Panic tightened her chest. "Timmy!" She grappled with her seatbelt. "Timmy, honey . . . where are you? ARE YOU HURT?"

Wind and rain and rumbling engine and boots scraping asphalt toward her. She tugged at her stubborn seatbelt, swearing, tugging harder . . .

It unlatched. She yanked the door handle but it wouldn't open. Jammed, maybe. She slammed it with her shoulder, jerked the handle and pushed again.

"ELLEN!"

She looked up and saw the bat swing; saw Danny's feverish eyes glittering in the night.

She screamed and dove into the passenger seat. Glass shattered, shards peppering her face. She ignored them, scrambling out the door and into the cold, wet ditch.

But Danny had beaten her there. She pushed herself off the ground, rolled over and yanked the .38 from her pocket.

Danny loomed above her.

"NO!"

She thumbed the hammer back.

Danny raised the bat high.

Her finger tensed on the trigger, and she hesitated, for just a moment . . .

Danny screamed in drunken rage, lurching toward her, swinging the bat down.

And she squeezed the trigger once, twice, three times. Danny jerked with each blast, dropping the bat, which hit the road with a wooden clatter and rolled away. He grabbed his middle, clumsily groping at the redness spilling there, muttering, gibbering, sagging to his knees.

He quivered, then slumped face-first to the asphalt.

Ellen dropped the gun, covered her face with her hands and sat there, rocking, as Danny's truck idled and sirens warbled down the road, coming from town.

14.

"By THE TIME I arrived on the scene that night you were nearly inconsolable, hysterical at Timmy's disappearance, insisting *something* had taken him away. But then you called us three days later and changed your story, telling us to end our search because Timmy was 'safe and in a better place.'"

I lean forward, hands clasped before me, trying to be gentle because I can see that recounting her ordeal is hard for her, can see it in her wet and glimmering eyes. "Why did you tell us that, Mrs. Danvers? What was that . . . thing you saw? Where is this 'better place?' I can't report any of this, can't ever speak of it to anyone. But I need to know."

so the Guardian may protect the Threshold

She nods, sniffing, and wipes both eyes with the heels of her palms. Composing herself, running a hand through her hair, she whispers, "I . . . I wasn't in a good place after that. I'd lost Timmy, lost everything. With Timmy gone there was nothing left to live for and I almost . . . "

She sucks down a deep breath, wipes her eyes again and bravely screws up her face and looks me in the eyes. "I was almost . . . "

***

. . . almost there, sitting on her old, ratty couch, rocking back and forth, crying, shoulders quaking as she cradles the Smith and Wesson in her lap, searching for the courage to raise it, to do what must be done, she's almost there . . .

Next to her on the couch sits the picture Timmy drew of him and the scribbled, fuzzy black 'Mister Nobody.' His imaginary friend, one he said talked to him in his sleep, the one he'd said was coming for him that night . . .

The thing in the road.

The thing she saw in the road, holding her son against its chest before she crashed. She hasn't shown the picture to the police; worried they'd think she's crazier than they already think she is, but she knows she's not crazy. She saw it, saw it standing in the road holding her son and she knows, somehow, that the police won't find Timmy, won't find *anything.* Timmy's gone and he's never coming back.

Ever.

So she swallows her sobs, clears her throat and sits up straighter, curling her right hand around the .38's grip, her finger pressing the trigger. Timmy's gone, she doesn't know where, doesn't know if he's alive or dead, and she doesn't care anymore, she doesn't . . .

She's got nothing left.

So she's done.

She raises the .38 and presses the muzzle against her temple, and even as she feels a hard ball of determination forming in her gut, she also feels a burning despair because she's about to become another Clifton Heights statistic, just another strange, unexplainable story that townspeople will shake their heads over and mutter about and then forget . . .

The television flicks on.

Static fills the screen, resolving into that report about the missing Utica girl, only this time with her picture: an angelic, cherubic face with a cute pixie nose and vibrant red hair in pigtails, a splash of freckles across her nose and cheeks and such vivid, bright green eyes . . .

Movement flickers from the corner of her eye.

A shadow sliding down the edge of the wall, something—someone?—hiding just around the corner in the hall leading to Timmy's room.

A hand?

And childlike, small fingers, spreading flat against the wall, and there . . . a head, with bright red hair and a vivid green eye, peeking at her . . .

And a red pigtail falls over a small shoulder, as . . .

No.

Can't be.

But it *is*.

The little girl missing from Utica, hiding in their dark hallway, engaging Ellen in a childish game of peek-a-boo, half a smile on her face.

Ellen starts off the couch with an inarticulate cry, the .38 dropping from nerveless fingers to thump against the trailer's thin carpet. She holds out her hand, steps forward, a thousand burning questions crowding her tongue . . .

But the girl darts from the hall, across the den, toward the front door, moving silently and more quickly than any child should and she's carrying something under one arm . . .

"Wait!"

Ellen's voice finally works and she moves on pure instinct, chasing the little girl who simply passes through the trailer's front door without opening it, as if she's made of mist or smoke or fog but Ellen's nothing more than a stumbling mass of reflexes as she lurches across the living room, jerks open the trailer's front door and stumbles down the steps. Dozens of thoughts and words spin through her head and a name jumps up, burning on a big white screen in her mind and without thinking *why*, she yells . . .

"Anne Marie!"

The little girl slides noiselessly to a stop on bare feet. She turns, standing at the parking lot's edge, cradling something against a body wearing a bright yellow nightdress with flowers on it . . .

And that something is Timmy's stuffed Thomas the Train.

Ellen Danvers stumbles to a halt, blinking. This is *her*. Without a doubt this is the missing Utica girl and here she is, standing at the edge of the Commons parking lot, barefoot, dressed in a sun-yellow nightdress, holding Timmy's favorite stuffed toy, Thomas the Train, under her arm.

Ellen opens her mouth but nothing comes out.

And the little girl smiles and says, "I just hadda get his Thomas, so he won't be lonesome no more. He'll be happier now. An he'll be seein you again, someday. Promise."

Before Ellen can speak the girl flickers away, past the parking lot and what Ellen sees there steals her breath away with an ethereal beauty she'll never forget, ever.

Five years ago the trailer park's owners cleared the adjacent plot with plans to build a playground. However, funding didn't come through and nothing was ever built . . . but there's a playground there now, one of the biggest jungle gyms she's ever seen, massive and sprawling, like those at an amusement park, like at Water Safari over in Old Forge . . .

And it's glowing, pulsing with a haunting yet beautiful phosphorescence, as if drawn with a fluorescent neon pen and there are children everywhere, clambering up ladders, climbing ropes, sliding down poles and slides, swinging off monkey bars, running across play drawbridges. Children everywhere; bright, glowing children.

And she hears—as breath on the wind—the distant and muted but joyous shrieks and cries of laughter.

The little girl carrying her son's toy disappears into the throng and though Ellen really can't distinguish one child from the next she somehow knows they're of different sizes, ages, race and culture . . .

And she knows that Timmy is among them and safe.

She sinks to her knees, sobbing for different reasons now, and when she finally stops crying and opens her eyes, the playground is gone, but she no longer feels empty or alone.

She feels at peace.

At last.

***

"I can't explain what I saw," Ellen continues in a hushed voice. "Can't explain what I saw in the road holding Timmy or what I saw three days later. All I can tell you is what I KNOW. What I feel."

I nod. "Your neighbor, Cassie Tillman . . . "

of course

" . . . called 911, reporting shots fired at about 9 PM. Deputies Potter and Shackleford arrived on the scene at Bassler Road forty minutes later, at approximately 9:40 PM. Danny Treemont was already down, shot three times in the gut by you. And the thing no one's been able to understand is how he could've taken or done anything to Timmy in that time span."

She nods, her green eyes remarkably clear. "There's the seatbelt, of course. Which never got hooked."

"Right," I whisper, "but forensics found no evidence that Timmy was thrown from the car. It *was* raining but not hard enough really, to wash away . . . "

"Dead," Ellen whispers, looking me straight in the eye. "If Timmy had been in that car when I crashed, his head would've smashed into the dash. He would've died. I know it."

With as much gentleness as I can muster—it's been a long, draining night—I whisper, "But we have no way of knowing that for sure, Mrs. Danvers. We really don't."

She shakes her head, eyes shining. "I saw some *thing* in that road before I crashed, holding Timmy. I SAW It, holding him . . . cradling him . . . in Its arms, right before an accident that could've very easily killed him. And then I saw . . . on that playground, I saw . . . "

She swallows and pulls herself together. "He was saved, Sheriff Baker. That's what I know, that's what I FEEL. Seconds before he was about to die, maybe real bad, Timmy was taken away and now he's in a better place where he'll always be safe."

Of course, what she says means nothing. Just like everything else in this town, like everything I've read tonight, there's no proof of what she's claiming. She's telling me another Gavin Patchett story. All I've got is a missing six year-old who, for all intents and purposes, has vanished without a trace.

And I don't tell her about the break in the Anne Marie Hauer case, which I heard on the radio on the way here. The boyfriend was found this morning in a hunting cabin out past Brookdale, sucking on a double-barreled shotgun, the back of his head spread all over the wall behind him. He'd left a note, confessing that . . . Mother of God . . . he'd been molesting Anne Marie Hauer for little over a year and the night the girl disappeared . . . when he was babysitting while his girlfriend was working . . . he went into her room, to . . .

But Anne Marie was gone, vanished from her bed, her bedroom window open, with no signs of forced entry.

Like she had *let* someone in.

Like Timmy Danvers had wanted to.

And the boyfriend fled in a panic because he'd known how it would look, and even though he'd been molesting her, in his own twisted way he'd never wanted to *kill* her, so—according to the note—that's why he'd run, and why he'd killed himself.

But I won't tell Ellen Danvers this. I'll not add any more fuel to the fire that's already burning so brightly in her eyes. She'll see it all over the news soon enough, and she'll make her own assumptions.

"Can you tell me anything else, Mrs. Danvers? Anything at all?"

She smiles sadly and shakes her head, as if she feels

sorry for me, somehow understanding that I'm grappling with affairs I'll never understand. "I'm sorry. That's all."

I nod.

Because what else is there to say?

I stand, replace my patrol hat and offer her a tired smile. "Thanks Mrs. Danvers. It was . . . illuminating."

***

I'm driving the long way home. Not straight back into town, but further down Bassler Road toward the interstate. I'm not sure why. Am I hoping for a glimpse of Jenny Tillman, walking down Bassler Road, flagging down unsuspecting motorists? Or maybe I'm expecting to see Jarred Simmons' truck broken down on the shoulder. Or, better yet, the ghostly shadow of Timmy Danvers. However, according to Ellen I won't see Timmy because he's in a better place now, like maybe Ann Marie Hauer.

Like my wife, too.

Or so everyone keeps saying, telling me she's in a better place, where she's no longer sick and suffering, her cancer a thing of the past, me not really believing because (before tonight) I'd always believed there *were* no other places, better or otherwise.

But I'm not sure what I believe, anymore.

They're just stories. Unsubstantiated in any way, and even Ellen Danvers' story can be chalked up to denial or depression . . .

Just stories.

But something haunts me as I drive down this road, letting myself be pulled by the instinctive hunch that Gavin's stories are *real* and yet not, that somewhere in the middle lies the truth . . .

But do I really want to know it?

A bright flicker dashes across the road.

A small figure running, and I catch a brief flash of yellow and bare feet blurring in the night.

I hit the brakes, park my patrol car and slide out the door. Something stays my hand, however, and I don't pull my Glock, just round the front of the car and shout, "Hey!"

And the little girl skids to a silent stop on the road's gravel shoulder. She turns and faces me and I know, without a shadow of a doubt—I'd know even without Ellen Danvers' description—that I'm looking at Anne Marie Hauer of Utica, NY, missing for three weeks, standing on the other side of the road in her sun-yellow nightdress.

And she's smiling. Just a happy, carefree little girl out for a lark. Not ghostly or glowing around the edges and she's not see-through or any of those other clichés. She just IS, standing on the other side of the road, shining, bright and happy, and for all I can tell . . . alive.

"Anne! Anne *Marie!*"

The voice sends chills down my spine, pulling my gaze to, of course, Bassler House.

And it's changed.

Not glowing or anything like that, but its windows—filled with whole glass—are ablaze, emitting rays of warm yellow light and there are shadows moving past them. Also, Bassler House is brand new.

Renovated.

Reborn.

And I have no doubt in my mind that a Google Image search for archived photos of Bassler House generations ago would produce pictures of a new and fresh and *good* house looking exactly like this one.

In the front doorway stands a dark figure, silhouetted by bright light. Tall, feminine, waving and calling Anne Marie's name again in a voice that freezes my bones. I catch just the barest suggestion of long hair, backlit by the glow coming from Bassler House.

Blond hair, perhaps. And on the air drifts the sounds of music, of play, of laughter and of singing.

Children singing.

"She loves you, mister. A whole bunch. An misses you, too."

I gape at the little girl in the sun-yellow dress. She smiles again, maybe whispers, "bye," then turns and dashes up the walk, faster than any child should. She slips past the silhouette in the door, into this new, transformed, *clean* Bassler House.

And the silhouette stands and stares for several long seconds that seem to drag on forever.

I stare back.

But I don't wave. I nod briskly and walk back to my car, because this is not for me, not yet, maybe not ever. But most assuredly, and I'm more certain of this than I've ever been about anything in my life: right *now*, this house and what's inside is *not* for me.

There's no sound of a door shutting, but the music and the laughter and the singing fade as I get into my patrol car. I don't look as I drive away, however, because I don't want to see what Bassler House has turned back into.

And as I drive numbly toward the interstate, I tell myself that wasn't my wife's voice I heard calling Anne Marie.

THINGS SLIP THROUGH

That wasn't Liz standing in the doorway.
It wasn't.
And mostly, I believe that.
Mostly.

The book is completed,
And closed, like the day;
And the hand that has written it
Lays it away.
Dim grow its fancies;
Forgotten they lie;
Like coals in the ashes,
They darken and die.
Song sinks into silence,
The story is told,
The windows are darkened,
The hearth-stone is cold.
Darker and darker
The black shadows fall;
Sleep and oblivion
Reign over all.

"CURFEW"—HENRY WADSWORTH
LONGFELLOW

CONNECT WITH KEVIN LUCIA

Clifton Heights always welcomes visitors, *The Skylark Diner* is always open and when he's not teaching or writing, Gavin Patchett is always there, ready to tell a story. Please visit and 'Like' the Clifton Heights page. Gavin will be waiting.

https://www.facebook.com/CliftonHeightsNY

Kevin Lucia's short fiction has appeared in several anthologies, his podcast "Horror 101" is featured monthly on *Tales to Terrify*, and he's the Associate Fiction Editor for The Horror Channel. He's currently finishing his Creative Writing Masters Degree at Binghamton University, he teaches high school English and lives in Castle Creek, New York with his wife and children.

He is the author of *Hiram Grange & The Chosen One*, Book Four of *The Hiram Grange Chronicles*. *Things Slip Through* is his first collection. He's currently working on his first novel. Visit www.kevinlucia.com and add him on Facebook:

https://www.facebook.com/kevinlucia
https://www.facebook.com/authorkevinlucia

CONNECT WITH CRYSTAL LAKE PUBLISHING

Website:
www.crystallakepub.com
Facebook:
www.facebook.com/Crystallakepublishing
Twitter:
https://twitter.com/crystallakepub

We hope you enjoyed this title. If so, we would be grateful if you could leave a review on Amazon, Goodreads, your blog or one of the many websites open to book reviews. And remember to keep an eye out for more of our books.

THANK YOU FOR PURCHASING THIS BOOK